THE
KEEPER'S
VOW

MEG ANNE

Cover Design by CReya-tive Book Design

Edited by Analisa Denny

Proofread by Dominique Laura

THE KEEPER'S VOW

ELYSIA
Grey Spire
Etillion
Talyria
Vyruul
The Queen's Aerie
Caederan
Endoshan
Emerald Ocean
Kiri's Palace
Tigaera
Daejara
The Mother's Tears
Sylverlands
Sea of Mist
Keeper's Catacombs
Bael
Holbrooke Estate
Broken Vale
Forest of Whispers
Ebon Isle
N
NW
NE
W
E
SW
SE
S

PART I
SHADOW-TOUCHED

"I love you as certain dark things are to be loved,
in secret, between the shadow and the soul."

Pablo Neruda

CHAPTER 1

LUCIAN

*I*cy fear arced down Lucian's spine as Effie crashed into him with the force of an enraged Talyrian. He grunted in pain, his head cracking into the rubble-strewn floor as he instinctively lifted his hands to protect his face.

She fought like a wild animal, all fang and claw, landing on top of him and immediately going for his jugular. No one so little—Shadow-touched or otherwise—should have the ability to knock a man of his size onto his arse, let alone keep him there. But he'd be lying if he said it wasn't a struggle to pry her slight body off of his. He couldn't remember having to work this hard in his life to break out of an opponent's hold. It just went to show that while her transformation was not yet complete, she was already infused with a Shadow's unholy strength.

As if underscoring her rapidly devolving state, little growls erupted from her throat as she gnashed her teeth, aiming time and again to tear into his vulnerable flesh.

"I don't want to hurt you," he managed, maneuvering his right arm between them, "but I will if it means keeping you whole."

His words were met with more wet growls.

"Fine. Have it your way."

He shoved her off, a feat that required far more effort than it should have, and she flew back into the desecrated bodies she'd been ravaging when he'd found her. With a snarl, she pulled herself up into a crouch and glared at him through the bloodied strands of her hair.

A shiver of apprehension danced across his skin as her expression shifted from malice to dark amusement. There was no question which of the two emotions frightened him more.

Lips parting in a cruel smile, she purred, "What's wrong, lover? Don't you want me anymore?"

The words were bad enough, but it was her voice that cut at him like the scrape of metal over glass. It was all wrong. A broken rasp that had no place coming from such a sweet mouth—even if said mouth was currently dripping blood.

Using the opportunity to assess his next move, Lucian raked his eyes over his charge. He barely recognized her. Physically, she appeared almost normal. If one discounted the sheer amount of gore coating every visible inch of her and the snaking black lines slithering in her milky eyes. But those were merely window dressing. The subtler, harder to pinpoint shifts in her were what inspired true fear. Like the odd, halting way she moved, almost as if she was no longer at home in the flesh that contained her. Or perhaps it was the aura of hatred that suffused the very air around her like some kind of invisible mantle.

The entire assessment took him less than a heartbeat to finish.

Lucian might be looking at Effie, but she was not who was staring back. A savage, blood-thirsty monster had taken over and it had no intention of letting go of its prize anytime soon. This was not a battle that could be won today. Not without a sacrifice he was unwilling to make. What he needed was time. The only way to buy that was to subdue her, and fast. The longer this went on, the worse it was going to be—for both of them.

Teeth clenched, Lucian pushed to his feet and eyed the discarded weapon a few paces away.

Following his gaze, Effie tsked. "Can you really kill me so easily,

Guardian? Just sink that blade of yours straight into my heart as if I mean nothing to you?"

A savage roar tore through him in immediate protest, but he kept his expression carefully blank. Let her call his bluff. He only needed to fool her long enough to tie her up. Then he could figure out how to save them both, because there was no doubt in the entirety of his being that if she was lost, so was he.

Stooping down, Lucian scooped up his blade. "Effie, if you can hear me, I need you to fight this, okay?"

The creature sneered. "Effie's not home right now."

"Fight, fledgling," he snapped, taking a step forward.

Her expression rippled, like there was some kind of internal war taking place within her that he was not privy to. Or perhaps that was just his fervent hope making him see something that wasn't there.

"There's nothing to fight except for you," she growled, slowly standing. "Your fledgling is dead."

"No!" The protest was ripped from him in a roar as he charged forward in a burst of speed.

She was ready for him, tossing a handful of dirt and rocks up into his face. Luckily, he didn't need his eyes to see. He pulled his power forth with no more effort than one used to take a breath.

His lips curled up as he lunged straight at her, the purity of her soul shining like a beacon and lighting his way despite her trick. Realizing she'd failed to stop him, Effie let out a keening shriek, but her outrage only fueled Lucian's determination. He would not fail. One way or the other, he was going to save her.

Even now with the corruption streaking through her in a series of thin black and gray strands, Effie glowed a pale gold. Her light was barely diminished, reinforcing his hope that it wasn't too late. If anyone was strong enough to fight against the corruption while he searched for a cure, it was her.

Sword arm raised, Lucian dropped his power. A slight widening of her eyes was the only hint she knew what was coming. He bashed the hilt of his sword down into the side of her head, not holding anything back from the blow.

The effect was immediate. Effie crumpled like a ragdoll, her eyes rolling back into her head as her body went slack.

Lucian winced, mentally apologizing as he caught her. Shadow-touched or not, she was still his. His eyes dropped to her face, and his heart ached. Eyes closed and features no longer twisted with menace, there was no trace of the being that was living inside of her. She could have been sleeping.

Swallowing, he adjusted her in his arms and forced the thought away. He couldn't afford to think like that. Right now, Effie was the most dangerous enemy he'd ever faced. Not because of the threat she presented to the world at large, but because of the threat she presented to him. To his very nature. It would be a battle with his deepest and most primal instinct at every step. He was going to have to do the impossible if he had any hope of surviving this—*her*.

A Guardian's primary objective was to protect at any cost. But how could he protect someone when *they* were the monster?

"Lucian?"

Kael's voice should have brought a wave of relief, but he knew his brother. He was not going to like Lucian's plan.

"Over here," he called.

Kael rounded the corner, his expression relaxing slightly when his eyes landed on the woman in his arms. "You found her. Is she all right?"

He didn't know how to answer that without lying, so he didn't.

Brows veeing, Kael stepped forward. "What is it? What's the matter?"

"We've got a problem."

Sparing a glance for the destruction around them, Kael let out a humorless laugh. "That's putting it mildly."

"Effie's Shadow-touched."

Color leached out of Kael's face, his jaw going slack. "What? When? We were all fine after the lajhár . . ."

"It must have happened before. When she was bit."

Kael's eyes shuttered, and he leaned heavily against the wall. "Fuck," he whispered. "Luc, I'm so sorry."

Lucian had known Kael long enough to know what direction his thoughts were heading. Hell, it would be where his would go had their positions been reversed.

"Don't," he gritted out.

"Lucian, you know what this means."

"Stop," he warned, feeling the throb of his pulse in his neck.

"We both know what needs to be done."

"Shut. The. Fuck. Up."

Kael's voice was soft, his green eyes filled with his own pain. "Do you need me to do it for you?"

Lucian growled and tightened his arms around Effie. "She's not to be harmed."

"You know as well as I do what's in store for her. She wouldn't want to become that."

"She won't."

"Oh? And how do you plan to stop it?"

"I'll find a way."

"Brother—"

"We're not having this conversation, Kael."

"But, Lucian—"

"Either help me find a way to save her, or stay the fuck out of my way. Those are your only two options."

Kael closed his mouth, his eyes assessing. "I recall a similar conversation not too long ago where you were on my side of this argument."

"And?"

"You spoke of mercy."

A muscle ticked in Lucian's jaw. "We weren't talking about *her*."

"Are you sure you're willing to put everyone else at risk for less than a sliver of a chance?"

"I'd risk anything to save her."

"Lucian, I care for her too—"

"Kael, this isn't a debate. Help me or fuck off. I don't care which."

His brother scowled, offended by the implication. "Of course, I'm helping you. That was never a question. I just wanted to make sure you were aware of the stakes. If we're going to set the world on fire, Luc, I want to make damn sure you're certain before you light the match."

Lucian allowed himself a small smile of thanks as some of the tension eased. He'd hoped Kael would side with him, but his brother's loyalty was to the realm first. Technically, so was his, but everything had shifted with Effie's arrival.

"For now, we need to find somewhere safe to keep her. Somewhere away from the others."

Frowning, Lucian nodded his agreement. He didn't like the idea of locking her up, but it was the safest thing for everybody involved. With the citadel gone, the last of the Keepers and townsfolk would need to regroup and decide what came next. There was no knowing how many of them were left or if the city could even be salvaged. They'd likely spend the rest of the day combing through the rubble and searching for survivors. He couldn't focus on that if he was worried about Effie waking up every two seconds.

Glancing down at her peaceful, albeit gore-splattered face he made up his mind. "I'll take her to the catacombs."

"You should do it now, before the others show. Less questions that way."

The warning had him shooting Kael a hard look. "We keep this quiet for now. I mean it, brother. No one else can know."

He lifted a dubious brow. "Just how long do you think we can keep her from the others?"

"As long as we have to."

"They're going to want to know what happened to her."

"So we tell them the truth. She fought bravely defending her home."

"And?" Kael pressed.

"And what?" Lucian asked, barely keeping the snarl out of his voice.

The other Guardian shook his head, making it abundantly clear how short-sighted he thought Lucian was acting. "You really think they're going to be satisfied with half of an answer?"

He let a fraction of the rage simmering within him rise to the surface. "If they were that concerned for her, maybe they shouldn't have left her behind."

"Fair enough. I'll buy you some time."

"Once I get her settled, I'll come find you."

With a nod, Kael turned and started to walk away. Pausing at the end of the hallway, he turned and glanced back over his shoulder. "Lucian?"

"Yeah?"

"For what it's worth, I'm truly sorry."

Lucian struggled to maintain his blank expression. It felt like someone had shoved their fist into his chest and ripped out his heart. "I know."

With a final dip of his chin, Kael left them. It was obvious he didn't believe they were going to find a way to save her in time. All he could see when he looked at Effie was sand pouring into the bottom of an hourglass.

But when Lucian looked at her, he saw the flickering promise of everything he'd ever wanted. She represented an entire lifetime of unspoken hope; his heart's deepest wish made reality by a woman who was so much more than she ever gave herself credit for.

The flame might still be there, but it was guttering, and there was no telling how much longer it would last.

THE CATACOMBS WERE tomblike in their silence, especially after the insanity of war. Set beneath the citadel itself, deep within the earth, they were all that was left of the Keepers' original home. Few, if any, remembered they were still here, and it had been millennia since anyone had need to visit them.

Until now.

Ignoring the thick webs built and abandoned by centuries of spiders, Lucian easily maneuvered his way through the winding chambers, the place still as familiar to him as the city above. But the air was heavy and thick, and breathing became almost painful the deeper down he went.

Reaching a room that had once been a bedchamber—and the first he'd come across that still had a door and functioning lock—Lucian stepped inside and carefully laid Effie's unconscious form down on what was left of the bed.

She didn't stir.

Even though he'd felt the soft gust of her breaths against his neck, he pressed his hand to the side of her throat, not convinced she was all right until he felt the steady thump of her pulse against his fingers.

He allowed himself a moment to linger, his hands running along the velvety column of her throat up to her jaw. Even battle-stained she was breathtaking. Not because of something superficial like the symmetry of her features, but because of the aura of fierce defiance she still seemed to exude even while unconscious. A warning, perhaps, for those that would seek to harm her.

Lucian's eyes fell closed, his breathing ragged.

His fledgling had been forged by fire, her life more difficult and painful than most of her friends would ever know. Her scars might be the only testament to her struggles, if one took the time to learn how to read them. Effie herself was carefully evasive with answers about her past, downplaying the horrors that had been heaped upon her— sometimes by her own parents. Where many would have crumbled, she continued to rise, each time stronger and more resilient than the last. And all with a core of unyielding kindness and quiet strength. He'd never met her like.

Her existence was a miracle, even if it had been preordained.

Opening his eyes, Lucian traced the curve of her lips. The curse of the Keepers was to be gifted with foresight but never know their own fate. It was a curse Lucian shared. He'd been informed he'd find his true purpose in Elysia, but had been given no clue when or where it would be waiting. No amount of bribery or threats had revealed anything further. Not even a name.

There was nothing in any world with more allure than a Guardian's true purpose. Once found, it superseded any prior vows or commitments. While it was not always a person, nor a relationship with romantic ties, a Guardian spent their immortal life searching to find and fulfill that. While Lucian had spent most of his life waiting for her—had even known to some degree that he *would* succeed in finding her—Effie had crashed into him like a wild storm.

He knew now that no amount of warning would have ever prepared him for her.

"M'vitra pour vestry. Non refert l'coût." The words of his native tongue came unbidden, pouring out in a guttural rush.

My life for yours. No matter the cost.

It was a Guardian's most sacred vow. There were no words, in any language, that held more meaning for him, and right now it was the only thing he had to give. Brushing his knuckles across her cheek, Lucian leaned down to press his lips to Effie's forehead.

"I'll find a way to bring you back, fledgling. Or I'll die trying."

CHAPTER 2

EFFIE

A low snarl echoed around the empty room as she pushed herself into a tight crouch. Thoughts were nothing more than fragments as Effie squinted into the darkness.

Cold.

Dark.

Hungry.

Safe?

A tentative sniff confirmed that she was alone, but it did little to calm the echo of rage pulsing through her. There was another's scent in the air. Faded, but distinguishable. An essence of midnight and musk.

His . . .

Guardian.

A deep, wet rumble filled the room as her anger spiked. He was alive; had left her here. Likely to rot.

Foolish male.

A dark grin stretched across her face as she climbed off the bed and crawled across the floor.

Never safe. Not from me.

Coming for you.

Pale light shone through a crack under the door, and she lowered her face down to peek out into the space beyond.

Empty.

A triumphant growl vibrated low in her throat.

She slid a hand up the pock-marked wood, searching for a handle. Her smile faltered when her fingers moved over cool but jagged metal.

Broken.

Wood thundered as she pounded her fists into the flat surface. The door shook and trembled, but it did not open.

Trapped.

Scuttling backward, she pushed herself into a corner of the small room. Her prey would return. She could wait. A spider in her web.

He loved this body. Would not harm it. But he would not be so lucky.

Blood would flow free.

And it would never be hers.

CHAPTER 3

LUCIAN

"What do you mean gone?" Ronan snarled, his blue eyes bloodshot.

"It's an obvious enough statement," Lucian replied in a low voice, not looking up from the dagger he was using to pick blood from his nails.

The other man let out a strangled sound that was a cross between a disbelieving laugh and a growl. "And you didn't think to keep looking for her?"

The sheer hypocrisy of that lone question sent Lucian's ire spiking. "I'm not the one who left her behind in the first place," he snapped, eyes shooting up to pin the Shield in place.

Twin patches of red bloomed in Ronan's cheeks and he had the grace to look away. Lucian knew it was a low blow. Effie's course had been set from the second she'd gotten bit, and nothing Ronan said or did after would have changed the outcome. Except, perhaps, not leaving her to face such a horrific fate on her own. Effie looked up to Helena's Shield, trusted him like a brother, and yet he'd left her when she needed a protector the most. For that reason alone, Lucian wasn't sure he could ever forgive the red-headed commander.

"Did you find a body?" Reyna asked, placing her hand on Ronan's back.

"What do you think?" Lucian returned, his voice just barely on the side of sounding human.

He'd anticipated the interrogation, but it did little to alleviate the bubbling anger inside of him. Each second they spent squabbling amongst themselves was another that Effie was left to deteriorate. He could not afford to let this carry on much longer, even if he was the one misleading them.

"How many of us are left?" he asked, twisting to face Kael.

The Guardian's green eyes were so dark they were almost black. "Just under thirty."

"Keepers?"

"Thirty total. Keepers *and* citizens."

Lucian's stomach dropped. "So few?"

"Aye."

His eyes closed, a shudder working its way down his body. So many lives lost. They'd been ignorant fools, all of them; their faith in the citadel's safeguards misplaced. They mistakenly believed their safety was assured since the citadel had never fallen before. But just because an attack had not come did not mean they'd been immune, they'd simply been untested. What an expensive lesson to learn. And now, due to their hubris, the Keepers had been all but exterminated and their sanctuary demolished.

As a Guardian, Lucian should have known better, should have been prepared for this eventuality. As far as he was concerned, he was just as much to blame for this attack as the one who initiated it. These deaths were on him.

Regardless of fault, or that the battle was over—for now—they couldn't remain here. Not when they were little more than sitting ducks waiting for the enemy to come back and finish the job.

"And where will we go?"

Lucian glanced at the hooded figure standing apart from the others. "Somewhere safe."

"The citadel was supposed to be safe."

The note of censure was unmistakable, and he bristled at the less than subtle dig. "No one is ever truly safe from betrayal."

A slow nod was his only response.

He spared the member of the Triumvirate a final hard glare before returning his attention to the bedraggled figures around him. Effie wasn't the only one missing from their ranks. Kieran hadn't been located either. Lucian wished he could muster some semblance of regret at the Dreamer's apparent demise, but the worm had been nothing but a pain in his arse for years. Good riddance. May the Mother have better luck with him than they did.

"We'll go to the Broken Vale," Lucian declared, the answer coming to him almost without conscious thought.

"The Vale? It's little more than a ruin. We'd be better off staying here," Ronan protested.

"Nothing is ever what it appears to be on the surface," Kael said.

"What the fuck is that supposed to mean?" Ronan snapped.

Kael quirked a brow. "The Vale is home to many survivors, if one only knows where to look."

"You fucking Keepers and your vague platitudes."

"It's a sound plan," Kael said, ignoring Ronan's grumbling.

Lucian gave the other Guardian a nod of thanks. Ronan was likely the first of many dissenters he'd have to deal with in the days to come. Shows of support like Kael's were the only way he was going to get anyone to agree to follow his lead.

"It's close enough that we won't have to travel for long. If we leave tomorrow, we should reach the Vale within a couple of days."

"Do you really think your people are fit for that kind of travel?" Reyna asked.

"We don't have a choice," Lucian replied. "The Kaelpas stones we still have aren't nearly strong enough to move everyone, even with our numbers so diminished. Sticking together and caravanning is the only option."

Kael shot Lucian a pointed look, which he ignored. He'd deal with how to move Effie when he had to. For now, they had other things to worry about.

"We need to salvage what we can," he said instead, rubbing the back of his neck as if it could do something to relieve the vise-like tension that had settled there.

"Is it even safe to comb through the wreckage?" Ronan asked.

"Probably not, but we have to risk it. Millennia's worth of prophecies will be lost if we don't try."

"They will be lost regardless."

Lucian scowled at the man hidden within the scarlet robes. "Would you rather we didn't bother?"

"By all means, search, but much has already been lost. The little you are able to recover will be less than a drop in the ocean."

"But it will still be more than nothing at all," he ground out, not appreciating his decision being questioned. If a member of the Three had something to say to Lucian, he damn well knew better than to air it publicly. The Triumvirate and the Guardians were supposed to be a united force, two sides of the same blade. How could they expect these people to put their trust in them when they seemed divided?

The robed figure shrugged. *"For all the good they've done us."*

Lucian clenched his teeth. The bastard wasn't wrong, but that didn't make him right. "If we abandon them, then all of this"—he held out his arms and moved in a slow circle—"has been for naught. What was the point?"

"Perhaps we've placed too much importance on the prophecies and not enough where it actually matters."

After all that had been lost, to be told that what he'd spent the last few centuries of his life safeguarding wasn't actually worth anything after all . . . It was too much.

Lucian's fragile hold on his temper snapped. He crossed the short distance between them in two swift strides, grabbing him by his robe and pulling his cloaked face forward. "You want me to strangle you, is that it?" he snarled.

"Try."

"Your runes won't protect you from *me*," Lucian bit out, slamming him against what was left of a bookcase as if he weighed no more than a sack of feathers.

"Perhaps not. But your vow will."

He let out a roar of frustration that bounced around the few remaining walls.

"Luc, let him go," Kael murmured, placing a warm hand on his shoulder.

Lucian shrugged it off. "Why should I?"

Kael's answer was immediate and filled with earnest sincerity. "These people need a leader they trust now more than ever."

"What good have any of the Triumvirate ever done for anyone?" he asked, lifting the robed figure a little higher off the floor.

"We have always done what we needed to."

"Luc," Kael said again, his voice holding a warning edge.

"Or have you forgotten?"

Blood pounding in his ears, Lucian lifted his other arm and slammed his fist into the bookcase. The last of the wood boards exploded into dust as he pulled his hand free of the wall. "I have forgotten nothing."

Letting go of the man's robe, he spun and stalked away.

"The Triumvirate and the Guardians will present a united front. Together we will lead our people to safety."

His shoulders tensed as he heard his earlier thoughts thrown back at him, but he didn't slow down. He needed to get away. There were too few of them left for him to risk anyone being the next thing he hit. Because the mood he was in? Whoever he hit wouldn't survive the blow.

"Luc? Where are you going?"

"Do *not* follow me, Kael."

He didn't let out the breath he was holding until the sound of footsteps behind him faltered. His chest was so tight it felt like someone was currently using it as a hilt for their sword. The pressure didn't abate as he walked away from the citadel's pavilion and back out into the devastation of the city.

The sky was black and orange, the few lingering flames casting their grotesque light on thick clouds of low-hanging smoke. The Chosen gifted with Air and Water were doing what they could to bank the last of the fire and push the smoke away, but it was a task for many and there were only a handful of them still standing.

Lucian moved slowly, still not wholly able to process the extent of the destruction. Just a couple of days ago, he'd strolled down this block with Effie on his arm. Now it was almost impossible to tell where the sidewalk had even lain. If he hadn't taken this path so many times before, he may not have been able to find his way now.

He wasn't aware he'd had a destination in mind until he came to a halt outside of the little art shop where Effie had fallen in love with his paintings. Desda, the shopkeeper, had been the one to convince him to put his work on display. For Lucian, art in all its various mediums had always been a way of purging the soul. There was so much he'd seen in his long life that he couldn't speak about. Art gave him the voice to tell his stories, no matter how dark or terrible.

With a sigh, he stared at the smoldering store. It hurt to see that part of him destroyed, but not as much as the thought of Effie locked away. He'd never had the chance to tell her he was the one who had made both the castle deck and the small leather-bound journal she loved so much. Or what it meant to him to see something he'd created so lovingly cared for by another. Now he might never be able to see the look of shock on her face when she learned his secret.

Lucian's fingers skimmed the small pack he'd tied around his waist. He'd made a point to grab the two items for her before joining the fight. Just in case. He hoped he'd have an opportunity to return them.

He started to turn away.

"Lucian! Thank the Mother you're okay."

He spun as Desda stepped around the corner.

"Des . . ."

She rushed over to him as fast as her bowed legs could carry her. Tears shone in her eyes as she pressed her gnarled hand to his cheek and grinned. "Guess the Mother didn't want these old bones just yet." Her smile dimmed as she eyed her shop. "I'm so sorry about all of your beautiful work, Lucian."

"Don't be."

"I'll just have to rebuild," she said wistfully.

"You know we can't stay here."

Ever the pragmatist, Desda simply shrugged. "So I rebuild somewhere else. The world needs to be reminded of the beauty and wonder that surrounds us. Especially after such terrible times."

"What people need right now is a roof over their heads."

"And I'm sure you already have a plan to make sure they get one."

"I might."

She squeezed his hand. "So where will we go?"

"The Broken Vale."

Her eyes widened, and she made the sign of the Mother.

Lucian lifted a brow at the uncharacteristic display. "I didn't realize you were so superstitious."

"Everyone knows it's a cursed place."

"Right now it's our best shot at survival."

She fell silent and looked around them. Straightening her shoulders, she gave a little nod, as if reaching some sort of decision, and glanced back up at him. "If you say this is our path, I trust you."

"Then gather up what you need. We leave at first light."

Desda held out her arms and gestured to her singed boots and threadbare dress. "This is all I have left."

Frowning, Lucian removed his cloak and wrapped it around her shoulders. "That will have to do until I can find you something more suitable."

She tightened the billowing material around her frail body and smiled up at him. "I could not love you more if you were my own flesh and blood, boy. Your mother would be so proud of the man you've become."

Her praise shamed him. He didn't deserve it. Not after such a spectacular failure. If he'd done his job, she'd still have her shop and all her earthly possessions.

"I'd be so lucky," he mumbled, his voice gruff.

Desda rested her hand against his cheek. "In every way that matters, Lucian, you're my family. I will follow wherever you lead.

Now, let's go. Best we focus on building our future instead of crying over our past, hmm?"

Throat thick with emotion, he nodded. "Best plan I've heard all day."

"You're not the only one with brains in this family, boy-o."

Her cocksure pose and accompanying smirk made him laugh, the sound foreign and rasping, but no less real. "I'm starting to see that."

"Better late than never."

He shook his head and held out his arm. "Careful. I might just put you in charge."

She grinned. "You couldn't handle it."

"Is that so?" he asked, helping her navigate the rough terrain.

"I wouldn't bother myself catering to fragile male egos. It'd be too much honesty for you lot to swallow."

Another bark of laughter rang out and Lucian felt some of the pressure in his chest ease, just a little. If he could still laugh, perhaps things weren't quite as dire as they seemed.

Perhaps there was still hope.

Perhaps.

CHAPTER 4

KIERAN

Spitting out a mouthful of sand, he wrapped the torn pieces of his tunic more firmly around his nose and mouth.

"It must be here somewhere," he muttered, eyes frantically scanning the horizon for something other than the yellow dirt he'd been wandering in for the past two days.

Since he hadn't planned on an extended trek through what was essentially a desert, Kieran didn't have any of the supplies that would have made such a journey tolerable. Namely water. Or food.

He'd gathered what he could find in the jungle before he'd crossed the border between the two lands, but it ran out on his first day, and he lost sight of the Mother's Tears—the river that bisected Elysia—around the same time.

Now, half-starved and beyond thirsty, Kieran was officially losing his mind.

The hallucinations were the worst of it. Tricking his eyes into seeing what couldn't possibly be there. Trees. Shelter. People. Time and again, he'd stumble up another sand dune in chase of something, only for the object in question to up and disappear. Never having existed at all.

Once a bustling center of trade, the Vale had been a desert oasis.

Bordered by both the river and the sea, it had been a hub of learning, a place where the Chosen could gather and share their goods and their knowledge. Now there was nothing left of it, save a few crumbling ruins and an endless sea of sand.

Jealousy was a cruel mistress. She couldn't abide others having what she coveted for herself. If ever there was a mantra that prophesied the downfall of the Vale, it was that one. A few centuries ago, war tore the oasis apart. What had once been a beacon of life and learning, gone overnight.

The irony of his situation wasn't lost on him. If Kieran was one to believe in karma, he might even say he'd deserved his current fate: to wander lost and alone in the remains of a ruined city—after escaping another he'd just singlehandedly destroyed—all because of his inability to accept his lot in life.

But Kieran knew what very few did. The Broken Vale wasn't just home to dust and dirt. It was also home to the sole gateway in all of Elysia. The same one he'd come through twenty-five years earlier.

The fact that the gate had been destroyed and that only a Gatekeeper had the magic necessary to open the door between worlds didn't matter. He was certain that if he could only find the it, he'd figure out how to get back home.

"It *has* to be here," he said again, a slight whine threading its way through his words.

He couldn't accept any other possibility. There was nowhere else for him to go.

His memory of his travels through the Broken Vale were spotty at best. He'd been too blinded by the hope that he'd finally find the woman from his dreams to pay much attention to his surroundings, but he knew the trip to the citadel had only taken three days. That meant he had to be somewhat close to the crumbling gateway.

Spinning in a slow circle, Kieran squinted in the distance, eyes straining to make out something—anything—in the endless yellow.

There.

He almost missed it, his eyes passing over the broken arch only to fly back and widen in frantic delight.

Heart stuttering in his chest, he let out a watery laugh. He'd found it. His lips were cracked and streaked with dried blood, but he didn't care. Smiling in sweet relief, he barely felt the painful tugging as the fragile skin split further apart. A wave of energy surged through him and he took off running, legs and arms pumping in a graceless sprint across the sand.

His flight slowed as he approached the spot where he'd just seen the familiar stone arch.

It wasn't here.

Kieran spun around, desperately searching for the pale gray stones he'd spotted from his perch on the dune.

There was nothing here but more sand. His eyes had played tricks on him once again.

"No!" The broken cry was torn from his throat, scraping the parched flesh like razor blades. He sank to his knees in the sand, the final shred of hope he'd been clinging to snuffed out. "No," he whispered, his hands sinking into the scorching sand as he hung his head in despair.

He was too dehydrated for tears, but that didn't mean he couldn't weep. His shoulders shook with the force of his tearless sobs, until he was no longer strong enough to hold himself up. Flinging his arms out on either side of his supine body, Kieran stared up into the cloudless blue sky and knew with absolute conviction that he was going to die here.

And not one person, in any world, would mourn him.

CHAPTER 5

LUCIAN

*L*ucian tightened the straps of his pack before setting it beside the single wagon they'd managed to salvage. Thankfully, two healers had survived the attack and had been able to take care of the others' injuries so no one had need of the wagon to travel. That meant Lucian could hide Effie inside of it along with the rest of the supplies they'd pulled together.

With that logistical nightmare solved, all that remained for him to do before setting off was to go free Effie from her cell and pray no one discovered her. He didn't hold much hope for the latter part of his plan. It was only a matter of time before his luck failed and the secret he'd been keeping was brought to light. But if the Mother was on his side, today would not be that day.

To that end, he'd convinced Kael to take the lead and get a head start with those traveling on foot. He would remain behind with the wagon and bring up the rear of the caravan. If nothing else, it bought him a little more time, maybe even a few extra days if that luck of his held out. Days he sorely needed but might not have. There was no way of knowing how long Effie could continue to fight off the corruption.

"You sure about this?" Kael asked for the seventh time that morning.

Lucian speared him with a look and didn't bother answering.

Kael released a heavy breath, crossing his arms over his chest and staring down at the tips of his boots. "All right, well . . . I guess we'll take off. No use wasting daylight."

"You know what to do if you come across signs of the corruption?"

"Circle around and send word via the Triumvirate's mental link so you know the new path."

Lucian nodded. "Right."

"Luc, I don't like splitting up."

"So you've said."

"These people aren't warriors," he tried again.

"That's what you, the Night Stalker, and the Shield are for. Besides, these people fought and survived once. They can do it again."

Kael scowled. "You're a stubborn arse, you know that?"

Lucian brought up a hand and squeezed the other Guardian's shoulder. "Love you, too, brother."

"Just . . . stay safe, all right? Don't take any unnecessary risks where Ef—"

He clamped down hard on Kael's shoulder, causing him to wince and correct his misstep.

"—*she's* concerned."

"I won't."

"She's going to be worse than the last time. Have you taken precautions?"

Lucian's only answer was a hard stare.

Kael shook his head and sighed. "It'd be easier to talk sense into a wall."

"I'm not far behind you," Lucian said, not acknowledging the aggrieved comment. "We'll plan on making camp at the border. If I don't catch up to you by nightfall, don't come looking for me. Keep going. Get these people to the Vale."

Kael pressed his lips together, looking like he wanted to argue.

"We've discussed this, brother. It's not safe to wander in the jungle, especially at night. Until we meet up again, you are in charge. These people and their safety are your top priority. You cannot let your loyalty to me sway you from your task."

"I won't," he finally agreed, sounding thoroughly put out.

Lucian understood the war waging inside of his oldest friend, but it didn't mean he would yield. Not on this. "And make sure the Triumvirate are seen walking beside the survivors. These people need to know that their leaders are with them."

Kael muttered something about scarlet hooded arseholes, and Lucian bit back a grin, understanding the sentiment if not the words.

"I'll see you soon, brother."

"Safe travels, Luc," Kael said, his expressive green eyes somber.

With a nod, Lucian turned and walked away. He didn't get far before a hand shot out and grasped his forearm. Spinning, sword already halfway free from its scabbard, he bit off a curse and resheathed the blade when he saw who'd stopped him.

"What?" he snapped, breaking free of Ronan's hold.

"Where are you going?"

"Gathering the rest of the supplies," he lied smoothly.

Ronan's eyes narrowed with challenge. "The last of them were loaded into the wagon an hour ago. What are you really up to?"

"None of your business," Lucian replied, his voice tight.

"I'm the Shield. In the Kiri's absence I am the senior person in charge—"

"Tell that to her Advisor."

Ronan scowled, but didn't miss a beat. "—and that means I outrank you. So spit it out. Now."

A muscle spasmed in Lucian's jaw. *I do* not *have time for this shit.* Leaning forward, voice dripping with something dark and not wholly sane, he snarled, "No one outranks a Guardian. Not even the Kiri herself has power over me or my brothers."

Ronan's blue eyes glittered dangerously. "Want to test the theory?"

"I've already kicked your arse once, Shield. I'd be happy to do it again."

Lucian's patience was frayed on his best day. Right now, with fear regarding what he'd face when he made it back to Effie eating away at him, he was hardly fit to be around. And that was true for people he actually liked. Ronan was pushing his luck by testing Lucian's control. Especially considering the man did *not* fall into that category. Not after leaving Effie behind.

The longer they stared at each other, violence and temper simmering between them, the better a brawl sounded. At the very least it would be a way to let off some of the tension thrumming through him.

Finally, Ronan let out a deep breath and shook his head. "I'm not looking to pick a fight with you."

"Pity."

"You're up to something. I want to know what. Especially if it puts the rest of us in danger."

"I told you, Shield. It's none of your business."

"Let me be the judge of that."

Lucian could practically feel time slipping away. There was nothing to gain by wasting more of it on this farce of a conversation.

He knew it was a risk, letting Ronan see Effie in her altered state, but the man was going to find out sooner or later. Lucian couldn't picture him *not* taking his side in this when he clearly cared about her.

But if he didn't . . . well, Lucian would deal with that too.

"You want to know so bad? Fine. Follow me."

Ronan's eyes widened, but he wasted no time catching up to Lucian's ground-eating strides. "Are you going to at least warn me about what to expect or am I going into this blind?"

"Don't push your luck, Shield."

He didn't speak further, but Lucian felt Ronan's displeasure building between them. His unease was palpable. As was his curiosity. Not that Lucian gave two shits about either. After what he did, the Shield could live with his questions awhile longer. Lucian didn't owe him a damned thing, least of all satisfaction.

They walked in silence for ten minutes, weaving through the destruction and taking a wide path around what had once been a courtyard. Lucian came to an abrupt stop once the path opened up into the remnants of a garden causing Ronan to crash into him with a muffled curse. The Guardian only just managed to bite back his smirk. Sometimes petty pleasures were the most satisfying.

Schooling his features and refocusing on the matter at hand, Lucian drew on his power, his eyes flaring bronze as he revealed the shimmering portal just ahead. The entrance to the catacombs was hidden in plain sight, just like everything else when it came to the Keepers. It didn't take centuries of living to learn that the less secretive something appeared, the less interest people had in poking around where they didn't belong.

A rose bush that was more thorns than flowers was the perfect hiding spot. Nasty looking enough to warn off anything that might be tempted to pluck a bloom, it deterred unwanted guests more successfully than a sign or gate ever could.

"After you," Lucian said in a deceptively courteous voice.

Ronan's eyes narrowed. "Is this a trick, Guardian?"

He let some of his pent-up anger filter into his words. "When I come for you, Shield, there's no mistaking it. I have no need for tricks."

The warrior's training was extensive enough he masked his reaction to the threat, but when his nostrils flared, Lucian knew it landed.

"Walk straight ahead. You'll end up in a dim hallway, just keep walking. I'll be right behind you."

"Doesn't fill me with confidence."

"Don't care."

Ronan gritted his teeth and did as he was told, tightening his hold on the hilt of the dagger strapped to his thigh—as if that would do anything to stop Lucian from completing a kill if that was his intent. He watched the redhead disappear between one step and the next, waiting two beats to ensure he was clear of the portal before following him. The hallway was dank and dark, the few torches Lucian had left burning now extinguished. Spotting one, Ronan set it ablaze with a flare of his power.

"What is this place?" he asked in a low, tense voice when Lucian strode past him.

"Catacombs."

"I thought they were a myth."

"Live long enough, Shield, everything turns into a myth."

"Don't much enjoy the thought of disturbing the dead."

Lucian contemplated telling him the truth—no one was buried down here—and just as quickly decided against it. "Then don't disturb them."

He knew he was being an arse, but it didn't lessen his flicker of dark amusement. Payback, in any form, was sweet. More than that, after the way things had been going lately, Lucian would take any win he could get. But his good humor was short-lived, and it guttered out just as quickly as it had appeared as they approached the room holding Effie.

No matter what Kael believed, there was no way Lucian could prepare himself for what came next. To anticipate what the sight of his fledgling, mindless in her bloodlust, would do to him. How it would shred him and test the very limits of his control. The most he could hope for was that she'd still be unconscious, and that was a bleak hope at best.

"I don't care what happens, you do. Not. Strike. Do you understand me?" Lucian asked, his voice a terse whisper.

Ronan eyed him before giving a single, swift nod.

He paused in front of the door, ears straining for any hint of movement behind it. If it had been a proper cell and not abandoned sleeping quarters, there'd be bars to peer through instead of solid wood, which would really come in handy right about now. The thought of going in blind made his skin crawl, but he didn't exactly have a choice. He supposed he should take comfort that the lack of visual intel worked both ways. He may not be able to see what was waiting for him on the other side, but neither could she.

Quit stalling, Luc. She doesn't have time for you to waste.

Releasing a tense breath, Lucian dropped his eyes to the twisted mound of metal that had once been the doorknob. Holding his hand just above it, he released his power only long enough to transform it back to its original state.

If Ronan was impressed by the act, he gave no indication of it.

Lucian supposed it took quite a bit to faze him. He'd likely witnessed far grander displays of magic while in the Kiri's service. Be that as it may, Lucian was also willing to bet the creature behind the door was going to blow Ronan's fucking mind.

Eyes closing briefly, he willed his heart to slow and his mind to calm. If he believed in the Mother, he might have asked her for strength. But he'd lived too long and watched too many die in the name of deities who cared nothing of their devotion—let alone their lives—to bother with such a fruitless endeavor. So instead, he sent his fervent prayer to the one person he *did* believe in.

Her.

Fight as long as you can, fledgling. I won't give up until one or both of us is dead, and I have no intention of dying. You know I'm a stubborn bastard. Nothing, not even this, will keep me from you now that I have found you. Don't give up on me.

Calling on his power, Lucian shoulder checked the door and sent it crashing open. He scanned the room, eyebrows knitting together in confusion when he didn't immediately spot her. Shock had his magic flickering out. Had she managed to escape?

He moved further inside, eyes sweeping the ground for a sign of her.

His mistake.

He never should have let his guard down.

An inhuman shriek echoed around the mostly empty chamber as the feral creature formerly known as Effie launched herself at him. The attack took him by surprise and Lucian staggered to the side as he caught her weight and tried to pry her off.

"Miss me, Guardian?" she crooned, licking up the side of his face before trying to sink her teeth into his neck.

Lucian jerked his head back, and shoved her face away from his, holding it there. "Can't say that I have." It wasn't exactly a lie. He hadn't missed the monster, only the woman whose face it was wearing.

Behind him, Ronan gasped in shock. "Effie? Sweet Mother have mercy."

"Not the time for praying, Shield."

"H-how?" Ronan stuttered.

"Not . . . the . . . time . . ." Lucian gritted out as the thrashing creature in his arms started landing kicks that narrowly missed his groin. "A little help, please?"

Stunned, Ronan shuffled into the room, his hands stretched out before him like he wasn't sure what to do with them.

"Grab her, dammit," Lucian ordered over his shoulder, still attempting to fully dislodge himself from Effie's hold while also not causing more physical harm than necessary.

Had it been any other creature, he would have tossed it against the far wall and dismembered it by now. He'd been a devout disciple of the 'kill first, ask questions never' school of warfare since the day he first picked up a sword. A Guardian tasked with protecting the defenseless had to be.

But this was no ordinary monster.

She was still his fledgling. Or at the very least he had to believe she was, because any other possibility was simply too devastating to bear. Which was why fighting her required a level of finesse he rarely, if ever, employed during battle. He didn't want to inflict lasting damage. He was already keeping a mental tally of every bruise he'd inflicted, hoping they'd live long enough for her to repay him for each and every one.

"Don't let her bite you," Lucian warned as Ronan moved into position behind her.

The red-haired commander froze when the creature lifted her gaze to meet his.

"What's wrong? Don't you love me anymore?"

A visible shudder worked itself down his body at her guttural rasp.

"Shield. Get your shit together."

Steeling his shoulders, Ronan's eyes slid away from Effie's monstrous visage. "What do you want me to do?"

"We need to immobilize her for travel. That will require bindings."

Effie let out a savage cry at his words, trying to twist her head to snap at his fingers.

Lucian spoke over her, giving her face another shove to avoid her snapping teeth. "I need you to help hold her still while I work."

She smiled then, a crazed sort of grin that had his stomach dropping to his feet. He felt her slipping further away by the second, the madness overtaking her piece by piece. Soon there would be nothing left to save.

He could hardly bear to look at her. Although his fledgling had always been fierce, the creature before him was something else entirely. A feral savage more akin to a wild animal than a human woman. Her face had already taken on a gaunt cast, and her cheekbones were more pronounced than they'd been the night prior. Even her body, which had always been softened with feminine curves, had started to change. There wasn't a damn thing soft about her anymore.

She was no longer a woman, but a weapon.

Lucian shuddered as the lines in her eyes slithered obscenely as if underscoring the point. He forced himself to look away, meeting Ronan's gaze over her head. "We'll start with her mouth since it's the most dangerous."

Effie cackled, drawing his attention back to her. "But I thought you loved my mouth, Guardian." She punctuated the words by licking her lips in what he assumed was supposed to be a seductive display, but the only thing the act gave rise to was the bile in his stomach.

"Shut up," he snarled, hating himself for letting her get under his skin. He was stronger than this, dammit.

But she was just getting started.

Effie raked her nails down his arms, drawing blood. She closed her eyes on a deep inhale and let out a groan that sounded entirely too sexual in its pleasure. "Delicious," she rasped.

Ronan moved fast, seizing her by the wrists and yanking her arms back. One of his hands easily held both her wrists behind her while he banded his other arm about her waist and pulled her free from Lucian's hold. The move might not have worked if she wasn't so distracted by the scent of his blood.

"Go. I've got her."

Lucian cast his eyes around, searching for the weathered blanket he'd seen when he'd been here last. He found the dirty garment crumpled on the floor, and held out a hand, using his power to weave it into something new.

In less time than it took to draw a breath, Lucian lifted heavy chains from the ground. In his other hand, he held up the last remaining scrap of fabric. Hefting the chains over his shoulder, he raised the makeshift gag and stepped back to the squirming woman.

"Don't you dare," the creature spat.

Lucian clenched his jaw.

"You wouldn't do this to someone you claim to love, would you?"

The pain caused by her words ripped through him, leaving part of him in absolute agony. It was because he loved her that he *had* to do this. Even so, he was guilt-ridden at the mere thought of it.

It's the only way, he reminded himself, taking another step toward her.

She went wild, thrashing in Ronan's arms as Lucian moved in. Ronan grunted when she smashed her foot into him, but otherwise remained still, his hold on her unbroken. She reared back, lifting both her legs in a frenzied attempt to slam them into Lucian's chest.

He moved fast, catching her before the blow landed by banding an arm around both her calves. Between him holding her legs, and Ronan at her back, Effie was trapped. The knowledge didn't faze her. She continued writhing like a worm on a hook. Chaining her was going to be difficult if they both had to keep her still.

Exchanging a look with Ronan over Effie's head, Lucian inwardly sighed. She wasn't making this easy. Not that Effie ever did. Instead of another wave of grief, the thought bolstered him. If that much of her true nature was still intact, all could not be lost.

Tucking the scrap of fabric into his belt, Lucian went to work wrapping the first of the metal chains around her feet. Since she needed to be able to walk, that required him to wind the links around each of her ankles, leaving enough slack to allow for some movement.

When the chains were looped, albeit loosely, Lucian tapped into his power once more, transforming the links into tight bands that fit perfectly around the creature's slender ankles. And even though it was a Shadow-touched he was binding, since it was Effie, he ensured that the insides of the metal cuffs were lined with the softest suede to minimize any chafing. It was the least he could do.

She squirmed in earnest as Lucian lowered her feet to the ground, the clinking of chains somewhat of a relief, even though it made her howl with rage.

"Damned convenient skill, that."

Lucian shrugged, not sparing Ronan a glance. "It has its moments."

"Brother, you just turned a sorry excuse for a blanket into a fucking length of heavy chain, and then changed portions of it into perfectly sized metal cuffs. I'd never have to worry about packing again."

Lucian shook his head, using his power to connect a length of chain to the piece that ran between her ankles. Once that was complete, he started raising it along the back of her legs, until his hand hovered just beside her wrists.

"I'm going to need you to adjust your hold so I have room to work," he murmured.

Ronan did as he was told, watching silently as Lucian repeated his trick with the chains around Effie's wrists. Even once she was fully bound, Ronan did not release her.

Lucian braced himself, taking a deep breath before rounding her and staring down into her sneering face.

"I hate you," she hissed.

"Likewise." And it was true. Lucian despised the being that had taken residence inside her. He couldn't wait to destroy it. "Which is why I'm going to enjoy this." Grasping the bit of cloth in his hand, Lucian grabbed her jaw and pried it open, tightening his grip to keep it locked in place as he shoved the gag in her mouth.

"Without something to tie around her head, she'll eventually find a way to spit that out," Ronan pointed out.

Lucian nodded, eyes already searching the floor.

"Can't you just wiggle your fingers and make something appear?"

He raised a brow. "I don't make things appear, Shield. I modify the nature of something that already exists."

"Oh."

Not spotting anything he could use, Lucian's eyes lifted to Ronan's single braid. Not waiting for permission, he simply grunted, "Sorry."

Ronan's eyes went wide as Lucian grasped the bottom of his hair and severed a chunk of it. It wasn't much, but the man bellowed as if he'd been burned. By the time Lucian's hand was held up between them again, the red tuft had been transformed into a long piece of fabric in the same color.

"You going to cry over a little haircut?"

Ronan glowered at him. "At least warn me first."

"Why? So you can try to talk me out of it?"

The other man silently seethed, nostrils flaring as he sucked in angry breath after breath. "Do you have any idea how long it took me to grow that out?"

"Stop pouting. Consider it your contribution to the task."

Ronan sighed, still looking thoroughly put out. "Not much I can do about it now."

Technically, Lucian could, but he wasn't about to waste his magic on something as superficial as a haircut. He had far more important matters to deal with.

He shifted his attention back to the woman growling low in her throat. Although silenced, the fiend had no trouble communicating the depth of her hatred. She stared up at him, brows low and nose scrunched in a silent snarl. Unable to withstand looking into that face for long, Lucian tied off the second piece of fabric, and moved to the side.

"Come on, let's go."

At first, Effie refused to budge, but Ronan had no issue tugging on the length of chain and threatening to drag her. Begrudgingly she fell into shuffling step behind him.

Lucian kept his eyes trained ahead, not wanting to add this to the other images that were already seared into his memory. He had more than enough of them to keep him awake at night. No use adding to the nightmares.

"What caused this?" Ronan asked after they'd taken a few steps.

"Shadow bite."

"But . . . when?"

"Before you arrived."

"Her scar." Ronan sucked in a sharp breath. "Are you telling me this whole time—"

Lucian gave a terse nod. "Yes."

"I don't understand. How could we not know?"

"Remember Tinka?"

Ronan took a shuddering breath as he connected the dots. "We mistook the symptoms, explained them away, when in reality . . ." He took a couple more steps before speaking again. "But that still doesn't explain how this is even possible. Rowena created Shadows by feeding off the souls of those she turned. That required Spirit magic. How in the name of the Mother are the Shadows replicating that? No one else alive, save Helena, has any claim to the Spirit branch."

It was Lucian's turn to fall silent, turning over the question in his mind. "Some of Rowena's initial spell must still run through the ones she personally turned. Like an echo . . ."

Ronan scrubbed his free hand down his face. "Are you telling me that the Shadows have access to Spirit magic?"

"No," Lucian said slowly, processing the answer even as he gave it. "I'm telling you that whatever tainted magic she used to turn the Shadows left a stain on those who remained after her death. That is the source of the corruption and why it continues to spread."

"I'm not sure I follow."

Lucian was only barely starting to understand himself. "Rowena fed off of her victim's souls. Since she is the source of all of this, it's my belief the corruption creating the Shadow-touched works in the same way. In order to take hold, it must first consume its host's soul, unable to fully claim them until the entirety of their humanity is destroyed. That is why some take longer than others to turn. The stronger they are, the purer their essence, the harder it is for the corruption to take root. Unchecked, it will inevitably win."

"Lucian, if her soul is gone—"

"It's not gone. Not entirely."

"But how can we save her if—"

Unable to stand hearing the words uttered out loud, Lucian cut him off again. "I don't know. But I intend to find out."

"Lucian." Ronan's voice was soft, filled with an emotion that only stoked the anger and pain the Guardian was trying so hard to ignore.

"Stop," he said, the word a threat as much as a plea.

He should have known it was futile. The Shield never backed down from a fight, he only altered the nature of his attack.

"If we don't find the answer in time . . ."

White-hot pain erupted in Lucian's chest, but his voice was devoid of emotion when he replied, "Then we do what needs to be done."

CHAPTER 6

KIERAN

The world tilted on its axis and Kieran groaned. He had no idea how long he'd been out this time. It could have been six minutes or six hours. Everything had become a blur, which meant he could just as easily be losing entire days now.

"He's still alive," an unfamiliar voice drawled.

Kieran tried to force his eyelids apart, but they were crusted shut. Somehow, he managed to open his right eye into a narrow slit, but the light was blinding after being cocooned by the dark, and the mysterious shape above him was indistinguishable.

"Leave me alone," Kieran said. Or tried to. It came out as an indecipherable slur. His voice dry and cracked.

Voices continued to speak above him, but he could only make out fragments of what they said. It was too hard to concentrate for long.

". . . dehydrated . . ."

". . . do with him . . ."

". . . get . . . base . . ."

He felt hands grab him by the shoulders, and a survival instinct he didn't realize he still had flared to life. Kieran had been waiting for death to claim him. Had been hoping for it. At least it would put an end to his misery. So why was he attempting to fight off the potential means of his death?

Weakly, he swiped at the hands that gripped him. The world shifted again, and Kieran's stomach rolled with it.

"Leave me," he tried to protest, but the words were lost.

The movement proved too much excitement in his current state, and oblivion claimed him once more.

THE GROUND BOUNCED AND SWAYED, jolting Kieran back to consciousness only long enough for his face to slam into something hard. A pitiful whimper managed to escape as he curled into himself, arms lifting to protect his head.

"There now. Just a bit further and we'll get you taken care of."

"Sydney!" a harsh voice snapped.

"He's in pain," the first voice protested.

"Until we know who we're dealing with, you'll stand clear, do you understand me?"

There was a muffled grunt of assent and then a hushed, "Sorry."

Before Kieran could dwell on why the voice was apologizing, something soft scraped against his leg and lightning sang through his veins. His body bowed off the ground as the burn consumed him, robbing him of consciousness.

WHEN KIERAN WOKE NEXT, he was in a room the color of the desert at night. Soft grays, dark greens, and deeper blues enveloped him, making him feel like he was lying beneath the stars, the last week a distant and terrible dream.

The complete absence of pain was the first thing he noticed. The second was the lack of dirt.

Kieran abruptly sat, looking around more closely. *Where am I? More importantly, how did I get here?*

The last thing he remembered was searching for the gate. He'd thought he'd found it the last time, but it had only been another of the Vale's many tricks. A mirage to torment an already broken man.

Fate was a cruel bitch. Promising him something, dangling that promise before him for centuries, only to snatch it away once he finally thought he'd found it.

First with Effie. Then with the gate.

Kieran swore softly under his breath, eyes drinking in everything while his thoughts raced, trying to piece together the fragmented memories that were beginning to surface.

There had been voices, which meant people. He'd been rescued? Or was it captured . . .

Standing slowly, Kieran walked around the room, his fingers trailing lightly over the dove-gray walls.

It doesn't look *like a cell.*

It was just an ordinary room. Plain. Unobtrusive. Like it was used for guests, or perhaps waiting for an owner to claim it and give it personality. There was one small table beside the bed he'd been lying on, a braided rug on the ground, and an empty bookcase standing against the opposite wall. That was it.

He spotted the door and moved swiftly, hand reaching for the doorknob. Locked.

Prisoner it is, then.

The breath left him in a whoosh, although he wasn't sure if he was disappointed by the discovery, or relieved. It wasn't exactly like he had anywhere else to go.

With nothing else to do for now, Kieran turned back to the bed, his eye catching something he'd missed before. His belongings were folded and sitting on the ground beside the bed. They'd been washed, and the small pack he'd been carrying was lying on top of the pile. His weapons were nowhere to be found.

Definitely a prisoner.

Retrieving the small bag, he opened it and peered inside, mild surprise flowing through him when he saw that nothing else had been taken. The few coins, stolen prophecy book, and journal the Keepers had given to him were still inside.

He remained hunched over the belongings, his fingers stroking the ancient leather mindlessly before he plucked the book from the pack. He didn't know why he'd kept it. Wasn't like the damned thing had been useful in the end.

Standing, he let the pack drop back to the ground with a soft thud and made his way back to the bed. Sitting down, he opened the book, riffling through the pages without really seeing any of them.

The tome fell open to a familiar page and Kieran scowled as his eyes landed on the string of words that had haunted him ever since he'd first discovered them.

The TMJ prophecy.

He never had figured out what prophecy those letters referred to. Or, if in fact, they were somehow tied to the Shadow Years and their markers.

Kieran slammed the book shut, frustration and anger overtaking the other mess of emotions within him. The taste of failure was like ash in his mouth. After everything he'd done, all in an attempt to win the heart of the woman he'd spent his life loving, he'd lost. None of it had been enough, and worse, he'd destroyed the only home he had left in the process.

Try as he might, Kieran could not ignore the tidal wave of guilt and pain that pummeled him. Sighing gustily, he leaned his head back against the wall, his eyes falling shut. At least if he'd died out there, he could have found some measure of peace. It would have been a relief to be free from the burden of feeling everything, all the time, all at once.

But even that path was closed to him.

Not even death wanted to claim him.

CHAPTER 7

LUCIAN

*R*onan made a better partner than he cared to admit. Between the two of them, they were able to keep Effie hidden from the rest of the survivors—not including the Triumvirate who knew everything. To that end, they took turns guarding the wagon, while Kael remained at the head of their caravan, leading the way into the Broken Vale.

But the time was swiftly approaching when Lucian would no longer be able to keep her existence a secret. His honor would not allow him to place the people of the Broken Vale at risk by bringing one of the Shadow-touched into their city. Not without their consent. He only hoped that when the time came, they would not turn her away.

The Keepers were well into their third day of travel, the humid jungle giving way to arid desert the day prior, and Lucian was ready for a warm meal and real bed. He'd roughed it before, countless times, but never had the emotional toll of his mission had such an effect on him. He was beyond exhausted, and sheer force of will was the only thing keeping him moving.

"You look like shit."

Lucian didn't bother hiding his scowl as he turned to the robed man beside him. "On my worst day, I am still a far cry better looking than you."

The sound of rustling leaves swirled around Lucian, which only deepened his frown. He'd been trudging beside the Triumvirate member Effie referred to as Mirror Two for the better part of an hour. If his patience was frayed before, it was non-existent now.

"So touchy, Guardian."

"Is there a point to your commentary or are you merely seeking to annoy me? I should warn you; it's working."

The rustling sound swelled.

"If you mistook that for anything other than a warning to tread carefully, then you are a greater fool than you realize," Lucian bit out.

"You need to sleep. You're of no use to anyone in this state, least of all your charge."

"I'll sleep once we are safely arrived."

"You know as well as I that it could be days before the members of the Valen Council accept our request for entry into their city. You go on like this much longer; you won't survive the summons."

"Did I ask for your opinion?"

"It's fact, not opinion."

"Don't recall asking for that either."

Lucian could feel Mirror Two's sigh like a gathering storm. The air between them grew heavy. It did little to calm the tempest already raging within him. He was doing his best to keep it leashed—to protect the citadel survivors from the backlash—but he wasn't sure how much longer he could last.

"How is our daughter, by the way?"

"Stop talking. Now."

"Or what? You going to strike me, Guardian? And how would that look?"

"Ask me if I care," Lucian hissed, staring straight ahead.

"We must keep up appearances, dear Lucian. You know how important it is, especially in times of crisis."

Lucian ground his teeth so hard, he could swear the other man heard it. He had more important things to do than worry about standing on ceremony.

"That's what you're for."

"You cannot forget your role in all of this. After all—"

"I am perfectly aware of my role."

These games he was forced to play grated. Yes, they served a purpose, perhaps even an important one, but any possible benefit to such games paled in comparison to what he would lose if he failed in his current mission.

Nothing else mattered. Nothing.

He had to find a way to save Effie.

"Are you? When was the last time—"

"Shut. Up."

The air grew thick once more, and it was difficult to draw a breath.

"You are not the only one who resents the weight of the chains that bind you."

The mention of chains brought Effie to mind, and Lucian's hand spasmed around the hilt of his sword. He didn't recall reaching for it.

"Do not forget your vow, Guardian."

"I've forgotten nothing."

"See that it stays that way."

Lucian glowered at Mirror Two's back as he picked up the pace and moved ahead to torment some other unsuspecting soul. He may have gotten the last word, but it didn't matter. Lucian had made three formal vows in his lifetime. The first when he became a Guardian. The second when he took his post in Elysia. And the third only days earlier.

Of the three, only the last one meant anything.

"How long are those arseholes going to make us wait?" Ronan asked, not for the first time as he took another bite of his meal.

"Don't you remember what happens when you enter someone else's land without invitation?" Reyna chided lightly.

Ronan's lips tipped up. "Hard to forget the day I met you."

Kael gave the pair an amused grin before answering Ronan's question. "They will make us wait as long as they want. The secrets of the Vale are almost as closely guarded as those of the citadel."

"You say this Council must decide whether or not they'll take us in?"

Kael dipped his chin in a nod. "The Valen Council."

"We're hardly a threat in this condition. What's the holdup?"

"Speak for yourself," Kael said.

"Is it a requirement of the Guardians for your arrogance to know no bounds?" Ronan asked, biting off the last of the meat on his skewer.

"Enough," Lucian said, interrupting the verbal pissing match before it could go any further. "This is their land. It will take as long as it takes."

"Don't those hooded bastards have any sway?" Ronan asked, craning his neck around as he searched for a sign of the Triumvirate.

"Where do you think they are right now?" Kael asked.

Lucian shot Kael a pointed glare. The Guardian ignored it, his smile stretching wider.

"They've been gone since we got here. Doesn't seem to be doing any good," Ronan muttered before reaching for his canteen.

Lucian lifted a brow. "We're still alive, aren't we?"

"Seems to me that a request from the Three—especially one made in person—should have expedited the process."

"Who said it didn't?" Kael asked.

"The point of the matter is this, regardless of where the Triumvirate have run off to, or what they're up to, these people aren't going to survive out here much longer. We've barely enough food to last us another three days, and that's already cutting back our daily rations. They deserve a place to rest and come to terms with all that they've lost. We all do."

Lucian stared past Ronan, the Shield's words sinking their hooks in deep. He wasn't wrong. Looking around, he eyed what was left of the travel-weary Keepers and their townsfolk. He spotted Desda offering what was left of her dinner to a man who'd lost his wife and daughter in the attack. These people needed a safe harbor. Somewhere they could start to rebuild what was left of their lives.

"If we do not hear anything by morning, I will go myself," Lucian declared.

Ronan gave him a nod of thanks.

Before Lucian could resume his own meal, a piercing scream shattered the night. His eyes fell closed, dread pooling in his stomach. He knew without looking what the cause of that terror-filled cry must be.

Effie.

Shooting to his feet, Lucian started running toward the wagon. *Please don't let her hurt anyone.* If she survived, that was a blow she would not recover from easily. Casualties during war was one thing. The mindless slaughter of innocents was another entirely.

Before he made it far, Lucian realized the crowd was running in the opposite direction, namely *away* from the supply cart. Never had he been happier or more relieved to be wrong. But if Effie wasn't the one causing the screams . . .

He didn't have a chance to finish the thought before more terrified shouting filled the camp.

"Attack!"

"They've found us!"

Some of the survivors drew their weapons, while others began dropping to their knees, prayers on their lips.

Lucian wasn't immune to fear, although it was rare for something to dig in deep enough to cause it. The possibility of another Shadow attack now, just when they were on the verge of finding a small measure of peace, was such a time.

He scanned the area around the camp, blood surging through him as he prepared for battle. As his heart thundered, his brows began to vee with confusion. There was no way for the Shadows to sneak up on them here. The desert was flat as far as the eye could see—broken up with small sand dunes here and there—but none tall or wide enough to conceal a body, let alone several. A surprise attack would have been all but impossible.

Completing his circle, Lucian found the source of the distress. Five figures dressed in shades of twilight stood on the edge of their camp.

The people of the Vale had finally arrived.

But where did they come from?

After the war that destroyed their city, the people of the Vale saw fit to let the rest of the realm believe them dead. They took to the earth, rebuilding their city beneath the ground. To say they were wary of visitors was like saying Effie was suffering through a summer cold.

After three scorching days, and two near-freezing nights, the Keepers were finally deemed safe. *Or safe enough,* Lucian mentally amended as he sheathed his weapon and strode through the gathered throng to join Kael.

"You were saying?" Kael muttered to Ronan as Lucian reached them.

Coming to a halt, Lucian found the answer to his question. The people of the Vale hadn't approached them from the desert. They'd risen from the ground. Just behind the five figures, the entrance to their underground city glowed with soft light.

"Stand down," Kael ordered, his voice booming through the night. "These people mean us no harm."

"You picked a hell of a time to come," Lucian said by way of greeting.

"It didn't seem fair for your people to suffer out here another night," the man in the middle said.

He looked vaguely familiar, but it had been decades since Lucian had cause to interact with one from the Valen Council, and it could easily be the descendant of a man he'd once met. The speaker had faded orange hair. It might have once been the same color as Ronan's, but time had softened its burn. His skin was near translucent in the moonlight, his eyes a pale gray.

Lucian quickly assessed the strangers flanking the speaker, starting with the younger woman beside him. She was perhaps half the speaker's age and shared his coloring and features. *Daughter . . . and possibly heir.* On her left another man hovered protectively in front of her, not bothering to mask the threat in his dark eyes. *And that would be her mate.*

To the other side was another male-female pair, although where the first couple had the aura of diplomats, these two were clearly soldiers. They did not have the sheer strength or size one usually associated with a warrior, but there was a calculating gleam in their eyes that Lucian recognized. That, combined with the wickedly sharp blades at the end of their polearms, painted a pretty clear picture. It had been a long time since Lucian had used a glaive, and he couldn't help but feel a professional curiosity about their weapons as his eyes returned to the speaker.

"I take it you've accepted our request for asylum," Lucian said.

The man dipped his head. "We have."

"I can't help but notice the representatives we sent to speak with you are absent."

"Already making themselves comfortable below."

Lucian's jaw clenched, but he did not voice his frustration.

Ronan let out a disbelieving laugh.

The speaker lifted a pale orange brow. "That's amusing to you?"

"Just seems to me that our comrades could have as easily been slain as doing as you say. It does not invoke much comfort that you have appeared without them."

The two soldiers at the man's side did not move, but Lucian didn't miss the way their grip tightened on their glaives.

The man's pale gray eyes glittered dangerously in the moonlight. "Are you insinuating that we are murderers, Shield?"

Ronan's eyes widened at the use of his title, but he did not back down. "No. Simply pointing out how this looks to the casual observer."

Lucian was inclined to agree, but he knew Nord. The youngest of the Guardians was as prone to breaking the rules as he was to following them. Often the one left behind while Kael and Lucian took care of various matters, he would absolutely take advantage of the opportunity to eat and bathe before the rest of the group.

Kael and Lucian exchanged a knowing look. Lips pressed together, Kael discreetly shook his head.

"We mean no offense, but it has been a trying time. I'm sure you can understand," Lucian said before Ronan could get them into real trouble.

The man glared at Ronan a second longer before his expression evened out and he nodded. "Of course. Your home was destroyed, your people slaughtered. It stands to reason that your manners would be lacking."

Ronan grunted.

"Gather your people and your belongings. Let's get you settled."

Lucian relaxed at the words, the tension melting from his shoulders as he turned to obey. His relief lasted for a second, maybe even two, before his eyes landed on the wagon. They may have overcome one obstacle, but a bigger, much riskier one still waited.

"Councilman," Lucian called over his shoulder.

"Yes?"

"There's something else we need to discuss."

CHAPTER 8

LUCIAN

The Councilman stared into the wagon, his face leached of the little color it retained.

"You want me to allow that . . . *thing* . . . into my city?"

"Her name is Effie."

Gulping, the older man blinked up at Lucian. "All due respect, Guardian, but that is no woman."

"She is a close friend of the Kiri Helena. We cannot simply abandon her."

"Be that as it may, Guardian. The risk is too high."

"You have my word that no harm will come to your people because of her."

Lucian could read the sympathy in the man's eyes as he replied, "You must care for her deeply, and I have no doubt of your skill, but—"

"Councilman, please . . ." Lucian's hand was wrapped around the other man's wrist. He did not beg. In his position, he rarely needed to. People often obeyed without question, and those that didn't quickly had a change of heart after a little *convincing*.

"How can you be sure your bindings will hold?"

"They have so far. None but a handful even know of her presence. I thought it best until we found a cure."

Effie chose that moment to let out a muffled growl and writhe in her chains. The Councilman flinched and scrambled away from the wagon.

"I don't know . . ."

"You have my word. You know that a Guardian does not give it lightly."

Lucian should have felt bad for placing such a decision at the other man's feet. If their roles were reversed, he would not be half as accepting. Not after what he'd seen in Caederan. Luckily for him, the Councilman had no such references to draw from. He only had Lucian's promise that Effie would not be a threat.

"She stays bound and locked in one of our holding cells at all times. *If* you find the cure you seek, you will perform any rituals locked in the cell with her. Until we are certain she has recovered, she will not set foot outside her cage."

Lucian fought a snarl at the word. It would not be the first time his fledgling had been locked away. And not just in the last handful of days. From what he knew of Effie's upbringing, caging was a form of punishment her parents utilized often. His options were few, but to have to agree to such a thing . . . it rankled.

Vowing to make it up to her if they got through this, Lucian gave a terse nod. "Agreed."

"Guardian . . ."

Lucian braced himself, the Councilman's tone warning enough that he would not like what the man was about to say.

"If you do not find a cure before her transformation is complete, I'll kill her myself."

Rage exploded through Lucian, and his voice dropped to little more than a savage growl. "Touch her and you better wish she's the one that ends you, Councilman. Because if she doesn't that means you'll have to deal with me, and I will not make it quick."

The older man blanched, and there was no missing the stench of fear as it rolled off him.

"If the time comes I, and I alone, will see to her. Do you understand me?" Lucian asked, stepping forward to invade his space.

"Y-yes, Guardian."

"Then it's settled. Show me where we'll be staying."

Gulping, the Councilman called over his shoulder. "Quin, Trinity, take our guests down to the holding cells. Then show the Guardian to his room."

The two Lucian identified as the soldiers peeled away from their perch by the tunnel. They'd remained behind after the last of the Keepers made their way down the ladder to wait for their leader.

Lucian bristled, not wanting them or their weapons anywhere near Effie, but there was no real reason to fight against it either. Sighing, he finally allowed his gaze to lift up to the chained woman. He'd felt her eyes boring into him the entire time he'd spoken with the Councilman. The monster that had taken residence inside of her was sly. Lucian knew that she'd been intrigued by his conversation, curious as to what he had planned for her. It was the only reason she was behaving.

He didn't trust that behavior to last. As soon as he went near her, she would lash out. It would not bode well for him if it appeared that he could not control her.

Heaviness settled in his chest. Lucian couldn't give the Councilman's guards any reason to attack. Without giving himself a chance to second guess himself, Lucian stepped into the wagon.

Effie began to squirm.

Not wanting to give himself away with his words, Lucian stared into the milky orbs that marked her as a Shadow-touched. He searched for any sign of the woman trapped within the monster, but came up empty.

Forgive me, fledgling.

Lunging forward, Lucian brought the hilt of his sword down on her temple. He tried to temper his strength, but he still grimaced when her eyes rolled back in her head and she slumped over.

It was as if he felt the pain of the blow himself. Every time he had to strike her it was the same. She might be the one on the receiving end, but he was the one suffering. He minimized the use of violence with her as much as possible, but it was a necessary evil. Logically, he knew it, but that didn't make it any easier. His soul was procuring quite the collection of scars. By the time this was over, it might be more tattered than the scrap Effie currently clung to.

Bending down, he lifted her up over his shoulder, trying to ignore the changes to her once lush figure. The corruption was spreading, of that there was no doubt. The physical transformation was the slowest, the process subtle but no less terrifying because of it. Each morning when he'd check on her, he'd find some new sign of her deterioration. Lucian was dreading the morning it was complete.

Sucking in a breath, he turned and dropped from the wagon as if nothing happened. He might be trapped in the midst of his own private hell, but no one else needed to know about it. That turmoil was for him alone. It was his penance for failing her in the first place.

"Let's go," he said, voice flat.

Quin and Trinity wore matching blank expressions. If they knew what the creature in his arms was, they gave no indication. Lucian was mildly surprised that the Councilman didn't see fit to fill them in. Perhaps that would come later, once he was well away from the angered Guardian.

"Where shall we find you once we're done, Vance?"

The casual use of the Councilman's name struck Lucian. So far, the people of the Vale had not officially introduced themselves. It could have been intentional or merely an oversight. When it came to members of the Valen Council, anything was possible. Even so, Lucian strongly believed it was the former, if only because it was something he would do.

"I'll be updating the rest of the Council. Meet us in the solarium."

Lucian was intrigued despite himself. "A solarium? Underground?"

The female soldier, Trinity, smirked. "Not familiar with the history of Val'don, Guardian?"

"Should I be?"

She rose to the bait, her smile fading, replaced with something far closer to a sneer. "Your ignorance is disappointing. I thought the

Keepers and their immortal guards were supposed to be people of learning."

Lucian shrugged. "And I was told the people of the Vale's hospitality was surpassed only by their innovation. With the bar you've set thus far, I'm not holding my breath for much in the way of the latter. Guess we'll both have to learn how to live with the disappointment."

Trinity's eyes narrowed.

Quin chuckled, causing the woman to level her scowl on him. "He insults us, and you laugh?"

"Trin, he's goading you."

Her eyes bounced between them before her expression cleared. "Oh."

Quin offered Lucian a friendly grin. "Our ancestors learned how to harvest the power of the sun with mirrors early on. As a desert people, life away from the sun was a blessing and a misery. Since then, we've fine-tuned many of their early tinkerings and made our own advancements, but that one has remained untouched."

"I look forward to discovering some of them during our stay. Perhaps it will help me find an answer to my own riddle."

Quin glanced at Effie. "Would that riddle have anything to do with what happened to her?"

He had to credit the man. There was no discernable fear or disgust in his voice. "Aye."

The soldier nodded. "Well then, let us hope you find the answers you seek."

"I find it hard to believe a Keeper would struggle to find answers to any question."

Lucian glanced at Trinity. "Alas, I'm not a Keeper with their access to prophecy and visions."

She let out a soft, disbelieving, "Hmm."

"Forgive my sister. She can hold a grudge longer than anyone I know."

"I have my share of experience dealing with wounded pride. I think I'll survive hers."

Quin laughed, but Trinity threw him an ugly look.

"I don't like you, Guardian," she stated.

"Stand in line. Not many do."

"I can see why," she hissed.

Lucian had to admit he was enjoying ruffling the woman's feathers. It reminded him of bickering with Effie and had the added benefit of blunting the edge of his temper. Trinity may not realize it yet, but she'd just found herself a new verbal sparring partner. He bared his teeth at her in the barest semblance of a smile.

Trinity's eyes went wide, and she stumbled slightly. His smile must have shown more of his true nature than he'd intended, he thought with a silent chuckle. *Good. At least now the woman realizes who she's dealing with.*

"Trin, enough," her brother said softly. "He and his people have requested sanctuary. They've suffered plenty without having to add your insults to the list."

Cheeks flushing at the reprimand, her eyes dropped to her feet as they reached the opening to the city below.

Peering inside, Lucian's eyes landed on an illuminated set of stairs that curved down, following the wall until it disappeared from view.

"Can you manage with her in your arms?" Quin asked with a raised brow.

Lucian nodded once. While the steps were steep, they would hardly present a challenge. He'd navigated worse while holding something far less valuable in his arms.

Trinity hadn't waited for Lucian to reply. She was taking the stairs two at a time, the top of her head already disappearing into the ground.

"After you," Quin murmured, waving Lucian forward.

His instincts raged against allowing an armed stranger at his back, but Lucian forced himself forward. For Effie, there wasn't much he wouldn't subject himself to. Especially when it was something that bought him another day with her. Or, if not with her exactly, at least it provided him with more time to find a way to save her. To find a way to bring her back. For that, Lucian would give anything.

The grief that was never far from the surface roared to life at the reminder of what was at stake. Not that he'd forgotten, that would be impossible, but with enough effort he managed to push it to the furthest recesses of his mind for a while. He had to. It was the only way he could continue to function.

If he let it, the pain would become a gaping chasm inside him, pushing him off the edge of sanity and straight into madness. There was no telling what he'd do if that happened. If he lost control and allowed the despair to take over. A man with his power? It wasn't a far leap to fear the worst.

A small shudder slid down his spine at the thought of losing control. Not just because of the irrevocable damage he would inevitably do, but because of what it would take to send him there. If Lucian gave in to the violence begging to be unleashed, it meant that Effie was gone.

Forever.

And if that was the case, no one would be able to stop him from tearing Elysia apart. That was no metaphorical threat. As a Guardian, he could weave together the strands of life, but so too could he break them. It would take less effort than releasing a sigh. With his power fully unchecked, Lucian could unmake the world.

"Guardian?"

From the exasperation fused into the title, it was clear that was not the first time Quin had called him.

Lucian was frozen on the second to last stair, his foot suspended in the air mid-step. Clearing his throat, he descended the last of the stairs and stepped to the side, making space for Quin to do the same.

Trinity was eyeing him, doing nothing to conceal the curiosity in her gaze. Lucian ignored it. Let her wonder. If she managed to stumble upon the nightmares that consumed him, she was welcome to them. Lucian sure as shit didn't want them.

He scanned the narrow hallway jutting off from the landing they were standing on. It had been decades since he'd last had reason to come to Val'don. So far, the hidden city was as unremarkable as it was unfamiliar. But the only constant in life was change, so that did not surprise him.

"I don't recall this area from my last visit," Lucian murmured when he felt both siblings' eyes on him.

"Val'don is like a hive. We are constantly extending its reach."

Lucian nodded, he remembered as much.

"This is one of the back entrances to the city itself. Go to the right; it will lead you to the residential wings by way of the dining hall."

"And the left?" Lucian asked, although given the Councilman's earlier orders he already had a pretty good idea.

"The left will lead us to the gaol."

Lucian felt his body tense, but managed to keep his face impassive. He knew Effie would have to be kept somewhere secure and guarded, but she was not a criminal. Not really.

"Let's go," he said finally, feeling a muscle tick in his jaw.

This time, Quin took the lead. Trinity was just behind Lucian, almost at his side, as if she was walking beside a friend and not escorting a potential threat. Any other time, Lucian might have appreciated the effort.

Ignoring his guards, Lucian focused on creating a mental map. He would need to know how to make it back here on his own. From the little he could see, this part of Val'don was more bunker than city. The walls and floors were the same muted gray, illuminated only by a string of lights that ran along the ceiling. As he watched, one of the lights brightened to a blinding white before flickering twice and dimming back to the soft orange of the others. Squinting, he tried to identify the source of the light.

"Star motes," Trinity murmured. Lucian's expression must have conveyed his lack of recognition because she added, "In ancient times, it was believed that the glowing motes were fragments of fallen stars. Now we know that they are just small bugs with the ability to light themselves up once the sun sets. The mirrors provide more than enough illumination during the day, and the star motes take over at night."

"How do the creatures stay alive if they are confined?"

Quin's answering grin shone with pride. "One of our more intricate advancements."

Lucian raised a brow, shifting Effie in his arms.

"Impulse based translocation."

Lucian blinked.

"Transverse orientation?" Quin tried again.

Lucian stared.

Flushing slightly, Quin explained, "It's similar to the atmospheric replication we use in the city proper, but on a much smaller more nuanced scale."

Fluent in over seventeen languages—many long since obsolete—Lucian had no clue what the other man was blathering about. It sounded like he was just stringing random words together.

"We found a way to use their natural instincts to our benefit."

"Why didn't you just say that to begin with?"

"I thought I did," the other man mumbled.

Trinity jumped in. "The star motes are drawn to the orbs. We were able to recreate the atmospheres found within their nests. Once the sun goes down, it emits a powerful pheromone that helps the star motes find their way home."

"Why would they need help when light literally shines out of their arses?"

"They're blind," Quin answered as if it was obvious.

"Go figure." Lucian shook his head. "All right, so you trick them into believing your orbs are their nests in order to light up your hallways at night."

Quin rubbed the back of his neck. "Basically."

"And during the day?"

"They come and go as they please. It's a perfectly harmless process."

Lucian wasn't sure manipulating creatures into believing they were home when they were actually enslaved was really harmless, but it wasn't his place to say. Mind snagging on something else that Quin said, Lucian asked, "And this is what you call atmospheric replication?"

Quin and Trinity nodded.

"You use it throughout Val'don?"

"Exactly. The earth was never meant to be inhabited in this way, at least not this deep below its surface. Our ancestors had to find a way to modify it so that our people could safely survive down here. That meant purifying the air and water, filtering out any harmful substances and increasing the amount of those we need, ensuring that the nutrients we needed to grow food were present in the appropriate amounts, and so forth . . ." Quin trailed off, looking uncomfortable under the intensity of Lucian's stare.

"And in all this time the land has never rebelled?" Lucian asked, impressed despite himself. He knew better than anyone the amount of magic required to make something resist its own nature.

"It might be easier to understand if we show you. Perhaps tomorrow?" Quin offered.

Lucian nodded his agreement immediately. "Yes, I think I would like to see how you've managed this feat."

There was an undercurrent of awareness that had pushed itself to the surface during the man's explanation. Lucian was practically vibrating with the force of it. Instinct informed almost all of his decisions; he would not ignore its pull now. He'd come here hoping for asylum, yes, but also for answers.

Somehow, the people of the Vale held the key, and Lucian wasn't leaving until he had it.

CHAPTER 9

LUCIAN

"Here we are," Quin said, standing outside a twelve-by-twelve cell.

A low growl sounded in Lucian's throat before he could stifle it. Three of the four walls were encased in jagged stone, the fourth was made of metal bars the size of his wrist. While its stone floors were surprisingly clean and it was larger than he expected, within it there was nothing save a bucket and a coarse-looking blanket.

Quin looked apologetic as he unlocked the door and swung it open. "We aren't in the habit of needing to . . . detain people who deserve grander accommodations."

Trinity's eyes were focused on Effie as Lucian crossed the threshold and carefully lowered her body to the floor. She clearly did not believe Effie fell under such a category.

"Who else besides you two holds a key to this cell?" Lucian asked, his voice low and angry as he stood to face them once more.

"There's only a handful of keys that will grant access to this part of Val'don. Councilman Vance holds one, my sister and I as the head of the security detail hold two more. The last are shared by those that rotate through the night guard shift."

"I am going to need those keys."

Trinity's eyes narrowed. "No."

"I wasn't asking."

Cheeks bright with anger, she opened her mouth, but her brother cut her off. "For the safety of our people, you must understand why we are hesitant to grant your request."

"If you think the lack of a key will bar my entry, you clearly know nothing of a Guardian's power. I want to ensure no one else has access to this cell. She looks harmless enough for the moment, but make no mistake, she is as clever as she is deadly. She will only grow more so as the days pass. I will not risk your people falling victim to her deception."

Quin paled, his eyes dropping to Effie's chains and lingering at the red scrap of fabric around her mouth.

"Yes, even chained and gagged she remains a threat."

"Do you not need to feed her?"

Lucian let his silence answer for him.

"If she is so dangerous, Guardian," Trinity spat, "why bring her here at all?"

Feeling every year of his age, Lucian's eyes met hers. "Because it is the only way to save her."

Trinity's expression softened, and though she didn't voice it, he could clearly see the question burning in her gaze. *Can she even be saved?*

"Very well, Guardian. If she is as dangerous as you say, we will agree to your demand."

Lucian gave Quin a nod of thanks. "Would you two mind giving me a minute?"

The siblings exchanged an uneasy look before nodding and moving back out the massive metal door that marked the gaol's entrance.

Dropping to a knee, Lucian crouched beside Effie's unconscious form. If not for the gaunt cast of her face, or dull sheen of her hair, he could have believed she was still whole. Still his.

Lucian brushed his knuckles across her cheek, leaning down to press his lips to her forehead. Eyes falling closed, he sucked in a ragged breath. It took everything he had left to lift his head up from hers and rise back to his full height. His heart demanded he stay and curl himself around her, protecting her in her vulnerable state. His mind shouted for him to get the hell away before she came to.

Although it tore him apart, Lucian exited the cell and shut the door. The click of the lock echoed around him, causing his jaw and fists to clench.

Even though she couldn't hear him, or care if she did, Lucian couldn't leave without promising, "I'll be back to check on you tomorrow." Swallowing, he silently added, *one way or the other, fledgling, this needs to end. I fear what will become of us otherwise.*

~

*E*FFIE

D*ISORIENTATION LINGERED,* momentarily muting the dull throb of pain that emanated from her arms and head. Something had pulled her from the darkness, but she could not say what.

Slowly, she took stock of her surroundings, starting with her body. The soft scrape against her wrists told her she was still bound, even without the all-too-familiar clink of chains. Her mouth was raw where the damp fabric had chafed the skin. Sucking in an angry breath through her nose, she rolled to her knees, eyes open into slits as she regarded her newest cage.

There. Something in the air.

Sniffing again, she struggled to make sense of the smell.

Damp. Earth . . . underground?

But that wasn't all. There was another scent in the air. It called to her, wrapped itself around her and sunk its claws in deep. It made her want to purr—no. Cry?

Confused, she whimpered. Nothing was making sense.

As awareness grew, her head throbbed, the pain slicing through the rest of the fog in her mind. A low growl sounded in her throat when she caught the unfamiliar scent again.

Midnight. Musk.

Her growl deepened.

She didn't like the way the scent twisted her emotions, making her feel weak and scared. Or that she couldn't identify it. In the end, it didn't matter. There's only one reason for another's smell to be in her cage.

It marked her captor.

Enemy.

The need for revenge built inside of her, bubbling up until it spilled over; the only thing she could understand. No one caged her.

Not unless they wanted to die.

Her eyes closed at the memory of tearing into tender flesh, the hot spray of blood dripping down her chin. Her stomach grumbled at the thought of metallic tang. *So hungry.* The need was nearly unbearable.

Another whiff had her groaning with savage want, the desire to sink her teeth into her enemy and until she was bloated with his blood all-consuming.

Delicious.

She crooned the word, mouth salivating at the thought.

This one would pay for his crimes, but not before she tasted him. She would not let him die until she feasted on his still-beating heart.

Scooting back, she pressed into the wall. Something sharp poked her and she shifted, her neck swiveling slowly as she eyed the jagged rock.

Another low rumble sounded, this one filled with satisfaction. There was little she could do about the chains, but it took only a few tries sawing the cloth against the edge to pierce through the gag around her mouth. She didn't stop when the rock raked against her flesh, just adjusted her position and continued with her slow progress. Soon the smell of her own blood filled the air, but it did not dissuade her.

She didn't stop until the fabric sagged and fell down her neck, collaring her like some kind of defiant necklace. Feeling vindicated, she spat the wad of cloth from her mouth onto the floor. Licking her cracked lips, she bared her teeth, the feral smile a sinister promise.

He would come and she would feast. A creature such as herself did not need use of her hands to be a threat. Her bite was her greatest weapon, and she'd just stolen it back.

Pressing herself back into the darkest part of the room, she waited. Her hunger and need for revenge thumped through her with each slow beat of her heart. Hours passed, the tantalizing aroma of her target—the focus of both her desires—her sole companion. It was a scent she memorized until she knew every facet of it. She would recognize it anywhere.

Now, even if he ran, she would find him. She would never stop hunting him. Not until he slaked the need burning in her veins.

He was marked, and only death would free him.

CHAPTER 10

LUCIAN

Impatience battered at Lucian, pushing him to walk faster even as his fingers fumbled to tighten the belt slung low on his hips. He'd lain in bed until he couldn't stand the silence—or his own company—any longer. He was beyond exhausted; the days since the battle merging together in one never-ending blur, but sleep never came. Not for him. When your soul was haunted, there could be no peace.

Quin had told Lucian to meet him in the commons when he was ready for his tour. That was where he headed now, his strides long and sure despite his restless night. Before Lucian reached the archway that signified the official separation of the guest quarters and the public areas, he was flanked by two men in scarlet robes.

Lucian ignored them. Or he tried to.

"Guardian."

"We require a word with you."

"It will have to wait."

"Lucian."

His name, so filled with exasperation, in the Triumvirate's serpentine hiss brought him up short. As a rule, the Three unerringly relied on the formality of titles; never names. At least not when they

69

were acting in their official capacity. It added to the mystique of their position, but in reality, it was just another link in the chain of duty that bound them. If their robes were donned, they were slaves to a law older than even them. But no one ever saw that. They only saw power. Feared it, even as they craved it for their own.

As if any knew what they really asked for . . .

"What?" he demanded, turning to finally face them. Not that there was anything to see, hooded as they were.

"We've come to join you this morning."

"We wish to witness this weave you spoke of."

Centuries of experience told Lucian there would be no talking them out of it. *Stubborn bastards.* It didn't stop him from trying. He was just as obstinate. "We don't even know if there's anything to find."

"That's not what you indicated in your report last night."

"You said they hold the key."

"Might," Lucian immediately corrected. "I said they *might* hold the key."

The figure on the right—Effie's Mirror Two—shrugged. *"For a Guardian it is one and the same. You would not have mentioned it otherwise."*

Lucian's jaw clenched and an angry breath hissed out between his teeth. "Why are you really here?"

Mirror One tilted his head as if the answer should be obvious. *"Is the potential solution to the corruption that plagues us not enough?"*

"When it comes to you, it is never that simple. Or altruistic," Lucian added, his voice bitter and tight.

They were here to play nursemaid. To ensure that Lucian didn't rush off to attempt something on his own. They didn't trust him. Nor should they. If he did, in fact, find the answer he needed during his tour of Val'don, he'd be down in the cell with Effie before anyone drew their next breath.

"Can you blame us?"

"You would risk much for something that could spectacularly backfire."

Lucian took a step forward, his face all but pressing into the shadowed depth of the other man's hood as the words poured from him. "Can you blame *me*? You know. You *know* what she is to me. What that means. Would you really try to stop me from saving her?"

"No, Luc. You know we would never stand between you and your true purpose."

"Then *why*?" he asked, his voice tortured.

"We need to be sure it will work before we can let you try."

Lucian let out a low growl. "We won't know if it will work until we try."

"And we cannot risk you becoming corrupted for the sliver of a chance."

"You are too powerful, Guardian. Under that kind of influence there's no telling—"

"Trust me," Lucian said, his voice menacing, "if she dies because we did nothing, I can tell you *exactly* what will happen."

The silence stretched between them as Lucian's heart raced and the sound of blood filled his ears.

"Consider us warned."

"But it does not change anything. We will come, and if we feel that the magic is sound, then you may attempt it."

Lucian laughed, but there was no humor in it. It was a dark, manic sound. "I am not asking permission. She is my responsibility. I will take whatever risk I deem necessary. No one, not even the Triumvirate, will stand in my way." He was practically vibrating with his fury. "You don't want to find out what happens if you try."

He was a hairsbreadth away from losing control entirely. Lucian forced himself to turn around, before the violence within him snapped free from its tether. He'd meant what he said. He would slay anyone that tried to keep him from her. That didn't mean he wouldn't regret it later, once sanity returned to him—if it ever did. He was already teetering on the brink of madness.

There was nothing left to say. They were at an impasse. The Triumvirate were determined to try to wrangle him, and Lucian had no intention of being restrained.

He stalked toward the meeting place, the whisper of robes brushing against the floor trailing his every step.

~

"GUARDIAN, I was just wondering when you'd make an appearance." Quin greeted him with a broad smile.

Still on edge from his confrontation in the hall, Lucian could only manage a tight-lipped one of his own in return.

Quin's eyes widened slightly when he saw the two members of the Triumvirate step into place beside him. "I didn't realize this would be a group tour."

"Neither did I," Lucian said, not bothering to hide his annoyance.

Rubbing his hands together, Quin pushed himself up from the desk he was seated behind. "Well, the more the merrier. Shall we be off?"

Lucian answered by stepping away from the door.

"I thought it best if I show you the hub"—he turned to look over his shoulder—"that's what we call the center of the city. It's where all the action is. It's also the best example of what you were asking about yesterday."

"Your atmospheric . . ."

"Replication," Quin supplied with a nod. "Exactly."

"You've found a way to recreate the atmosphere from the surface."

Quin's back stiffened at the intrusion in his mind, but he forced an answering smile. "Yes."

"How?"

"Well, that's what I wanted to show you. I think it's easier to understand if you can see it."

Lucian's brows dipped, but he followed the man further into the city. Val'don was coming to life around him. With each step, the sounds of people going about their day grew louder. The simple gray interior gave way to architectural marvels that would have been impressive above ground. Down here, they were miracles.

The city was sprawling, stretching far past what Lucian's eye could see. He'd been to Val'don before, but never this deep into its heart. He had no idea what the people of the Vale had been hiding.

"Welcome to the real Val'don," Quin murmured, pride shining in his eyes as he watched them take in all his city had to offer.

The earth had been excavated, towering buildings scattered along its surface, with more shops and offshoots dug into the walls that encircled the whole of the city. In its center, shooting all the way from the ground up to the . . . *sky.* Lucian blinked, shocked at what he was seeing. A massive structure, its numerous archways illuminated the same brilliant blue of a midday. Its details were beyond intricate, the delicate domes and spires seemingly made from glass.

"How?" he breathed, echoing the Triumvirates' earlier question.

"What do you know of our powers?" Quin asked.

"Not enough, apparently."

Quin chuckled. "The strength of my people has always been our adaptability. We were always willing to learn about other cultures, take what they had already perfected and use it as our own. It is what originally incensed the Chosen and had us declared one of the Forsaken. They did not like that we *desecrated*"—Quin rolled his eyes —"what the Mother had seen fit to gift us."

Lucian rubbed his chin, the story sounding vaguely familiar.

"What they call desecration, we call advancement. In its basest form, our magic is tied to nature. Using what we learned from others, we were able to modify that power, strengthen it."

"Modify?"

Quin nodded, eyes bright. "Outside of Elysia there are many practitioners of magic. It is not something they are born with, as we are, but something that they can call upon and control. They use a series of spells or rituals to tap into the power of the world around them. Using their spells, we are able to harness and employ our natural gifts in new and amazing ways."

"If you already possess power, why would you need to tap into other sources?"

Quin gestured to the city thriving below them. "You see what is possible when hundreds combine their strength. Now imagine what is possible when each of those people is capable of what you see before you on their own."

A current of foreboding skittered through Lucian at the possibilities. In the wrong hands, such power could be catastrophic.

If the low cast of the voices in his mind were any indication, the Triumvirate shared his concerns.

"Dangerous to play with such forces."

"If they were to lose control . . ."

Quin's expression did not change, so the Triumvirate had not broadcasted their thoughts with him. His smile did falter slightly, however, when no one seemed to share his enthusiasm.

"We take every precaution when performing new rituals," he rushed to assure them. "We do not want to put our citizens at risk. We only seek to find advancements that make all our lives better."

Lucian nodded, his eyes narrowed thoughtfully as he peered at the city.

"Water, for example. There were many underground streams, but the runoff from the destruction above had tainted them. We found a purification spell that allowed us to provide fresh drinking water. With it we've been able to filter out what does not belong. The same with the air and the earth. With the added boost from the ritual, we need only strengthen the magic every decade or so."

Could it be that simple? Lucian's mind was racing, his attention riveted on the man before him. "Where do the impurities go?"

"The Nether," Quin said with a shrug.

Lucian went completely still. "Nether?"

Quin's eyes bounced between them, shock registering briefly on his face when he realized they were not familiar with the word. "Surely you jest?" He laughed uncomfortably before sputtering, "H-how could you not have heard of it?"

"Humor us," Lucian said.

Cheeks tinged red, Quin explained, "It is a world tied to our own, existing alongside us, connected as counterbalance."

The longer he spoke, the faster Lucian's mind spun. Fragments of ancient text fluttered through his mind as a tornado of emotion tore through him. A solution was just out of grasp, but not for much longer. This was it. He was on the precipice of discovery.

"It is the birthplace of nothingness. If our world is one of life, the Nether is one of death."

Breath stuttered from his lungs as answers came crashing into being. "For everything there is balance . . ." he whispered.

"Fire and Water."

"Air and Earth."

"Spirit and . . . Nether," Lucian finished.

Power blazing forth, Lucian cast his eyes over Val'don, truly seeing it for the first time. The strongest of the Chosen could see the various elemental powers as colors, but for Lucian, life in any form was comprised only of golden light. That's why the threads of onyx liberally streaking through the city stood out in such sharp contrast. It was nothing like the inky black dissonance of the corruption, but it was similar enough that Lucian finally understood where it had originated. Unlike the corruption, these onyx threads were not seeking to destroy. They were part of the weave itself, existing in perfect harmony.

More explanations fluttered at the edges of his awareness, but there would be time to explore them later. For now, Lucian needed to make sense of what the presence of onyx threads meant.

"You've learned how to harness Nether."

Quin's brows pulled together in confusion. "No."

"No?" Lucian asked, snapping his attention back to the soldier.

Quin flinched at the power pouring from his eyes, but Lucian did not pull it back. He wasn't done with it yet.

"There is nothing to harness. The Nether is a void. Nothingness. It is where we send that which we do not need."

"That may have been true . . . once," Lucian murmured.

"I-I'm sorry?"

"Did your ancestors use the Nether to help with their excavations while building Val'don?" Lucian asked instead.

Quin shrugged. "I'm not sure. It's possible."

"If that's so, then they sent *something* into a place where *nothing* should exist. They warped its purpose, and in doing so, created something new."

Quin was shaking his head. "Anything that goes into the Nether is destroyed. Nothing can exist there. It's impossible."

Lucian hummed low in his throat. It was clear Quin believed what he was saying, but that didn't make it true. Lucian was staring at the proof of the opposite right now. As with all magic, the Nether had left its trace. While it may have come from the void, when called into their realm, it too was transformed. Called into being. Now it was part of the weave.

"What do you see, Guardian?"

Lucian ignored the question, still focused on Quin. "I'm going to need you to show me the spells you used. The ones that cast out the impurities."

His answering nod was a sharp jerk. "Sure. I just need to notify the Council. They maintain all of our records."

"You do that." When the man didn't move, Lucian bit off a growled, "Now."

"R-right, I'll be right back."

Lucian watched him retreat before addressing the Triumvirate's earlier question. "The Nether is interwoven in the very essence of this place."

"How is that possible?"

"When the people of the Vale called it forth during their rituals, intentionally or not, they called the Nether into *being*. Transforming it."

"They gave it substance."

"Aye. Its presence here indicates that something tangible has been cast out. It is the echo of what once existed, although invisible without a gift such as mine."

"You think we can utilize the Nether."

"To cast out the corruption?"

"It makes sense, doesn't it? At its core, the corruption is based in Spirit. Nether is its balance. If we cannot use Spirit to combat it, as Helena does, we will use Nether."

"Do you really think it will work?"

Lucian gestured behind him. "They've already proven that it has. You heard the man, whatever is sent into the void is destroyed. Similarly, whatever fragments of Nether that were called into our world have been spelled into being. Each world has its own natural laws, which supersede any others, so while the Nether is a void in its natural state, here it is given substance and woven into existence."

"Guardian, that only solves one problem. Removing the corruption only keeps it from spreading. It does not undo the effects."

"Anything with substance can be altered," Lucian said, his eyes glittering as a smile stretched across his face. If there was anything a Guardian understood, it was the art of transformation.

"Lucian . . ."

"I know how to save her."

CHAPTER 11

KIERAN

Kieran stood from the table, leaving his plate for someone else to deal with. After days of solitude, he'd finally been allowed to leave his room. Apparently he'd been deemed safe enough to allow outside. That didn't mean the people of the Vale welcomed him.

Quite the opposite.

They gave him a wide berth whenever he walked among them. He was a stranger, and his claim of amnesia did little to invite trust.

Not that he cared.

All that mattered was making sure no one could associate him with the massacre in Bael.

Head down, Kieran made the trek back to his room. Now that he'd been granted his freedom, he found he had nothing to do with it.

The sounds of a whispered, albeit heated, argument reached his ears. Kieran glanced up, keeping his face carefully neutral.

"You offered to do *what*?" the female shrieked, her hands fisted at her sides.

"What is the harm, Trin? You know better than anyone that seeing a spell hardly means you know how to perform it," her male companion replied calmly.

"That's worse! They are going to dabble in something they don't understand. Here. In our home. They're as likely to bring the entirety of Val'don falling down around us as they are to actually be successful in their endeavors. Who knows? Maybe that's what they've been intending all along," she finished with a hiss.

Kieran frowned. It would seem he was not the only one visiting the Vale. Inching closer, he dropped to his knee and pretended to retie his boot.

The man snorted. "As if the Triumvirate would come in person if that was their intent. Their people are *suffering*, Trin. They are the victims."

Kieran was frozen in place, his heart pounding in his chest, and his fingers started to tremble. They were here. The very people he was trying to escape. *Did they track me? Do they know?*

"The Guardian is merely seeking a way to save that woman," he continued.

"What do we even know about her, besides the fact that she is clearly dangerous? Councilman Vance wouldn't have insisted on locking her up otherwise."

The man laughed again. "Did you see how slight she was, Sister? Barely larger than a child. I am sure they exaggerated so that we would toe the line."

Kieran peeked through the curtain of his hair in time to watch the woman cross her arms over her chest. His entire body was quaking, his lungs struggling to draw in air. There was only one woman with that description the Guardians would be worried about.

"As if the Guardian would need to exaggerate to get his point across. Did you see how she was bound? Tiny or no, no one his size wastes time with chains that big—or a gag for that matter—if they are not trying to contain an actual threat."

His thoughts were fractured, the words swimming around in his mind without making any sense. *The way they were talking, Effie . . . but that would mean . . . No!*

A horrible, keening wail filled his mind. He threw out a hand, trying to catch himself before he toppled over. *What have I done?*

He'd sought to punish her and ended up condemning her to a fate far worse than death. In his rage, Kieran had managed to destroy the one thing he'd ever truly loved.

Gasping, he pushed to his feet, staggering as he started forward.

"Hey, are you okay?" the man asked.

Kieran waved him off, heading for the only exit he'd managed to locate during his wanderings.

If the Keepers were here, if they'd figured out what he'd done . . . He couldn't stay. He didn't *deserve* to stay. If she was gone, there was nothing left to live for anyway. If he was condemned to die for his sins, better he risk his fate at the hands of the Mother than leave himself to face the wrath of the Guardians.

Maybe the right thing to do would be to turn himself in, to allow Lucian to tear him limb from limb, but Kieran never had managed to learn how to do the right thing. He was too selfish, driven by desire and ruled by his emotions.

His thoughts were spiraling, each new one making less sense than the last. The only thing he knew was that he needed to get out.

Now.

There was no time to gather his handful of belongings. If he had any hope of surviving this—not that he was sure he even wanted to— he had to leave.

So Kieran did what he did best.

He fled.

CHAPTER 12

LUCIAN

The Councilman stood with his arms crossed, his expression, while not openly hostile, was hardly friendly. There was entirely too much suspicion in his narrow-eyed gaze.

They'd spent the last twenty minutes going back and forth. Lucian was about to slam the man's face into a wall and simply take what he needed. He probably would have already, if he didn't need someone to translate the intricate symbols scrawled in the slender book sitting on the table in front of them.

"Let me just get this clear. You want to blindly test one of our spells on your *charge*, in the hopes that it fixes whatever has taken over her."

Lucian clenched his jaw. "I already told you. It would not be a blind test—"

"Oh, so you've done this before, then. You know exactly what the outcome should be?"

"I seek to remove what does not belong. Your head guard has already indicated that you have at least one powerful purification spell. That, combined with a Guardian's innate abilities, should be more than enough to revert whatever the Shadow's bite has accomplished."

Vance canted his head, his eyes unreadable. "Based on what you've told us of the Shadow-touched and the corruption working its way across the realm, I don't see how—"

"You don't have to. Just give me what I need and let me be on my way. I am wasting time she does not have."

"Have you even considered what will happen if you're wrong?"

"It is a rare enough occurrence that I am willing to risk it."

Something that could have been amusement flashed in the other man's eyes, but it was gone too quickly to know for sure. "You would risk her life on it?"

"Aye," Lucian bit out, hardly daring to breathe.

The Councilman sighed. "I guess that tells me everything I need to know."

Finally.

Lifting the book from the table, he started to flip through the pages. "It is not mere purification you seek. You mean to neutralize and expel. This one"—he twisted the book around and tapped a finger on a page —"is the one I recommend."

Lucian reached for the book, but Vance tugged it just out of range.

"I feel I would be remiss not to remind you that this is a life you are playing with. While I do not doubt that the spell will work—or your considerable power—we've never had to worry about the potential consequences of accidentally removing something vital. And well, frankly, you've never done this at all."

Leaning forward so as to look him straight in the eye, Lucian unleashed the grief that had consumed him since discovering what had become of Effie. "Do you really think that given everything we've been through to get her here, I would fuck it up now?"

Vance's eyes went wide with shock. "You're in love with her," he whispered. "I didn't realize."

"Love is for mortals. It is far too simplified an emotion for what happens when a Guardian finds the one who makes his soul sing."

Eyes cloudy with confusion, the Councilman asked, "A mating bond?"

Lucian sighed, not about to debate the intricacies of the *fuj d'âme* with him. "If that helps you understand the depth of my devotion to her, then fine. Call it what you will. Can we get on with this now?"

"Of course, Guardian. Let me gather what you will need."

His knees almost buckled with the force of his relief, but Lucian remained upright. If he'd known invoking the mating bond would have had the Councilman jump to aid him, he would have claimed it as soon as they arrived in the Vale.

Vance placed a few colorful jars on the table, speaking as he worked. "I will go with you and help set up—"

"No."

"No?" he repeated, hurried movements pausing as he risked a glance at Lucian. "But it's the safest way. One thing out of place—"

"I cannot allow you to set foot inside that cell, Councilman. You will tell me what I need to do."

Vance wanted to argue. It was obvious in the pursed set of his lips, but he must have seen the futility of it because he simply grabbed a piece of parchment and started sketching what appeared to be a map.

"You will be amplifying your own power by invoking the elements. These items are physical representations of each of them. They need to be placed in precise locations throughout the cell before you begin."

Lucian peered at the jars more carefully, trying to discern what they contained, but the contents were unfamiliar.

"The colors correspond with the elements. I'm assuming you are aware of the pairings."

Lucian gave a sharp nod, barely managing to keep from rolling his eyes.

"Good." Gesturing to the map again, Vance placed his finger beside one of four dots and started moving it in a circular fashion. "One by one, starting from the northern point, you are going to open the jars and do the following." Vance mimed pouring something into his hand and pressed his closed fist first to his forehead, then to his lips, and finally to the center of his chest. "As you do so you will repeat the following words: *apertum, roboro, incipere.*"

As he spoke, Vance performed the motions again, one word for each of the three gestures. Once he was done, he looked at Lucian expectantly.

"*Apertum, roboro, incipere.* I got it."

"After you complete your circle, you will move to the center of the room where your girl should be placed before you begin. Then you will start the final invocation. It is imperative you enunciate these words exactly as I show you. I've written them here phonetically for you as well."

Lucian glanced at the paper and nodded to show that he understood. "Pour out the jars, say the words, then what?"

The Councilman looked mildly aggrieved. "Then with any luck the force of the elements will be yours to command. While you speak the words, you will need to picture in your mind that which you wish to eliminate. You will repeat the invocation five times, each time imagining that the impurities are being pulled out of the source."

"I can do you one better," Lucian said with the ghost of a grin. "I don't need to imagine anything. I'll be looking right at it."

Vance blinked. "Well, yes, I suppose that will be more effective."

"So that's it; that's everything? Sprinkle some dust, mumble some words, picture the corruption leaving her body and it's done?"

"Not quite. After the final repetition, hold the image of what remains in your mind. Focus wholly on it until you are certain that is *all* that remains. Then, and only then, will you release the elements."

Lucian shrugged. "Sounds easy enough."

The Councilman's voice took on the air of a teacher attempting to impart a serious warning. "The process may sound simple, Guardian, but you will be channeling incredibly potent magic. One wrong uttering, and things will get away from you. That much power…the results could be catastrophic. So you cannot lose focus, not even for a moment."

"I won't."

Vance studied him, his eyes searching Lucian's face before he finally said, "All right then." Packing away the map and the jars, he held them out to Lucian. "May the Mother aid your quest."

"The Mother allowed this to happen in the first place. So if you don't mind, I'd rather leave Her out of it."

If he was scandalized, the Councilman did not show it. He merely dipped his head. "Then I shall see you when it's done."

~

LUCIAN STOOD outside of Effie's cage, hands braced on the bars. She was no longer lying where he'd left her. He lifted his eyes from the scrap of red and peered into the darkness at the back of her cell.

"I know you're awake."

A soft snarl sounded at his words, the clinking of chains overloud in the relative silence.

Lucian braced himself. He wasn't entirely sure what was waiting for him inside, but he knew it was going to haunt him long after he was done here.

"I'm coming in."

Why he felt the need to announce his next move he couldn't say, except that if he talked to her like she was still human, it made her seem like less of a monster.

There was another clink before a slow continuous melody filled the cell. It took him a heartbeat to catalog the sound as chains running against stone.

Closing his eyes, Lucian filled his lungs with air. Before he could save her, he was going to have to disable her.

Again.

He had a feeling this time it wasn't going to be a simple matter of knocking her unconscious. She was lying in wait, a predator ready to strike. Perhaps he shouldn't have made Ronan and Kael wait for him down at the other end of the hallway. Three against one were certainly better odds, but he'd wanted privacy for what he was about to do.

Lucian lifted his head, anticipation spiraling through his veins. When he opened his eyes they swirled with bronze fire and a grim smile curled his lips.

No one said he had to fight fair.

Power surged through him and between one breath and the next, Lucian walked through the bars as if they were no more substantial than smoke. If she somehow managed to take him out, he didn't want her to be able to escape.

Chains jostled as she shifted, mirroring his steps in some macabre imitation of a dance. Barely any of her essence's natural radiance was left. Instead of the intricate and blinding light he'd seen the first time he'd looked at her, there was only pulsing darkness filled with a dozen flickering golden beads. It was almost like staring at the night sky as the stars slowly faded from view.

It was worse than he realized. Barely anything was left of her.

He was out of time.

Shuffling footsteps echoed around them as she took the first step toward him. Lucian ran his fingers along one of the bars, pulling a section the length of his forearm free and hurling it at her in one fluid motion. As the piece of metal flew through the air, he continued to manipulate it. By the time it reached her, it was flattened and curved, its pointed ends sliding through the wall behind her as easily as if it were made of butter. The only thing stopping it from sliding straight through the rock was Effie's throat—and Lucian's power.

There was a garbled shriek as she realized she was trapped, his metal collar kissing her neck and locking her in place. Howling with rage, she started squirming in earnest.

Lucian ignored her and turned to pull Vance's bag of ingredients through the bars. Checking the map a final time, he started setting things in place. That much handled, he glanced back at Effie. He needed to get her from the wall to the floor without getting close enough to allow her to take a chunk out of him.

She bared her teeth at him as he crossed the cell to stand in front of her. Lifting his hand, he ran it along the cool surface of the metal, careful to stay out of range of her mouth. As his hand moved, so too did the band. It stretched and thinned until it covered Effie from neck to nose, leaving just enough room that she could still draw in breath.

It took only a finger running along the edges one at a time to sever the metal where it had sunk into the wall. As the pseudo face plate started to drop, it transformed once more, no longer metal, but cloth. Moving quickly, Lucian pressed her head to his chest and snatched the ends of the thick fabric in his other hand before they could fall, tying them off in a knot.

All of this happened in the span of a few heartbeats. The creature, realizing she'd been neutralized once more, started growling low in her throat.

Lucian did his best to ignore the savage sounds even as the hair along his arms and neck stood on end. He couldn't help but wonder what would be left of her even if the spell worked.

Using his left hand, Lucian reached behind Effie's back and found the thick length of chain that connected her wrists to her feet. With a sharp tug, he broke the chain in two and pulled her away from the wall. The force of his pull had her body spinning sideways as her arms followed the chain's momentum. She tried to fight it, her feet tripping over themselves as she struggled against his hold. Bound as she was; she was no match for Lucian's strength. She managed to regain her balance and stagger alongside of him instead of being dragged, her wet snarls beneath the gag a testament to her rage.

Once they reached the center of the room, he turned to face her, releasing the chain and giving her shoulder a firm shove that sent her flying back. She hit the ground hard, her head cracking against the stone floor. Lucian dropped to his knees beside her, leaning over her supine form, his arms outstretched in anticipation of his next move when she snapped her head forward, slamming it into his nose.

He grunted in pain, hot blood spurting down into his mouth. "It's going to take more than that to stop me," he warned her, his voice garbled from the blood.

She reared back to headbutt him again, but he caught her by the hair, pulling her head back far enough to bare her throat. She continued to thrash beneath him, attempting to use her legs to land several awkward kicks to his body but bound as she was, he dodged her easily.

Using his free hand, Lucian manipulated the chain still connected to her wrists, severing it so that her arms could come out from under her. Needing both hands for what he intended, he released his hold on her hair.

Effie didn't waste a second. She knifed up, but he was faster. Pressing his torso against her, he used his not insignificant bodyweight to press her flat against the floor. He could feel the heat of her damp breath puffing against his neck as she snapped at him behind her gag.

Fingers curled around each of her wrists, he pushed downward, using his power to sink the metal wrapped around her arms until it fused with the earth on either side of her body. Rising to his knees, he shifted his attention to her ankles, repeating his actions, not bothering to sever the chain that connected her feet together.

With a sigh, Lucian finally dropped the hold on his power and sat back on his heels. Effie wasn't going anywhere. Not until he allowed it. She was bound to the floor, the rock and metal fused so completely there was no telling where one ended and the other began.

She glared up at him, her brows dropping lower over milky eyes with slithering black lines.

Lucian's heart thumped erratically in his chest. "Now," he said, his voice a savage rumble, "it's time to take back what you stole from me."

CHAPTER 13

LUCIAN

"*Incipere,*" Lucian murmured, lowering his hand and placing the final item on the floor, briefly wondering how Vance had come across a phoenix let alone abscond with one of its feathers.

As it had with each invocation he'd performed, a surge of energy swept through the room, this one tasting of cinders and causing sweat to bead across his brow. But unlike before, this time *his* power also answered the call.

Rushing to the surface in a frantic burst, it arced from his hands and flew upward. Unused to it taking on a physical form, Lucian stared in wonder as the golden energy swirled along the ceiling, fusing with the other magics he'd summoned until they were one brilliant, pulsing mass of light. With no frame of reference for whether this was normal or even supposed to happen, he had to force himself to refocus and keep going.

The fresh scent of blood and the putrid stench of corruption filled the air telling Lucian that while he'd been busy invoking the elements, Effie had not ceased in her efforts to escape, futile though they were. She'd grown so desperate, not even splitting open her flesh was a deterrent. The creature had no care for the skin it wore. The body was a means to an end. Namely *his* end, if it had its way.

As he stared at her, another flickering light winked out, devoured by the emptiness of the corruption. He let out a derisive snort, darkly amused by the truth. She meant to destroy him, while he desperately sought to save her. A few hours more, she'd have her wish without having to do a goddamn thing. Because once the final light guttered out, he'd beg for the oblivion the fiend offered.

Without Effie, there would be nothing left for him to fight for. He'd have failed at the one thing he'd been born to do. Protect her, at any cost. Even if the cost was his life.

Lucian gritted his teeth as he returned to his place beside her, more determined than ever to destroy the abomination before it consumed what was left of his fledgling. Recalling the words Vance had painstakingly written down, he prepared to perform the final part of the ritual. Not sure what to do with his hands, he held them flat, one hovering over her forehead and the other just above her heart as he zeroed in on the area within her that seemed devoid of all light.

"Et quod solum remanebit."

As soon as he uttered the final syllable he gasped, feeling as though he'd been struck by lightning. His spine arched, his head flinging back as the power that had gathered in the room plunged itself straight into his heart. He could barely breathe through the pain of it, let alone think. It felt as though he was being unmade, the power taking away his form and scattering what was left of him into the heavens.

Chest heaving, Lucian somehow managed to open his eyes. Was it his imagination, or had some of the darkness ebbed?

Encouraged, he resumed his position and spoke as clearly as he could manage, *"Et quod solum remanebit."*

This time he was expecting the surge of liquid lightning running through his veins. He bit off a cry, but not before the taste of blood filled his mouth. If possible, it hurt worse than the first time. Never in his millennia walking the worlds had he experienced pain such as this.

Gritting his teeth, his pulse pounding wildly in his neck, Lucian focused harder on the slithering darkness, willing it to separate itself from the dull strands of light that were starting to reappear where Effie lay.

"Et quod solum remanebit."

The final word was barely formed before he was crying out in excruciating agony, the sound torn from his throat as if white hot blades were being shoved into every inch of his flesh.

His hands dropped to the floor, his body shaking so violently he feared he would not be able to push himself upright.

Is this supposed to happen?

Pink-tinged sweat poured down his face as he struggled to clear his mind. He could do this. For her, he could bear anything. Nothing would be worse than the anguish he'd succumb to if he lost her.

Eyes fluttering open, he sucked in a ragged breath and held his trembling hands over her body. There was still entirely too much corruption moving through her, although now it resembled smoke caught in a glass orb more than an inky stain.

"Et quod solum remanebit."

Lucian fell to the floor, his body spasming like Effie during one of her visions. He had no control over his limbs, the muscles straining as the power filled him. It was too much for one body to contain, even an immortal one. If he did not release it soon, it would kill him.

With a roar, he pushed himself up once more. His limbs continued to quake, but when it came to a battle of wills, Lucian was unmatched. He would not fail her.

This time he could not manage to lift his arms, so instead he rested his palms against her forearm. Head hanging down, he ignored the searing pain and followed Vance's final instruction. He called an image of Effie to mind. His favorite one.

It was one he'd painted many times, although he would never admit it to her. It was the night she'd first seen him, when the halus bane had held her in its grasp. She'd glared at him, oozing haughty defiance and feminine wrath, her eyes practically glowing beneath their sooty lashes. Her chin had been jutted up so that she could meet his gaze, allowing her to achieve the effect of looking down her nose at him even though he towered over her. The wind had picked up the heavy mass of her hair, flinging it around her like some kind of golden nimbus.

She had been an avenging angel.

Fierce.

Fearless.

Perfect.

His.

He'd known it even as it terrified him. From that moment on she owned him. What started that night had only grown more potent as they'd gotten to know each other. Each layer she'd revealed after, intentionally or not, only bound him tighter.

He'd gloried in her courageous spirit from the start, but he'd lost himself utterly when faced with her unwavering compassion. She was unmatched. Steel forged from pain and tempered with kindness.

And she . . . was . . . his.

Eyes snapping open, Lucian roared, *"Et quod solum remanebit!"*

His eyes rolled back in his head, and he fell to the ground in a graceless sprawl. Light poured from his body, and even through closed eyelids it seared him with its intensity. Wave after wave of the brilliant energy crashed against him as it filled the cell.

There was no telling how much time had passed when Lucian was finally able to reopen his eyes. The room was deathly silent, none of the overwhelming power remaining. Hardly daring to breathe, he called his power up once more, a broken sob escaping when he saw the blinding luminescence that was Effie. The thin strands of onyx threaded throughout did nothing to dilute the radiance of her spirit.

"Effie," he croaked, barely able to speak. "Fledgling . . ."

A pulse fluttered strong and steady in her throat, and her petal pink lips were slightly parted. Body still shaking, he removed all trace of her bindings, hauling her up into his arms and clutching her against his chest.

Raining kisses along every inch of her he could reach, he continued to brokenly murmur her name. "Please. Open your eyes."

Pulling back slightly, he stared down into her face. His lungs seized when her eyelids began to flutter, and when twin pools of the brightest blue blinked up at him, he began to openly weep.

His heart expanded, the joy almost painful in its intensity, only for her to shatter it completely with her rasping words.

"Who are you?"

CHAPTER 14

LUCIAN

She continued to blink up at him, her eyes wide and guileless. It hurt to look at her, to hold her, but after everything, he couldn't bear to let her go. Closing his eyes, Lucian tried to bury his emotions somewhere far inside himself. Somewhere deep enough they'd allow him to finish what he'd started.

He'd known this was a possibility. That even after the corruption was removed, there could be lingering effects. He'd been preparing for the eventuality, but he didn't want to make this choice for her. She may never forgive him.

There was a whisper-soft touch against his cheek, there and gone, and then her tentative voice. "Why are you crying?"

Lucian swallowed and forced his eyes back open. Not sure where to even begin answering that question, he opted for an oversimplified half-truth. "You've been very sick, sweetheart."

Her brows furrowed. "I have?"

Still feeling as though his heart had just been ripped out from his chest, he could only manage a nod.

"I don't feel sick . . ." she murmured.

"I'm glad to hear it, but we still have a little more work to do."

She seemed content to trust him and was in no hurry to leave the circle of his arms. For that, he was grateful. He didn't know if he'd be able to comply if she asked him to release her. His emotions might be locked away for the moment, but tremors were still racing through his body. He was in no state to open up the floodgates of his power once more.

But he had to.

No matter the cost. The promise echoed through his mind lending him strength.

Breathing deeply through his nose, Lucian emptied his head of all other thoughts. There would be time for them later. For now, he had a job to finish. He'd clearly healed her body, and he'd seen for himself that her essence was intact, but the corruption had stolen something. The only way to determine if he could repair the damage was to figure out the extent of the loss.

"Effie?"

"Hmm?"

The faintest tendril of relief unfurled within him. *She remembers her name, at least. So her mind is whole; that's something.*

"What's the last thing you remember?"

Her eyes took on a faraway cast, and she blinked in confusion. "Waking up," she answered finally.

"Not how you got here? Not who I am? Not the citadel?"

She shook her head, looking apologetic. "Should I?"

Even though his heart screamed *yes*, Lucian forced himself to smile and reassure her. "It's just the side effects of your illness."

"But you can fix it?" Her voice was so full of trust that it shattered whatever pieces of his heart remained.

"Aye, sweetheart, I can fix it."

"But you don't want to?" she asked, her lips dipping into a frown. She looked so lost, so small in his arms, but still she managed to see straight through him.

His answer was immediate. "Of course I want to. It's just . . . the *treatment* is permanent. It should be your decision whether to undertake it or not."

"Will it give me back my memories?"

Swallowing, he nodded. "It will."

A blush suffused her cheeks as she admitted, "I think I would like to remember you."

It hurt to breathe, and it took every ounce of control he had left, but Lucian managed not to crush her to his chest.

"We are"—she seemed to struggle for a word—"important to each other. Aren't we?"

Unable to meet her gaze, Lucian lifted a hand to brush a stray curl off of her forehead. "What makes you say that?"

"I may not recall your name,"—she lifted a hand and rested it against her chest—"but I remember you here. I feel . . ." She pressed her lips together, at a loss for words once more.

It might have been selfish, but Lucian *needed* those words. It may be his only opportunity to ever hear them come from her lips. "What do you feel?"

It was her turn to take a deep breath, her confession bursting from her in a rush. "*Everything*. When I opened my eyes and saw your face, it was like coming home. Peace, and warmth, and joy. And then I noticed your tears and that hurt. I-I think the only reason I'd feel those things, and for you to be so upset I was unwell, is if we meant something to each other."

Lucian briefly closed his eyes, his arms tightening around her. "Yes," he finally managed. "We are important to each other."

"Then what are you waiting for? If this treatment will help me remember you, then do it. I deserve to know the man who makes me feel all of that."

He groaned. "You don't know what you're asking me to do."

"Yes, I do."

He tried to shake his head, but she stopped him with another soft brush of her fingers against his cheek. "Please."

"Okay," he agreed, unable to deny her anything. Especially when his heart longed for the same. "I'm going to need you to lie back, all right?"

She nodded, and Lucian finally dropped his arms, watching her settle herself back on the ground. "Like this?"

"Yes. Perfect."

As he started to draw on his power, Effie let out a soft gasp. "Beautiful."

He blinked at her. "What's beautiful?"

"Your eyes. They're glowing."

Lucian wasn't sure if he wanted to laugh or cry. Her honesty cut almost as deep as the loss of her memories, if only because it underscored how much was at stake. "Close your eyes for me," he whispered, his voice strangled.

She obeyed immediately and even that hurt. Since when did his fledgling ever do anything he asked without a fight? Her unconditional trust was a gift he did not deserve.

Not when he'd been deceiving her since the day they met.

Palms resting on his thighs, Lucian let his power build around him. As it did, memories began to gather and swell in his mind. Memories that did not belong to him, but were no less his because of how they were obtained.

Memories he'd discovered in another place . . . while wearing a different form . . . and answering to a different name.

A name she'd gifted him.

Navy runes broke out across his skin, flaring with the same metallic brilliance as his eyes. Lifting his hand, he pressed his palm against the center of her forehead and then opened the telepathic connection that would irrevocably link them.

Effie's body bowed up off of the ground, her mouth opening on a silent gasp as she received not only her memories, but a power that would transform her more completely than the corruption ever had.

Lucian's power.

Smoke's power.

A Guardian's power.

PART II
GUARDIAN

"And as she fell apart,
her shattered pieces began to bloom –
blossoming *until she became* herself
exactly as she was meant to be . . ."

Becca Lee

CHAPTER 15

EFFIE

If she still had a body, Effie couldn't feel it. She was formless, existing in a state of consciousness that occurred outside any mortal definitions. For the first time in her life she was truly free.

Thoughts and voices swirled around her in a vibrant wash of colors she'd never seen before. Curls of silver caught her attention and she focused harder on them, bringing them into sharp and stunning relief. As she watched, more of the misty curls took shape until she was surrounded by thick clouds of smoke and enfolded in a cocoon of contentment.

As the clouds formed, one of the indistinguishable voices that had been murmuring in the background became clear.

"Effie."

Warmth exploded from her center . . . if she had a center. It was hard to know without a body.

This voice she knew, absolutely. Although it was altered somehow. Less insubstantial than usual. No longer just smoky echoes of a campfire, but rich with layers. Both crackling fire and delicious heat.

"Effie." The voice was impatient, but also amused. As if it knew she was distracted.

She tried to call out, only to be brought up short. How was she supposed to answer without a mouth?

"You need only think and I can hear you, fledgling."

Two faces obscured by the smoke floated into her view, blurring and merging as they fought for her attention. Before she could place either one, a discordant note vibrated throughout her consciousness, interrupting her musings. Only one person ever called her fledgling, and he'd never spoken in her mind before.

"Lucian? Am I dreaming?"

"No."

"Then how?"

"You know the answer, sweetheart."

And she did. It was right there, as if she'd summoned it. One man with two faces. They were one and the same.

"Smoke."

"Yes."

More of the pleasant numbness faded away, leaving her mind feeling crowded and heavy. It was hard to focus under the pressure. She struggled against it, preferring the weightlessness of before.

"You can't fight it, Effie. But if you let me, I can show you how to mute it."

"Yes," she eagerly agreed. Anything to keep from being smothered under the strain.

"It helps the first time to visualize it. I want you to imagine a bowl or chalice. The object doesn't matter so long as it's a vessel that needs to be refilled."

As he spoke, a bronze goblet took form. It was old; tiny fissures snaking through its metallic surface.

Lucian's startled laugh, a deep, husky rumble, moved through her like growls of thunder. Or maybe it was lightning, and she was the rod that channeled its unrelenting force. There was another rumble.

"Focus, fledgling. And try for something a little more substantial, please. The goal is not to lose that which we pour into it."

With a thought, she smoothed out the small cracks in her chalice, patching them with molten gold.

"Good. Now we fill it up."

"With what?"

"Everything that makes you Effie."

"As opposed to everything that makes me someone else?"

She felt his amusement as clearly as if it were her own. She wanted to burrow down in its warmth and stay there.

"The first transformation is always the most difficult. It is hard to imagine ourselves as a series of defining moments or relationships, but when you learn to embrace the things that created the person you are, it's easier to pull them close and be *them once more."*

"Is that supposed to make sense?"

"It will in time. For now, just do as I say."

"How can I obey something I don't understand?"

Lucian sighed. It wove through her, giving her form only long enough for her to feel the rush of breath like a caress. Mind-speaking this way was beyond intimate. In this state, she was wholly exposed, any mental barriers she might have once had obliterated. They were connected so completely it was as if they'd become one.

"When I am Smoke, I need to let go of Lucian. I send away everything that defines him—"

The words should have been jarring. The secret they so casually revealed deserving of further exploration, but she was interested only in contradicting them. *"Not everything."* Surprise—Lucian's—rippled through her. *"Pieces of him remain."*

"Well, we are the same in the end. Elements of us will always be connected."

"So, it's not just an illusion? Smoke's body?"

"It is . . . and it isn't. It is simply another form I take when required. Two sides of the same coin. As a member of the Triumvirate, Smoke is bound by different rules. There are things I can do—and be— as Smoke that I could never accomplish as Lucian."

"I'm still not sure I understand."

"It's okay. You will, I promise. For now, the only thing you need to do is focus."

"Okay." She was happy to let it go for now. Attempting to unravel

the paradox he'd laid upon her was too confusing. Trying only served to bring the chaotic swirl of thoughts pressing in on her once more.

There was a beat of silence and then another gentle prompt. *"Think of your favorite possession. An item that brings you joy or great comfort. Something special, but perhaps only to you."*

A small, intricately tooled leather journal immediately sprang to life in her mind. Her Keeper's journal. The one he'd given her.

Once again, his shock and delight over her response worked through her. Instead of giving voice to it, he simply said, *"Good. Now place your journal into the cup."*

Visualizing the items side by side, there was no way the journal would fit in the chalice, so she imagined it shrinking until it slid inside the empty bowl.

"Very good. Now take a favorite memory and do the same."

She was following his instruction before his words fully registered. The recollection rose unbidden, causing little flickers of heat to shimmer and spark. In it, Lucian's eyes bore into hers as he told her he wanted more than just her body. Not waiting to see what he had to say about that revelation, she imagined the cup filling with liquid, his face reflected along its wavering surface.

"Now something less pleasant. Something you wish you could forget."

Too many memories vied for attention at the almost apologetic order. There was Darrin's charred body. Kieran's hateful words. Her mother's sneering face as she told her she was worthless. Each memory hurt, but it was a dull ache, like a splinter that had sunk so deep the skin had already grown back to cover it. For each she imagined them as drops of rain, falling out of her and back into her chalice.

She didn't stop there.

Understanding now what she needed to do, she recalled every beautiful and equally hateful moment from her life, calling them to the surface so they could pour out of her and back into the vessel that was soon overflowing. With each new one she added, her body solidified, and the weight of all of the foreign thoughts and voices faded away until she was all that remained.

Whole once more, Effie opened her eyes.

CHAPTER 16

EFFIE

The first thing she noticed was the way the flecks in Lucian's dark irises glowed. They weren't the usual bronze, but an incandescent gold that was practically blinding in its intensity. She squinted automatically, trying to shield her eyes as he stared down at her.

"H-hi," she rasped, her voice rusty with disuse.

His entire body shuddered at the sound of her voice, and he let out a strangled groan. "Welcome back."

She almost asked him where she'd been, but the memories came flooding to her, sparing her none of their horrific details. Not what she'd become—or the soul-shattered look of Lucian's haunted gaze every time he'd visit her.

Pushing herself upright, Effie's head swam with the knowledge. A quick check of her body showed that none of the previous weeks' ugliness touched her. She was as whole and pure as if she'd been reborn. And in a way, she had been.

"Lucian . . ." That was all she could manage. There were too many questions demanding answers.

He lifted one of his scarred hands and ran his fingers along her cheek. She could feel the velvety drag of it deep in her core. Her breath stuttered out in a rush.

"I'll tell you everything you want to know, but first—"

She didn't need him to finish his sentence. Effie was already leaning forward, pulling his face down to hers until their lips crashed together. Desperation fueled them, their kiss a mere echo of the all-consuming need thrumming through their veins.

Answers could wait.

She'd been trapped; a prisoner taken hostage by the darkest parts of her soul. Everything that made her whole had been stolen—her memories, her humanity, her love. But even then, even faced with the monster she'd become, Lucian hadn't given up. Instead, he gave her back everything that had been taken from her. In the wake of that truth, nothing else mattered.

Only Lucian.

Only this.

His hands were everywhere: hauling her closer and pressing her body into his, running along the length of her back, diving into her hair. She was no better; the need to feel him—all of him—making her movements frantic. Desperate.

Lucian let out a low groan as she slid her hands beneath his tunic and scraped her nails up his stomach. His muscles bunched and flexed beneath her soft touch, but it still wasn't enough. Distantly, she thought it may never be enough. Not when it came to him.

Her breath came in little pants, her heart thundering as he tore his lips from hers and worked them along her neck. His mouth reached her scar and hovered just above the surface, his breath puffing out in warm gusts.

"Don't . . . you . . . dare . . . stop," she gasped, digging her fingers into his shoulders.

His answering laugh was primal, spiraling through her and calling to everything that was female inside of her. "I couldn't if I tried," he whispered, tracing the edges of her ear with his tongue.

"Good," she managed, her voice breathless.

"I just need a second," he said, giving her another skin-tingling kiss before pulling back.

He disentangled himself, grasping the discarded blanket from the far corner of the cell. Before she could ask what the hell he was doing when they were so clearly in the middle of things, his eyes flared bronze and the dingy cloth transformed into a pristine blue quilt. He laid it on the ground beside her before leaning down to lift her in his arms.

"Where were we?" he whispered, carefully setting her down along the velvety surface, the soft down far more comfortable than the stone floor. She had to admit it was worth the delay.

Lucian resumed kissing and licking her neck. Her eyes fell closed as his fingers ran along the edges of her shirt. His touch was whisper-soft, but it left a trail of fire in its wake. She pressed into his hands, craving more of the sweet burn.

As if he could read her mind, or perhaps just her body, he skimmed his palm over her torso, electric tingles her only warning as her clothing dissolved.

"You and your tric—" she broke off in a moan as his hand returned to claim her breast. The gentle friction of his skin rubbing against her tender flesh was exactly what she'd been craving.

But still it wasn't enough.

His mouth followed his hands, hot and demanding as he kissed down her pebbled flesh. It was hard to form thoughts, let alone words, as he took her nipple into his mouth. He gave a sharp tug, his teeth scraping gently against her sensitive peak.

She moaned, her fingers diving into his hair. Her legs clenched together, trying to ease the growing ache he'd created as desire washed through her, but it only made her more desperate.

"Liked that, did you?" he whispered, flashing her a wicked grin.

It was hard to form words let alone a meaningful comeback. He must have read the need in her expression because his eyes darkened and he resumed his slow exploration of her body. When his lips brushed against her center, her spine arched off the blanket on a silent groan.

Lucian ran his hands up her legs, the gentle scratch of his calloused skin adding a delicious friction. When he reached her thighs, he paused, and Effie reluctantly opened her eyes to find out what he was waiting for.

His eyes burned into hers, searing her with their intensity. Never looking away, he slowly pulled her legs apart. Heat flamed in her face. She should have felt vulnerable being so wantonly displayed, but it only made her burn hotter. Once she was fully spread beneath him, Lucian dropped his gaze and the hunger on his face nearly sent her over the edge, Her inner muscles clenched in a silent demand for him to fill her.

As if he could hear the call of her body, Lucian lowered his head, his eyes lifting to hers as he groaned her name. Not breaking eye contact, he ran his tongue along her core, the sweet pressure too much for her. Effie shivered, the wet glide of his tongue reverberating between her legs. Her eyes fluttered closed, and she lost herself in the feel of him as he played her body more masterfully than a musician, his symphony composed of her soft cries of pleasure.

Liquid desire surged through her veins, igniting her even as need continued to pool within her. She whimpered, her body chasing something she didn't know how to ask for. Lucian was there, his hands on—and in—her as his voice filled her mind.

"That's it. Just let go."

Her hips shifted, bucking of their own volition as they followed the gentle command. He continued to stroke her with his tongue, one hand pressing down on her belly while the other curled up into her, rubbing against a bundle of nerves that had tiny stars exploding behind her eyes.

Lucian growled in satisfaction as she spasmed around his fingers and the vibrations sent her careening off a cliff. Her back arched off the blanket as the world unraveled around her. For the second time that day, she floated in a sea of consciousness, sparks of pleasure continuing to flicker on the fringe of her awareness.

Before she could even comprehend what happened, Lucian's lips were at her ear, his voice a deep rumble. "I'm not done with you yet."

A grin stretched across her face as more happy tingles sparked inside of her body. She barely managed to open her eyes in time to see Lucian's clothes answer to the same fate as her own. A small gasp of wonder left her lips as he knelt between her legs.

If she was cast from moonlight, he was kissed by the sun. Golden skin stretched over cords of muscle with a dark sprinkling of hair that only enhanced its natural radiance. She eyed him hungrily, drinking in the sight of his powerful body looming over hers, his eyes hooded, his cheeks flushed with need.

Need for her.

The knowledge wrapped itself around her, giving her a siren's confidence as she reached out to take him in her hand and guide him to her center, her desire for him an ache that wouldn't be denied.

His breath escaped him in a hiss as she stroked his length, reveling at the silk and steel feel of him in her hand. Her name was a tortured moan as it left his lips, and Effie felt it ring through her body as she lifted her hips up, pressing the tip of him against her.

"Please, Lucian. Don't make us wait any longer."

His eyes were barely more than bronze slits as he grabbed her by the hips and shifted her position.

"Please," she moaned. Her eyes rolled back as he circled his hips, dipping the barest inch inside of her.

"What do you need?"

Whatever she intended to say was gone. The words lost in a haze of pleasure.

He slid in a little further, her inner muscles fluttering as they stretched to accommodate him. "Tell me," he demanded, his hands flexing into her skin.

Effie forced her eyes open, swallowing thickly as she looked up at him. If there was any piece of her heart that was still her own, it was lost in that moment. She was hopelessly and irrevocably his. Somehow, she managed to find the words to tell him what her soul recognized long ago.

"You—just you, Lucian."

His eyes closed at her confession, his throat bobbing as his fingers dug in almost painfully. Several heartbeats passed before he opened them and looked at her again. When he did, his irises flared with the full force of his power. Just like the first time he'd used it on her, she was consumed by the overwhelming feeling of experiencing everything all at once. Lucian chose that moment to slide the rest of the way inside of her, joining them completely in one hard thrust.

The feeling of him inside her was so exquisitely perfect that it was almost too much. She couldn't help the moan of pleasure as it was torn from her lips, her body pulsing around his.

"Are you all right?" he asked, veins straining in his neck as he held himself perfectly still, letting her adjust to his length.

"Oh yes," she breathed, her eyes peeling open just long enough to see the flush of pleasure her visceral reaction caused. "More," she demanded, her hands running down his spine to grasp the full globes of his arse.

Lucian gave her a feral grin and flexed, every wonderful inch of him pressing into the most secret places within her.

Effie exploded around him, his name a sob on her lips as the world turned into a ball of pure light. It was unlike anything she'd ever experienced, but she only had eyes for Lucian. He was made of glowing strands of golden energy, and it was the most devastatingly beautiful thing she'd ever seen.

I'm seeing his essence, she realized once she returned to herself. *Is this what he meant by fuj d'âme*, she wondered as she drank in the beauty that was Lucian's soul.

"It is," he confirmed, leaning forward to claim her mouth with his. Weaving fingers through hers, he deepened the kiss, pressing their joined hands to the ground on either side of her head. *"And it's only just begun."*

He rocked his hips back as Effie wound her legs around him, locking him in place as she let out a low growl of protest.

His responding laugh was both tender and potently male. *"Let me love you, Effie."*

"Well when you put it that way . . ."

He chuckled against her lips, the laughter ghosting through her mind like the sound of rustling leaves. When he pulled out again, she didn't fight him. Instead, she focused on the sensations rolling through her like an oncoming storm. Recognizing them as the promise they were, Effie gave herself over to them. To Lucian.

He activated every single bundle of nerves with each toe-curling thrust of his hips. She never knew it could be like this. So aware of—and unable to control—her body. He milked every cry from her throat, every single shiver, and still he demanded more. It wasn't until she was desperate with need, her body quaking beneath him, that he finally increased the pace, driving into her with a mindless purpose.

"Lu—" she gasped, not even able to finish his name as he propelled them both toward release.

This time when she came apart, Lucian was right there with her, his consciousness mingling with hers as they floated somewhere above the golden threads of their physical forms. There was no telling how much time passed as they existed there, their souls' very essence entwined in a way few must ever experience.

She didn't have the words to explain the all-encompassing bliss searing through her in that one endless moment. It was perfection, and just as she expected, now that she knew what it meant to truly be with Lucian, she would never be the same again.

Sometime later, head resting on his chest and legs tangled with his, Effie sighed.

"Now that we got that out of the way, I think you have some explaining to do."

CHAPTER 17

EFFIE

*L*ucian stiffened only for a second before letting out a low chuckle. "Maybe this is a conversation best suited for clothing."

She tilted her head just enough that her chin pressed into the smooth expanse of his chest so she could give him a half-hearted glare. "Clothes just make it easier for you to escape."

"Maybe you haven't noticed, but we're locked in here."

Effie rolled her eyes. "That didn't exactly keep you from getting in. I doubt it will pose a problem."

Her Guardian's gaze was warm as he stared back at her. A soft smile played around his lips, softening the usually stern lines of his face. "After everything we went through to find our way back to each other, leaving your side is the last thing on my mind."

Her heart tumbled through her chest, Lucian's raw honesty an exquisite kind of torture. It hurt to know how much he'd—they'd—suffered, even as it soothed the worst of the sting. Effie's throat grew tight, and she blinked back the unexpected wetness in her eyes. Love was not a strong enough word for what she felt for this man. She'd loved before, and that emotion paled in comparison to whatever storm he invoked inside of her.

Catching one of the tears before it could fall, he brushed it away. "What do you want to know?"

"Everything," she said, her voice adamant if not slightly warbled. "What did you do to me? How did you manage it without becoming tainted? Is it permanent? Am I like you now? How are you Lucian *and* Smoke? Why didn't you tell me?"

He cut off her flood of questions with a kiss, his chest rumbling with laughter as he cradled her head with his hand and pulled her back down to lay atop him. "Where would you like me to start?"

"How did you stop the corruption? From what I remember, I was worse off than Tinka . . ."

"After the citadel fell—"

Effie shivered. Some part of her knew the citadel had been destroyed but hearing him say it so matter-of-factly made the loss real.

"—we moved the survivors to the Vale. Besides being the safest place to regroup, I knew that there was a chance they might have access to magic we weren't aware of—their use of it is what got them exiled in the first place. So while it was a long shot, I wasn't going to miss the opportunity. Thankfully, it paid off."

"They knew how to remove the corruption?"

"No, well, not in so many words. When they made Val'don their home, they utilized a number of spells and rituals to both magnify their innate powers and also help make their underground city livable. I borrowed one of their spells, using it to amplify my power and send the corruption inside of you elsewhere. Once it was gone, your body was healed but your mind . . . well, the only way to make you whole required me sharing my power with you. Since there was no longer a risk of my being corrupted, it was a simple matter of transforming your essence."

"Why do I feel like you're leaving a lot of things out?"

Lucian snorted. "I'm not intentionally hiding anything. It's a lot to try to distill down into one simple explanation."

Effie bit back a retort, her mind struggling to make sense of all that he did—and didn't—say. "Okay fine. So you used some kind of spell and sent the corruption where?"

"The Nether."

"The what?"

"It's a world that exists alongside this one. A shadow realm, if you will."

"Shadow—"

"Not those kind of shadows."

The adrenaline rush that had surged up at the word died back down, though her heartbeat still felt slightly erratic. As if he knew, Lucian ran a soothing hand along her spine and feathered his lips over the crown of her head.

Bolstered, as always, by his silent support, she hazarded another question. "Is that even safe? Wouldn't the other world be at risk?"

Lucian made a frustrated sound. "The Valen Council can probably explain it better than I can, but in a word, no. Nothing can exist there. Not even the corruption."

She made a soft humming sound as she let that sink in. In finding a way to save her, Lucian may have also stumbled across the solution they needed to repair the realm. She wasn't about to pretend she fully understood what he'd done, but she couldn't exactly argue with the results either. She was here beside him. *Her*. Not some mindless monster. That was all the explanation she really needed.

Curious if she'd only imagined it, Effie asked her next question in her mind. *"Can you hear me?"*

"Yes. When you project the thought directly to me I can, just as if we were speaking out loud. Or if we're touching. As long as I focus, I can hear whatever you're thinking."

She frowned, not sure how she felt about him having access to everything as it ran through her mind.

"As a rule, Guardians respect others' privacy. We only take thoughts when granted permission, but if it makes you feel better, it works both ways. You have the same access to me."

"I guess that will have its benefits."

"Somehow I figured you'd enjoy that part," he said aloud.

"Is it the same for all Guardians?"

"The telepathy? Yes. You'll be able to mind-speak with Kael and

Nord or any of the other Brothers, should you happen to meet them. Although, our link will be stronger than most since it is my power that is responsible for your transformation."

"And what about non-Guardians like Ronan or Reyna? Can I speak in their minds now?"

"Technically, yes, although it is a skill reserved for the Triumvirate, so we only use that ability when we take their forms."

Her frown returned. "Why *do* you take those forms?"

She heard Lucian's mental sigh as clearly as if he'd released it. "The physical forms of the Triumvirate, as grotesque or off-putting as they can be, are reflections of the position itself. Blind to the lies of the flesh, silent so that we may better hear the truth, nameless so that we serve only the desires of those we are bound to. But it is a practical thing as well. If we all look the same, it is easier to replace a member as needed."

Nudity forgotten, Effie sat up, her eyes wide and her mouth agape. "Replace members . . . you mean you three haven't always been the Triumvirate?"

"Kael, Nord, and I are the seventh iteration of the unit known as the Triumvirate. The weight of the prophecies we carry becomes too great a burden after a millennium or so. Thankfully, the Brotherhood of Guardians is a vast network. While we share the same power, all of us have our own unique set of skills. As such, we rotate through positions that best suit us."

Had she not been so shocked by the admission, Effie would have appreciated how Lucian kept his eyes trained on her face. As it was, her mind was whirling, questions coming almost as fast as his answers.

"So were you sent here because you have visions?"

"No. Our power allows us to take the visions of others, and we have perfect recollection of all the ones we personally claim, but we do not have the gift of prophecy ourselves. Kael, Nord, and I were selected by the head of the Brotherhood for our ability to sense patterns and draw logical conclusions about links between what others have Seen. That combined with our military experience made us ideal candidates."

"Will I still have visions now that I . . . now that I share your power?"

Lucian shrugged. "I cannot say for sure."

She could feel the truth of his answer buzzing through her, but still she felt the need to ask, "You don't know?"

"I've never made another Guardian before."

"So why—" Effie broke off and shook her head, the answer to that one obvious. Lucian attempted the transformation because he thought it was the only way to save her. "So is that what I am now? A Guardian?"

He nodded, his expression both tender and fiercely proud. "The first female one, at that."

She bit down on the inside of her cheek as she mulled that revelation over. "Are you going to get in trouble?"

He gave her a pointed look. "Do you really think I care?"

She laughed. "No, I guess you wouldn't." There were still so many questions, and her head was throbbing the more she tried to process everything all at once. She was a Guardian . . . she may not have visions anymore . . . the Guardians *were* the Triumvirate . . . Lucian was Smoke.

Mother's tits . . . Lucian is Smoke.

Her eyes were wide when they met his once more. "So . . ."

He peered up at her with fathomless eyes, his mouth and mind silent while he gave her a chance to choose her words.

Effie's cheeks burned as she realized just what the connection between the two men meant. Lucian knew *everything*. He'd lived her past through the memories Smoke had acquired. He was the one she'd revealed her feelings to, the one who warned her to have more faith in her Guardian. She should have been embarrassed about such a clumsy confession, but after all they'd been through it wasn't like she wanted to keep anything from him anyway. Besides, her feelings for Lucian certainly weren't a secret any longer—if they ever had been to begin with.

Suddenly, it wasn't so hard to picture them as one and the same. Smoke had always been her mentor, protecting and guiding her as best he could. As Lucian, he'd done the same, albeit in a more hands-on way. Both versions of him challenged her, accepted her, believed in her. Lucian, in any form, gave her the space to grow and evolve, while being exactly what she needed to achieve it.

In the end, the face he wore didn't matter. She'd take him any way she could get him. Although she'd be lying if she didn't admit she had a definite preference for this form.

Lucian's eyes glittered as he followed her line of thought, his smile turning wolfish. "I wish I could have told you sooner. I was bound by my vow to keep the secret."

"But you don't have to keep it now?"

"You're a Guardian. The rules no longer apply to you."

"Not to me, but to everyone else."

She could feel Lucian's regret, his voice full of apology as he said, "No one outside of the four of us can know who or what the Triumvirate really are."

"I understand. Your secret is safe with me."

"*Our* secret," he corrected. "You're one of us now."

"I don't feel any different," she said, but even as the words left her lips she felt the lie of them. There was something new, foreign and yet familiar, running through her. It was just out of reach, like a forgotten name.

"You will. Your power is still banked."

"Banked?"

"You have to call it forth; activate it."

Effie held up a hand, staring at it hard like it was going to change before her eyes.

Lucian laughed, weaving his fingers through hers and bringing their hands to his lips. "It might take a few tries, but you'll learn how to access your power. You have the rest of your immortal life to practice until it's as easy as drawing a breath."

Immortal life.

Immortal.

The breath left her in a whoosh. Just when she thought she knew everything, something still managed to shock her. "I think that might be all the answers I can handle for now."

"It's a lot to take in."

"You're telling me."

"Usually we have a chance to prepare ourselves for what the change means and come to terms with it beforehand." His smile dimmed slightly. "You're not upset with me? For making the choice for you?"

She could feel the waves of his guilt and uncertainty crashing into her and any teasing response she was about to utter vanished. Pressing her free hand over his heart, she looked straight into his eyes. "You saved me, Lucian. From a fate more horrible than anything I could ever imagine—and given my past, that's saying something. So no, I'm not upset. Not even close."

He studied her, his eyes moving over her face as if searching for any hint of dishonesty.

"More than that," she continued, leaning down until their noses almost touched, "I'm grateful."

"Grateful? For the power?"

Effie shook her head, her eyes dropping to his lips as she whispered, "I don't care about the power. I spent years without any to speak of and made peace with it. No, Lucian, what I will never be able to stop thanking you for is that now I can spend lifetimes loving you instead of just what's left of this one. The endless possibilities that come with an eternity spent beside you is worth more to me than anything."

She kissed him, her heart near to bursting as he took over, weaving his hands through her hair and deepening it. Thoughts and feelings, both hers and his, merged in her mind. Need clawed at her, her hunger for him rising once more. Just as quickly as it built, a thrum of tension sobered her, cutting through the fog of her desire.

"What's wrong?"

"Someone's coming."

Lucian sprang up, the scraps of clothes that had been littering the floor forming around their bodies almost instantly. He held a hand out and Effie grasped it as she got to her feet. He shifted, using his body to shield hers as footsteps sounded down the hall.

"Luc, you alive?"

He visibly relaxed. "It's just Kael," he murmured..

"Great move. If he's not, you just gave the bloodthirsty fiend a heads-up we're coming."

"And Ronan," she added, a part of her growing defensive at his use of the word fiend. Even though that's exactly what she'd been mere hours ago.

Stepping forward, Lucian grasped the cell's door and pulled it open with no more effort than he'd used to help her stand. The subtle flare of bronze in his eyes was the only sign he'd called and released his power.

"I told you it wouldn't stop you."

He winked at her over his shoulder as he called out, "Here."

"Luc, thank the Mother," Kael said, coming into view. Seeing her, he stopped dead, gaping as wonder filled his green gaze. "You did it."

"Effie . . ." Ronan breathed, looking shaken.

"It's me," she said, smiling up at him. Her smile faltered as he continued to stare.

"Your eyes."

Her brows veed, not understanding what he was referring to. She glanced up at Lucian, seeking an explanation.

"They're like mine and Kael's now."

Her expression cleared. That made sense, those metallic flecks of color ringing their pupils were the only physical manifestation of a Guardian's power. With everything else going on, she just hadn't gotten around to really processing what any of this meant.

"Surprise," she said weakly.

Ronan swept her up in his arms, his grin nearly splitting his face in two. "I can't tell you how relieved I am to see those big blue eyes again."

Effie hugged her friend tight, realizing he wasn't put off by her becoming a Guardian at all. He was simply overcome with relief that the thing that most clearly marked her as Shadow-touched was gone.

Lucian not-so-subtly cleared his throat, and Ronan finally set her down.

"So the spell actually worked," Ronan said.

"Obviously," Lucian replied dryly.

"Play nice."

Kael's muffled laughter told Effie he'd overheard the thought she'd intended for Lucian.

"I'm going to need to figure out how to get the hang of this. It could get embarrassing fast . . ."

Kael's smile grew as his voice filled her mind. *"Welcome to the club, little warrior."*

<h1 style="text-align:center">CHAPTER 18</h1>

<h2 style="text-align:center">EFFIE</h2>

"Council's in session. We should go and request an audience so that we may tell the others. They'll want to know that the spell was a success." Ronan's voice boomed with the force of his enthusiasm.

"It can wait. Effie should rest; she's still adjusting," Lucian said.

"Effie is right here and can speak for herself," she said with a scowl. "And for what it's worth, I feel fine."

Lucian's expression was blank, but she could feel flickers of his concern.

Kael reached out and squeezed her shoulder, his dimples flashing as he gave her an indulgent smile. "Luc is right, as much as it pains me to admit. You're likely running off of pure adrenaline right now. I know I was after the change. Trust me, you're going to crash. Hard." Eyeing her carefully, he added, "Sooner rather than later."

"I'm not a child. You can't send me to my room and order me to take a nap."

Ronan and Kael laughed, but Lucian just continued to look at her. She had no doubt he'd try to do just that.

"Speaking of rooms, do I have to stay down here, or do I get to—"

"You're staying with me," Lucian answered before she could finish.

Ronan raised his brows but remained uncharacteristically silent.

"Well, the Council can wait, but we should probably meet up with Nord." Kael glanced at Lucian for approval.

"He was going to be my next stop after getting Effie settled, but seeing as how she's just going to argue until we bring her along, we might as well save ourselves the headache."

"Hey, I'm standing right here. I'm not Shadow-touched anymore, remember? Both my hearing and my comprehension are near perfect again, so feel free to include me in the conversation."

Kael at least pretended to look apologetic, Lucian didn't even do that much. His expression was fierce as he brushed the back of his fingers against hers, his voice a husky caress in her mind.

"I just got you back. You can't be mad at me for wanting to keep you to myself for a while."

Cheeks heating, she ducked her head. *"Well, why didn't you just say that?"*

"I thought it would have been obvious."

Effie sighed. More time curled up with Lucian sounded a lot better than being paraded around an unfamiliar place before a bunch of strangers. Or relative strangers, as the case may be. Too bad she'd already insisted she wasn't tired. Changing her mind now would only raise questions. No . . . the only way to save face was to go along with them and hope it didn't take too long.

"Where is the skulking blond giant?" she asked, hoping her voice didn't convey the depth of her disappointment.

Kael snorted. "Oh, he's going to love that description."

"Likely in his room," Lucian answered. "Shield, why don't you lead the way?"

With a nod, Ronan obeyed.

Once his back was turned, Lucian continued speaking privately to Effie, *"Nord has been keeping up appearances as the Triumvirate."*

"By himself?"

"With two of the three of us preoccupied with finding a cure for

you, he didn't have much choice. Although, he's managed to keep people unaware of our absence."

Effie's eyes darted to Lucian in silent question.

"Nord is a master illusionist."

She didn't realize Lucian had been speaking along the Guardian's public link until Kael added, *"His weaves are so detailed, not even we can tell whether it's really one of our Brothers wearing the robes."*

Effie shook her head, trying to think back to all of the times she'd interacted with the trio and wondering if it had just been Nord and his illusions.

Lucian answered her question before she could voice it. *"He didn't bother with the illusions at the citadel. The Keepers were used to the Triumvirate coming and going as needed. It wasn't uncommon for only one or two of us to be present for long stretches of time, or even for all of us to occasionally leave. Outside of Bael, however, it's a different story. The realm needs to see the Triumvirate intact."*

They walked a little further in silence, Effie barely paying attention to her surroundings. *"So . . . if Lucian's Smoke. Whose Mirror One?"*

"Depends on the day," Kael replied, his mental voice amused. *"Usually me, though. As our leader, Lucian practically always takes point. Nord and I just stand wherever is most convenient. That said, tradition dictates that as second-in-command, I stand at his left. So, that is where I generally end up out of habit."*

She hadn't realized there was a ranking system in place between the men, although that, too, made sense. Lucian was clearly used to being in charge and practically everyone deferred to his judgment.

"Don't think this means I am going to let either of you boss me around," she informed them primly.

Lucian's voice was as dry as fallen leaves as he replied, *"Expect you to break tradition? I would never . . ."*

Her fist shot out and slammed into his bicep almost without conscious thought. The resulting pain was immediate. It would have hurt less if she'd tried to punch a wall. Shaking out her hand, she scowled up at him.

"Now, now, fledgling, use your words."

Before she could reply, Ronan halted. While she hadn't been paying attention, they'd left the identical gray hallways and arrived in a new, much more spacious wing. It was decorated in red and gold and filled with expensive-looking furnishings. She almost felt as if they'd stumbled through a portal and ended up in the Palace.

"So this is where they keep the welcome guests," she murmured.

Kael laughed. "Don't feel too bad, little warrior. We were almost your neighbors in the gaol that first night. Lucian wasn't exactly on his best behavior."

"Making friends, were you?" she asked him with a knowing grin.

Lucian speared her with his eyes. "I had more important things on my mind."

She knew he wasn't upset with her teasing, but the wound was still too fresh for both of them. Smile fading, Effie took his hand in hers and squeezed.

"No one can blame you for that, Brother," Kael said.

"And fuck 'em if they do," Ronan added, giving Effie an affectionate look, though his next words were as much for Lucian as they were for her. "Because of you, all of us were spared a devastating loss."

Tears pricked her eyes and she looked to the floor, overwhelmed by the force of the men's joint emotion.

The door beside them swung open. "You planning on knocking anytime soon, or are you just going to stand out here gossiping like a bunch of fishwives?"

Lucian sighed. "Nord, you remember Effie."

Effie glanced up, the brusque greeting startling her out of her emotional reaction. It was the first time she'd seen the third Guardian without his Triumvirate robe, and the effect was devastating.

He filled the doorway, one hand on the door, the other on the doorframe, both hands decked out in rings. He was easily as large as Lucian, but light where he was dark. His thick blond hair fell in waves down his back and a full beard covered the bottom half of his face. His eyes were a blue so pale they were almost white, except for the azure flecks that ringed his pupils.

"H-hi," she stuttered, intimidated despite herself.

Nord took one look at her and shifted his attention to Ronan. "Leave us."

Ronan's brows lowered and color tinged his cheeks, but before he could reply, Effie placed a hand on his arm and nodded. "It's all right. We'll meet up with you later."

"I'll go check on the others," Ronan said tightly, pressing a chaste kiss to Effie's forehead and then throwing a glare in Nord's direction as he walked away.

Nudging the door open further, Nord stepped out of the way to make room for them. Kael moved into the sumptuous chamber first, Effie trailing behind him. Lucian entered last, shutting the door with more force than strictly required.

"Looks like you have some explaining to do," Nord said, his eyes landing on Effie's face once more.

"You knew I intended to save her," Lucian said, crossing his arms.

"Save her, yes. Turn her? Well now, that's something else entirely, isn't it?"

"Don't be an arse," Kael said, plopping down in the room's lone chair.

Nord shot him an exasperated look. "You two have been traipsing around, free to come and go as you please for months, all the while leaving me to do the grunt work, and you don't even have the decency to fill me in on the plan?"

"You would have tried to stop me," Lucian said, resting one of his hands lightly on Effie's waist. Despite the gentleness of the touch, there was no mistaking the act for anything but what it was: a claiming.

From the lift of his brow, Nord didn't miss it either. "Nay, Brother. I wouldn't have stopped you. You know as well as I that a new Guardian hasn't joined the ranks in centuries. It's cause for celebration. Especially knowing the world of shit you're going to find yourself in once the others learn about her." For the first time, Nord's lips curled up in a smile and his eyes shone with amusement as he turned to address Effie directly.

"Welcome to the Brotherhood, little sister."

~

EFFIE STIFLED A YAWN. They'd been talking for hours, and she was well past exhausted. Kael had been right. When the adrenaline finally left her, she'd crashed, hard. Unfortunately, the three men didn't seem to notice that it was all she could do to keep her eyes open.

Kael was still sprawled in his chair, one heavily muscled leg tossed precariously over its wooden arm. An arm that, under the weight of said leg, looked about as substantial as a toothpick. Effie couldn't help eyeing it occasionally to ensure that the entire thing wasn't about to collapse under his bulk.

Lucian was sitting on the edge of Nord's bed, one foot braced on the low metal railing, the other flat on the ground. She was beside him, her legs not quite long enough to touch the floor. In her defense, that was because the bed was massive. She had a feeling—although she dared not to interrupt them long enough to ask—that Nord had used his Guardian's power to enlarge it to better fit his towering frame.

Since bringing her back, Lucian had not stopped finding reasons to touch her. She wasn't certain he even realized he was doing it. It was like he needed to keep subconsciously reminding himself that she was real. For the moment, his leg was pressed against hers, although if she shifted too far away, he would shadow the movement until they were connected again. She'd been amusing herself whenever the conversation got too tedious to follow by seeing how long it took him to realize she was out of reach.

Now was such a moment. Effie had just pried her fingers out from beneath his, only for his hand to slide across the blanket until his pinky covered hers once more. She bit back a smile and let her eyes return to Nord. He paced the length of the room, pausing only when he wanted to make a particularly emphatic point.

"All this time, the Valen Council was sitting on the answer we were searching for and no one even realized it," Nord muttered, shaking his head and causing his hair to toss about like a Talyrian's mane.

"Well, we were focused on trying to better understand the problem.

It's hard to know what the solution is when you don't know even that much," Kael reminded him.

Nord hummed his agreement. "So now we need to perform the ritual on a larger scale across all of the infected land."

"While also seeking out any other victims," Kael added.

"As much as I like Effie—and am glad that you managed to save her—we can't just go around turning everyone into Guardians," Nord said, stopping to glance at Kael.

"We couldn't even if we wanted to," Lucian said, the sound of his deep voice so soothing she wanted to give up her fight with consciousness.

Nord and Kael looked at Lucian expectantly.

"Why not?" Effie finally asked when it became clear no one else was going to.

Lucian's eyes warmed her as he met her inquisitive gaze. "Because I was able to restore what was lost. Without having access to the memories of those who've already started to become Shadow-touched, there's no way to do so. We could save their bodies, but there's no way for us to salvage their minds."

"But even if you didn't make them Guardians, couldn't you at least cast out the corruption to save them? Even without their memories people could lead meaningful lives."

Lucian took her hand, the empathy shining in his gaze almost painful. "It's not just about the memories, Effie. I barely survived that ritual."

Hearing him say it so plainly rendered her speechless. For Lucian —arguably the strongest, most powerful man she'd ever known—to admit such a thing, it must have been close indeed.

"The drain on my power . . . I've never come close to that kind of burnout."

Nord and Kael gasped. Effie's eyes shifted to their horrified faces before shooting back to Lucian. "Burnout?" she asked, afraid of his answer.

His lips drew down in a frown. "If a Guardian burns out, the void left by the missing power inside of them will demand to be filled. It will pull on their very life force until nothing remains."

"It's a painful way to die," Nord muttered, his expression haunted.

"Lucian—" she started, shaking her head when she couldn't find the words. The risk he'd taken to save her; it was almost impossible to comprehend.

"Is it?" he asked, his eyes searching hers. *"If our positions had been reversed?"*

Her answer was immediate. *"I'd have done anything to save you, no matter the danger to myself."*

He squeezed her hand, his countenance equal parts tender and fierce. "The drain on my power notwithstanding, the control required to channel the foreign elements through my physical body was damn near impossible. I could hardly think through the pain, let alone concentrate on what needed to be done. If I hadn't been so single-mindedly focused on saving you, I would not have survived it. My need for you carried me through the ritual almost as much as my magic brought you back. That is not something that can be replicated for just anyone, let alone a stranger."

Effie nodded, although she was still miserable at the thought of not being able to save potential survivors. "No . . . I guess not." Sighing, she looked around at the others. "At least we can do something about the land."

"That's only half the battle," Lucian said gently. "What good is saving the land if those abominations continue to walk among it? The Shadows need to be hunted down and exterminated for good, otherwise nothing we do is going to make any bit of difference in the long run."

Nord and Kael nodded their agreement.

"Will the spell you found work on them?" Effie asked.

"I don't know," Lucian said, frustration giving his voice a sharp edge. "In theory it should, although I doubt it's going to be simple, even with multiple people to channel the overflow of power. When I saved you, I only had to pluck out that which did not belong. The Shadows are creatures of pure corruption, there's nothing left of them to save so we would need to send entire beings to the Nether. There's no telling what will happen, or if it's even possible."

"We can always deal with them the old-fashioned way," Kael offered.

"Sure, we can kill them, but until we hunt every last bastard down there's no telling how many more they'll create in the meantime. And you can be sure that as soon as we come for them they will go to ground." Lucian scrubbed a hand over his face and groaned. "Ideally, our first strike would be our last."

Effie didn't need the men's combined years of military experience to know that was wishful thinking. The Shadows were already scattered across the land. Worse, no one had the first clue where to find them. It would take years, maybe longer, to hunt each and every one of them down. How many more would die in the meantime?

Heavy weight settled in her neck and shoulders. The stakes were too high. They could not afford to fail, but it was looking more and more like there was no way they could win.

Lucian took her fingers in his, pulling her attention back to him. "Look, we're clearly not going to solve this tonight. Let's get some sleep, regroup tomorrow, and see what the others have to say."

"It's going to be at least another week before we can start our hunt anyway," Kael said as he started to stand.

Effie raised a brow. "A week?"

"We cannot just dump our people here and take off. They are still reeling. Once we are certain they are settled, then we will go," Lucian explained.

"Besides, it gives you time to play with your new power," Kael added with a grin.

"Perhaps in that time you can also convince the people of the Vale to assist in your cleansing efforts," Nord said.

Lucian looked skeptical. "We can ask, but I wouldn't hold my breath."

"Don't give them a reason to say no," Nord suggested.

"If my arriving with a Shadow-touched woman in chains didn't convince them, I'm not sure what else I can show them."

"No one truly saw what her being Shadow-touched meant," Kael said thoughtfully. "Maybe they just need to see what their future will be if we lose."

A shiver of foreboding sent goosebumps erupting down Effie's arms. "They already know . . ." She hadn't realized she spoke out loud until she felt the weight of three stares leveled on her. That alone would have been overwhelming before her new empathic connection to them, but now it was practically unbearable.

"What do you mean?" Lucian asked.

Effie's voice was strong, despite the fact that her stomach rolled with unease. "Everyone knows about The Shadow Years. The people of the Vale may no longer consider themselves part of the Chosen, but that does not make them exempt. If you tell them several markers have come to pass, they will join us. They'll have no choice."

The silence in the room took on a weight of its own. No matter what else happened, or what other battles they managed to win, it would always come back to that. There was no escaping what would happen if the last marker came to pass. So while they could fight the Shadows, and perhaps even repair the land, those things were just a smokescreen keeping them from addressing the actual threat.

Until they found a way to stop the prophecy from coming true, no one would ever be safe.

CHAPTER 19

EFFIE

"Just concentrate, you can do this."

Effie opened one eye and glared at Kael. "If you tell me to concentrate one more time, I will geld you."

Nord snorted with laughter as Kael's grin faded. He held up his palms. "Just trying to help."

She would have felt guilty if they hadn't been telling her the same thing for the last four hours. Well, three days and four hours. No matter how many times the other Guardians tried to explain it, she had yet to successfully access her power.

At least on purpose.

It would surge forth unbidden as it willed, usually in response to some kind of extreme emotion, and she didn't seem to have any trouble with mind-speaking. Although the latter seemed to be more of a passive ability than anything that required actual effort.

To say she was frustrated would be a gross understatement.

Lucian promised her that her power was there, not that she needed him to convince her of that. She could feel it, like an itch just out of reach. The problem was she didn't understand *how* to reach it. She'd tried envisioning it as a golden thread she needed to unspool. She'd

137

tried calling it forth, beckoning it as one does a skittish animal. She'd tried meditation and clearing her mind of everything else. When all of that failed, she'd resorted to begging.

She'd actually started pleading with her power to just put her out of her misery and hurry it up already.

Not shockingly, that too failed.

So here they were. Three days and four hours later. No closer to unlocking the riddle.

Lucian's hand pressed comfortingly against her lower back, his silent strength and unwavering support a balm to her fractured patience.

"This is stupid. It's not working."

"You're being too hard on yourself."

"Did you have this much trouble the first time?"

Lucian's mind fell suspiciously silent, and Effie let out a low snarl, her eyes flying open once more. "Why is this never easy? First the Mother-cursed visions and now this! You all can take your power and shove it straight up your—"

Lucian's arms wrapped around her, pulling her into his body as his lips pressed against her neck. "Peace, Effie," he whispered against the sensitive skin. "You're forgetting that all of us were trained prior to the change. We spent years learning about the gifts we'd acquire and how to use them. By the time we actually spoke our vows and underwent the transformation, it was practically a formality."

"Exactly," Kael chimed in. "You're expecting too much too soon."

"We don't have time for me to waste figuring it out. In case you've forgotten, we're in the middle of trying to save the world from eternal damnation."

Lucian's hands dropped to her hips, and he turned her around to face him. "You were an asset to our side before you became a Guardian, Effie. That hasn't changed."

"But think of how much more I could *do* now."

He silenced her with a gentle kiss.

"Might I make a suggestion?" Nord asked, causing the couple to begrudgingly break apart.

"Has the answer to that question ever stopped you before?" Lucian replied mildly.

Nord grinned, his smile looking roguish behind his beard. "Perhaps we're going about this the wrong way."

"By all means, enlighten us," Lucian muttered, taking Effie's hand and leading her to the chair he'd vacated earlier.

"Maybe one of us should show her what it's like."

Her brows veed with confusion. "I've seen Lucian access his power before."

"No, not watch us as we gather our power, but experience what it actually feels like, specifically the first time."

Kael nodded his agreement, while Lucian merely looked thoughtful.

"It could work," he eventually agreed.

"At the very least, she'd have the memory of the experience to draw from during her next attempt instead of blindly trying to make the connection," Nord said.

She was intrigued by the possibility, although she wasn't sure how they were expecting her to accomplish this feat. As the Triumvirate, the Guardians used their telepathic powers to experience the Keepers' visions. However, that required them to *use* their power. How exactly was she supposed to pluck memories from their minds in an attempt to better understand how to access her power when she couldn't access it in the first place?

"Uh, guys . . ."

Lucian must have already picked up on the direction of her thoughts, either that or she'd unconsciously projected them. "Our power connects us, remember? You don't have to do anything. I can simply recall the memory, and you'll be able to experience it as if it were your own."

"Really?"

The men nodded.

"Oh . . ." She'd known they could carry on conversations in their minds because of their power, but she hadn't understood the full scope of what that connection allowed.

Lucian squeezed her shoulder. "Would you like to try it?"

"Might as well. Not like it can make me do any worse, can it?"

His lips twitched up in a smile, but he had the decency not to outright agree with her assessment.

"I'm happy to share—" Kael broke off at Lucian's look. "Right, you're up."

Nord snickered and leaned back against the wall, his arms folded over his chest and one foot propped up behind him. Kael remained seated, his attention returning to the few books of prophecy they'd been able to recover from the citadel.

"Do you need me to close my eyes or anything?" she asked, looking up at Lucian.

"You don't need to, but it might help you focus."

"Here goes nothing," she muttered, wrinkling her nose at him before closing her eyes.

Lucian chuckled and brushed his lips against her forehead. As he pulled back, an image started to take shape in her mind. It started as a dark blue cloud, the mist dissipating as images unfolded before her.

As the picture crystalized, his thoughts merged with her own. As they did, she was struck by the sensation of being in two places at once. It was then Effie realized, she would not be mere witness, but a participant. Even though she could feel her physical body sitting in the chair, so too was she kneeling in the center of a tiled room. The chill from the floor permeated the thick leather of her pants, but it wasn't enough to mute the dull throb of pain caused by kneeling for hours. Despite the ache, her—Lucian's—body was frozen in place, without so much as a muscle twitch to expose his discomfort.

Anticipation swelled, as footsteps echoed loudly in the silence of the room.

"Initiates, rise."

Soon the footsteps were replaced by the rustle of fabric as a dozen men rose in unison. From her position in the front, Effie could not make out any of the others around her, except as hazy outlines in her periphery.

"Through your studies here you have proven yourselves worthy of bearing the incredible power, and with it, the responsibility of the Brotherhood. Henceforth, you are a Guardian of life—in all its forms. Above all else, your primary duty is to maintain the balance. Together we are the beacons, protecting those unable to save themselves and guiding the ways of man to ensure the continued survival of all. Do you so solemnly swear?"

Pride rippled through her as Lucian's deep voice rang out with a resounding, "Aye!"

"Come, then, and make your tribute."

Lucian was the first to step forward. A man with black hair liberally streaked with silver and familiar umber eyes grinned as he approached.

"Your mother and father would be proud of the man you've become, nephew."

Ancient grief rose in response to the words. Even though the emotion was not Effie's, it lodged itself in her throat, making it almost impossible to breathe.

Those dark eyes missed nothing. "Aye, feel the sorrow, Luc. Hold it close. 'Tis your reminder of what we stand to lose when the balance is broken. Now, make your offering and step from this dais as a full Brother."

Since being transformed it had been almost impossible to ignore the teasing allure of his gift. It called to him, a siren song that would have been irresistible if not for the iron-clad control he'd been taught. Instead of giving in to its call, he'd pushed it to the furthest corner of his mind, into a place hereto reserved for memories he chose to ignore. He could still feel it there, but it was no more than a dull hum.

Giving in to it now brought with it a heady sense of release. Electric tingles were already racing through his veins, eager to be unleashed. Lucian focused on the buzz of power, allowing it to fill his lungs and explode throughout his body.

Waves of power continued to build and crash within him until he could no longer separate himself from the sensation. The raw vitality was not just surging through his blood; it had taken over completely. He was no longer contained by something as insignificant as flesh; he was pure, unbound energy.

Light exploded around him, the world no longer a series of shapes and colors, but one breathtaking sea of golden light.

The part of Effie that could still distinguish herself from Lucian's memory recognized his dull hum as the itch she couldn't reach. Following Lucian's example, Effie concentrated on the sensation and took a deep, calming breath. Understanding how he'd pushed the buzz away until it was a distant thought, she reversed the action. No stranger to compartmentalizing that which she did not want to remember, Effie pictured a door. One that was made of impenetrable metal and locked with several thick padlocks. As she continued to breathe deep, the imaginary locks began dropping to the floor with loud reverberating thuds. With each crash, light began to pulse along the edges of the doorway, growing in intensity until the last of the locks fell away.

Her breath quickened, the hair on her arms and neck standing on end as what had laid dormant flared to life within her. Silently, the door swung open, filling her mind with more of the golden glow until there was no differentiation between the light and her consciousness.

Power did not simply exist within her, she *was* power.

Pure.

Potent.

Endless.

It filled her, finally alleviating that relentless itch. As the magic swelled within her, her awareness shifted. She was still connected to Lucian, but no longer tied to a single memory. New images assaulted her, brushing up against the edges of her consciousness like playful cats begging for attention.

Lucian's voice sounded all around her, as inconsequential as floating dust motes and as powerful as a storm. *"It's all right."*

A rush of emotion, not all of it hers, surged through her as her Guardian's entire life began to replay all around her, all at once. There was no rhyme or reason, simply Lucian and the events that had made him.

His past stretched out before her, moments taking shape like ink dropped into a pool of water. They swirled and converged, no less complete for their transience. Entire centuries passed this way in a matter of seconds.

She experienced them with an odd kind of duality. First, as if his memories were her own, but also simultaneously as the woman in love with him. Her heart broke with his loss while her pride rejoiced at his accomplishments. Wonder filled her at the discovery of his artistic gifts, and jealousy reared its head at those that had known pleasure at his hand.

No one event took precedence until Effie's own face was reflected back at her. She recognized her tangle of curls and her overly large blue eyes, but this was not her face as she'd ever seen it. Without the filter of her own insecurities, it was like seeing herself for the very first time.

From there, the floodgates were opened. Effie was looking at herself through Lucian's eyes. Each image colored by his reaction to her. She felt the acidic bite of his fear as she sprinted toward a Shadow, the purple flames of Shadow Fire burning in her eyes as her mouth opened on a savage battle cry. Then there was a flare of frustrated amusement warring with begrudging respect as she refused to be left behind. That was followed closely by the burn of unfulfilled desire as their bodies moved against each other on the shower floor. Before she could catch her breath, she was consumed by bone-numbing grief as she looked up at Lucian with milky-white eyes.

The intensity of it shocked her back to the present.

"How do you stand it?" she stuttered, her body trembling from the onslaught of his past.

"The power?" he asked, his deep voice ragged, the memories as fresh for him as they were for her.

She swallowed and shook her head. "The knowing. How can you carry the weight of all you learn without succumbing to the burden?"

Lucian's eyes flashed with understanding, the bronze flecks momentarily overtaking all other color. "You learn how to close yourself off from all but that which you are seeking. But there will be times when you find yourself a slave to the power, helpless to do anything but absorb everything regardless of your own will. That you can only endure."

She shuddered as she remembered Smoke's reaction to her past; the tormented sound of his voice in her mind as he revealed what it had cost him to relive it through her. Now she understood. The inescapable horror of living through someone's pain and not having a way to process or purge it.

"It is part of the balance," Lucian explained.

Effie nodded mutely. The man from his memory—his uncle—had said that Guardians maintain the balance. She'd misunderstood at first, thinking he spoke of something as simple as good versus evil. But what he'd really meant was the cost of a Guardian's power. Their gift came with a price. Immortal they might be, and granted the ability to transform the world around them, but that did not make them immune to the darker side of nature. If anything, they were more intimately aware of it. Souls may be beautiful—stunning even—in their purity, but no one was untouched by the cruelty of pain or desperation. In order to be worthy of the beauty, they had to also experience the sting of despair.

She had no doubt only the strongest among them could withstand it.

All of this she expressed without speaking, her eyes never leaving Lucian's as she fought to control the unexpected tempest his memories had unleashed within her. They were a part of her now, just as hers were part of him. Because of it, they were united in a way not even death could unravel.

Lucian cupped her cheek, the gentle scrape of his thumb against her skin as tender as his whispered words. "And now you know."

Her heart ached with equal parts joy and sorrow. He wasn't just referring to how to tap into her power, but also what she'd learned about him and what he felt for her in the process. She hadn't doubted he loved her. No man would willingly go through hell and back to save a woman he didn't love. What she hadn't realized was just how long he'd been waiting for her.

There was one memory, so well-worn and faded it was clearly a favorite. Effie had been confused about how that could be since they'd only just spent hours wrapped around each other in the prison a few nights past. Given her newfound understanding of sharing and taking prophecies, she now recognized the vision for what it was.

Kieran might have dreamed of her, but he wasn't the only one to know before she was born that their fates would be intertwined. Someone had told Lucian Effie was coming, gifting him with only that one moment as proof of what he could have if he was brave enough to fight for it. Miranda had broken every rule to give Lucian that piece of his future, but her love and hope for her granddaughter had made her bold.

Her grandmother's words, spoken to Lucian so many years ago, passed between them. *"She will need you, Guardian. The Mother is generous, but Her most precious gifts never come without cost. See what can be, and know what will be lost if you fail."*

Taking Lucian's hand in hers, Effie pressed it over her heart. "All this time, you knew . . ."

His dark eyes burned with emotion. "I hoped. No future is certain, and when I saw—" he broke off, his voice so rough he had to continue along their link. *"If the Triumvirate know anything with certainty, it is that a Keeper's vision is simply one potential path. A single choice can determine what comes to pass. I was told not to fail, and when I found you in the citadel after the attack, I feared I already had. But I had to try. For decades all I had was the promise of you, but then I met you, and it was only then I could truly appreciate what my failure would mean."*

It was a battle not to cry, but somehow Effie managed. There were no words she could give him that would do justice to the gift he'd just given her. But Lucian didn't need them. Connected as they were, he already knew.

Taking a deep breath, she glanced around the room. "I guess I get my rule-breaking tendencies from my grandmother."

Nord and Kael had remained silent, providing her and Lucian with the illusion of privacy, but at her words they burst into laughter. It wasn't long before she joined them, her shoulders shaking as she chuckled.

Grinning, Lucian leaned forward and pressed his lips to hers. "Thank the Mother for that."

CHAPTER 20

EFFIE

Now that Effie had discovered how to tap into her power, it was much easier the second time. There was no need for her to picture a door opening within her mind. It was as Lucian had promised, all she had to do was breathe and envision her lungs expanding with power. Her Guardian gifts came eagerly, crackling within her like unformed bolts of lightning.

"There's something I still don't understand," she murmured, reveling in the feel of power surging through her veins.

"Just one thing?" Kael asked with a playful lift of his brow.

Effie shot him a look. "Okay, lots of things, but just one thing in particular at this exact moment. Better?"

Kael flashed her his dimples. "Much."

She rolled her eyes and turned her attention back to Lucian, who managed to successfully hide his amusement behind a look of polite inquiry.

"What would you like to know?"

"You told me once that the Triumvirates' runes help contain their power. If a Guardian's power is the same thing, shouldn't I have runes, too?"

"What makes you think you don't?"

Effie held out her clearly unmarked arms, looking from them back to the Guardians. "Wouldn't I . . . feel them or something?"

Lucian gave her one of his enigmatic smiles. "What do you remember of the transformation?"

Her brows dipped as she thought back. "Not much, really. The sense of floating and then you telling me to fill the vessel—I'm guessing my body was the literal vessel."

He gestured to himself and then each of the other Guardians in turn. "Our physical forms are a manifestation of how we remember ourselves before the change."

"So I don't really look like this anymore?" Effie asked with a frown as she looked down at her body.

"You do, because that is the form that you chose," Nord interjected.

"I'm sorry, was that supposed to be an explanation?" Effie asked, her voice deceptively sweet.

Lucian was still laughing when he wrapped his arm around her shoulder, pulling her in close. "What do Guardians do, Effie?"

She blinked up at him, feeling like she was back in school and had just found out there was a test she'd forgotten to study for. "Uh . . . guard?"

Kael folded in two, his laughter coming in snorts. "She's not wrong."

Effie crossed her arms, feeling seconds away from a full-blown sulk. "You know, when you guys referred to me as your little sister, I didn't realize that meant I had actually acquired a bunch of annoying older brothers." Despite the peevish cast of her voice, the thought actually warmed her. It was nice to have a family in more than name.

Lucian tugged on the end of one of her curls. *"You better not be referring to me."*

She raised a brow. *"You may not be brotherly, but you are certainly annoying."*

"As long as we have that sorted," he replied with a wink that had her stomach turning to jelly.

"I wasn't trying to be vague," Nord said, once he managed to stop laughing. "Nor was Lucian, believe it or not."

"That's a first."

Nord gave her an indulgent smile. "I think you're confusing us with our alter egos."

"Is there really that much of a difference?"

Between one breath and the next, Nord transformed into Mirror Two, his body stretching into its inhumanly skeletal form as navy runes broke out along his pale flesh. *"You tell me."*

She blinked up into the twin pools of black that had once been his eyes, her heart beating erratically in her chest. "Mother's tits, I'd forgotten how unsettling you three were."

"Even me?" Lucian's question rang through her mind.

Effie spared him a glance, her expression softening. *"I didn't notice the surface as much with Smoke. He was just my friend."*

Lucian's eyes grew heated, but there wasn't a chance to say more.

Nord released his illusion and shrugged. "You have to admit it's an effective visage."

She shook her head at his casual assessment. Effective really wasn't the word she'd use.

"When we are reborn into our power, there's a moment when we exist outside of any physical trappings. That was the feeling of floating you experienced. As the final part of our transition we choose the form that will contain our power, our body, if you will. Naturally, we return to what we know, although it is possible that we can make modifications—transformation is at the heart of our power, after all."

Her head was starting to hurt. "So did any of you make *modifications*?"

The men shook their heads.

"Why mess with perfection?" Kael asked, unable to keep a straight face.

Effie let a ripple of begrudging amusement flicker through their link as she asked, "Can I really change my appearance?"

"Don't go getting any ideas," Lucian said in her mind, his eyes narrowing.

"You can create the illusion of any form you choose, and that is what everyone else would see, but the core elements of who you are will never change," Nord said.

"So you're saying I'll always be short?" she asked, making a face.

Lucian laughed. "Don't be so disappointed. I happen to think you're the perfect size."

She gifted him with a smile. "But what does any of this have to do with runes?"

"All magic leaves a trace, even ours. Our runes are the evidence of our transformation from human to Guardian."

"Although," Kael interjected, "they have the added benefit of allowing us to maintain a physical form."

The image of locks on a chest appeared in her mind, and for a second she wasn't sure if the analogy was her own, or gifted to her from one of her fellow Guardians. "I guess you were telling the truth when you told me the runes contained your power," she murmured, glancing back to Lucian.

"I may not have always been able to tell you the entire truth, but I did my best to never outright lie," he said with a small smile.

She stared at her completely human-looking arm, giving it a little shake. "So where are they?"

Lucian ran a tanned finger down the exposed skin of her forearm. "Use your power and see."

It took a second for his words to register over the tingles racing along her skin. Blinking a few times to clear her head, Effie closed her eyes and inhaled. When she opened them once more, the world was bathed in shimmering gold.

Lucian moved to stand behind her. He wasn't touching her, but his body radiated heat, which enveloped her as he leaned forward to whisper in her ear. It was distracting enough that her vision flickered, the world of light momentarily replaced with its mundane counterpart.

"You're not helping," she muttered, fighting for focus.

"Yes, I am," he purred. "You're just not concentrating."

More tingles followed his words, causing her to suck in a shaky breath. *Will I ever stop being so affected by him?*

"I hope not," he replied, startling her.

"I really need to learn to control that better.*"* Lucian's low chuckles caused her stomach to clench. *"Arse."*

He only laughed harder and ran his palms down each of her arms until his fingers were threaded with hers. "Focus, fledgling."

This time she was able to mostly ignore his presence as she looked around the room with her Guardian-enhanced vision. Now the breathless feeling in her chest was caused by the beauty that filled her eyes and not the man standing behind her. Nord and Kael glowed like twin beacons from their post by the door. She couldn't help but smile as her eyes moved over them.

It was incredible, this ability. The world was not comprised of shapes and colors, but of pure, radiating light. Even so, she could discern each individual item in the room. The threads of life that ran through objects such as the bookcase or bed might be dim in comparison, but they were no less spectacular for it. It was the difference between the white-hot blaze of the sun during midday, or the almost silvery glow of the moon at night, and every shade in between.

Her breath caught on a giddy laugh as streaks of sunlight moved through the spider-web-thin strands of gray that comprised the walls. The mice looked like shooting stars, their tiny hearts pulsing a blinding white as they scuttled past.

"Amazing," she breathed.

Lucian's hands returned to her shoulders, grounding her. Lifting her arm, Effie looked at herself for the first time. Her limbs were a network of shimmering white-gold strands. As she twisted her limb this way and that, she made out the snaking runes. Instead of inky blue, they were a stunning shade of silver, transparent but impossible to ignore.

A soft "oh" of wonder left her lips as she raised her eyes and made out the same ghostly shapes on both Nord and Kael. The runes had always seemed a bit eerie, nothing like the masculine beauty of a jaka —the warriors' tattoo that branded both Ronan and Von—but now, seeing them in their true form, she was drawn to the ethereal markings.

Effie turned to face Lucian, suddenly desperate to see what he looked like with the trappings of mortality no longer between them.

It hurt to look at him, he shone so brightly. Like staring up at the sun. If she was white-gold, Lucian was liquid metal. The core of each thread white while the edges shimmered a lovely, burning bronze. It was almost the same color as the flecks in his eyes, but more potent. Everything about him in this form was *more*. Lucian had always called to her on some subconscious level. First as a protector, and then simply as a man. But that paled in comparison to the effect he had on her now. Perhaps because she knew she was as close as she'd ever be to seeing his soul, and it was breathtakingly beautiful.

Her feelings were a complicated tangle as she stood before his glowing form. She felt equal parts unworthy and utterly at peace. As if she was in the presence of some holy figure. But this was Lucian. The man who knew her as well as, if not better than, she knew herself.

Desire spiraled through her, making her more aware of her physical body and its reaction to him. It was hard not to reach out and touch him, pull him to her and remind herself that he was in fact real.

Lucian's hands spasmed on her shoulders, his fingers digging in as she stared up at him. The pressure in her chest grew painful, and Effie realized she'd forgotten to breathe.

The outline of his runes shimmered, and her fingers itched to trace them. Lifting her hand, she murmured his name, still concentrating on his runes when a thundering knock sounded on the door. Effie blinked and the world was dark once more. For one long second, she couldn't see anything in the sudden gloom. She was utterly disoriented, her body feeling ungainly and cumbersome in the abrupt absence of her power.

Lucian let out an angry hiss. "Get rid of them."

Nord's eyes were wide, staring pointedly at Effie. *"How do you suggest I do that without anyone catching sight of her?"*

"Effie, I need you to hide your runes," Lucian said, his voice low and insistent in her mind.

She blinked up at him. *"What?"*

Worry flickered in his dark eyes. *"Your runes. While you were accessing your power you managed to manifest them. You need to undo it."*

The knocking sounded again, even more impatient this time.

"Undo it? I don't even know what I did in the first place."

Panic was making it hard to breathe. She absolutely could not be caught with her runes on display. She'd been a Guardian for a few days, and she was already about to give away one of their most closely guarded secrets.

Before Nord or Kael could say anything, the door started to swing open. Lucian moved fast, grabbing her by the wrist and pulling her body behind his. As he did, she felt heavy cloth settle around her head and shoulders. He'd managed to conceal her with a cloak in the space of a heartbeat, although it'd happened so fast she hadn't seen what he'd used to make it.

"Apologies for the interruption, Guardians, but there's someone that's insisting on speaking with you."

A muffled, clearly feminine voice was muttering something indistinguishable from just beyond the distressed-looking speaker.

"Now really isn't the best time," Lucian began.

His worry lapped at her. It was a mirror of her own. From behind the folds of her hood, Effie watched a pale hand wrap around the messenger's arm and pull the boy back.

No longer muffled, her heart stopped when the voice spoke again. "Trust me, they've been waiting for me long enough."

Helena. Ronan's messages must have finally reached her.

The Kiri had arrived.

CHAPTER 21

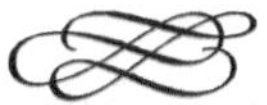

EFFIE

"**W**here is she? Where's Effie?"

Effie's mouth opened, a response on her lips as her body prepared to launch itself in her friend's arms, only to come up short. The flash of scarlet in the corner of her eye reminded her just in time why Lucian hid her in the first place.

Am I still runed? How do I check without alerting everyone to the fact I'm not actually a member of the Triumvirate? Or explain what I'm doing pretending to be one of them in the first place?

"I'm right here," a soft voice called.

For the second time in as many minutes, Effie's heart stopped. There, just beside Kael where Nord had been leaning against the wall, stood . . . well—*her*.

While Lucian had sprung to action robing her, Nord must have cast an illusion to take her place and thereby maintain the pretense of their meeting.

"This isn't your first time doing this . . ."

None of the Guardians' expressions betrayed them, but Lucian managed an infinitesimal shake of his head.

Completely oblivious to the tense undercurrent, Helena threw her arms around fake Effie. "I'm so sorry it took me so long to get to you. Can you ever forgive me?"

She couldn't help her mental snicker as Nord awkwardly hugged Helena back. The Guardian almost reminded her of herself. He clearly wasn't used to physical affection, and she hadn't been either for a long time. Her friendship with Helena and her Circle had changed that.

"There's nothing to forgive. I'm just so glad to see you," Nord-as-Effie replied.

Helena pushed back, her aqua eyes searching the illusion's face. "Do you promise? I feel horrible."

She watched Nord grin and gave an involuntary shudder. It was entirely too bizarre watching this impromptu portrayal of herself.

His voice filled her mind. *"You can feed me your responses through our link."*

She jolted, the unexpected convenience of their abilities momentarily rendering her speechless. She hadn't even thought about trying to carry on an actual conversation with her friend via her proxy.

"It will give her less of a reason to doubt the illusion's authenticity, but due to the strength of her power we shouldn't draw out your reunion. She might see through what others would not." That was Lucian; forever cautious and protective.

"Don't beat yourself up," Effie replied, hearing Nord repeat the words as soon as she thought them. "How could any of us know Rowena's death wouldn't be the end of it?"

Helena frowned, her lovely face darkening with self-recrimination. "*I* should have known better. Nothing that bitch did was ever by half-measure. Of course she would find a way to mock me from the grave."

Effie felt a pang of grief. They'd both suffered terrible losses because of the impostor queen. Not wanting to dwell on it, she changed the subject. "Can you tell me where you were?"

Helena's cheeks darkened in a guilty flush. "Von and I took a bit of a honeymoon. We spent the last few weeks visiting the pride in Talyria."

Talyria. No wonder the messages didn't reach them. How exactly was one supposed to communicate through a Talyrian?

"Not even you could have known what would happen. I'm glad you and your Mate got to spend well-deserved quality time together. Mother knows you earned it."

Helena flashed her twin a grateful smile. "You're sweet to say so, Efs. But look at what we came home to. I'm so sorry you've had to bear the brunt of this burden alone."

Effie felt the unexpected urge to cry at Helena's use of her nickname. She hadn't realized how much she missed having her friend around until this precise moment. It wasn't until Lucian cleared his throat that she remembered Nord was awaiting her response.

"Not alone. The Guardians are wonderfully capable."

She could feel Kael and Lucian's amusement at that response. It was almost a direct contradiction to what she'd spent the last month telling them. But only because they were as likely to annoy her as they were to impress her.

Helena glanced at Lucian and Kael, her gaze flickering with iridescence as it passed over the real Effie's robed figure. She stiffened, fear sparking at the small display of her friend's power, but Helena only looked curious as she studied the two Guardians and lone member of the Triumvirate.

"I am in your debt," Helena said formally, addressing Lucian as if she could sense he was the one in charge.

Effie bristled. *"I'm standing here disguised as a damned member of the Three and she* still *knows you are the true power. Shouldn't she at least acknowledge me or something?"*

Lucian's laughter brushed against her mind. *"Don't take offense, fledgling. Your Kiri is no fan of ours. She despises the Triumvirate almost as much as you did in the beginning."*

"I never despised you," Effie corrected immediately, frowning beneath her hood. *"I just hated that you could never say anything plainly."*

Lucian bowed his head, hiding the smile her admission caused as he replied to Helena, "A debt we do not accept, Kiri. You are not the sole protector of this realm. It is as much our responsibility to address the threats to Elysia as it is yours."

Helena's lips twisted. "You should tell my Advisor that because he has been preaching otherwise for years."

The others chuckled while Effie fought against a laugh. He wasn't even present and Timmins still managed to end up the brunt of a joke.

"Did you come alone?" The thought was practically blurted, Effie only just realizing that Helena was standing in the room without any of the men from her Circle hovering protectively behind her.

Helena turned to face Effie's double, giving her a lopsided grin as she shook her head. "As if any of them would allow it. Von is upstairs with Ronan getting brought up to speed. Kragen and Joquil are on their way from the Palace, but Timmins stayed behind."

Effie watched Nord give a small nod, realizing he'd sensed the gesture from her as easily as her words. *"This is so weird."*

Lucian risked a brush of his hand against her arm.

Helena's expression sobered. "We have much to discuss, you and I. I want to hear all about your visions, these Shadow-touched you've discovered, and everything that has come to pass since you left us. Ronan said you've been unwell, but I have to say, you look wonderful." Helena's gaze turned thoughtful, a small smile lifting her lips. "It would seem that being amongst the Keepers has been good for you."

For the first time, Effie was thankful she was hidden behind the cloak so that Helena could not witness the blush her words caused. While being one of the Keepers had definitely challenged her and helped her grow, it was no secret that the real reason she was standing here was because of Lucian. And not just because he'd saved her. The effect he'd had on her had taken root long before she became a Guardian. She owed him more than she could ever repay.

Nord chuckled, picking up on the direction of her thoughts, but he did not embarrass her by repeating them. Instead he gave a small shrug and remained silent. Effie could have kissed him.

"Perhaps before the two of you catch up, we should meet with the Valen Council," Lucian interjected smoothly. "There is much that has happened, and still more that needs to be done. It would expedite things for all of us if we could discuss matters with all relevant parties present."

Helena sighed. "You're probably right. I've already insulted the Council by insisting on finding Effie first. I didn't even bother with introductions before bossing that poor boy around." Helena looked over her shoulder at the messenger still waiting in the doorway. "Sorry for that."

The boy shrugged, his cheeks pinkening. "No apology necessary, Kiri. I am happy to be of service."

"He keeps looking at her like that, her Mate is going to pummel the boy." Kael's amusement coated his observation.

"As would you. A man might understand another's appreciation of his woman, but he'd never let puppy love like that go unchecked for long, especially not when she's his Mate," Lucian mused.

Effie eyed the messenger more closely. He'd been flustered before, but he was clearly smitten with the Chosen's queen. Not that she blamed him. Helena was impossible to ignore. It had nothing to do with beauty—although she had that in spades—and everything to do with the unmistakable energy that flowed from her. It was the Mother's power, empathy and love encased in raw magic and absolute strength.

One couldn't help but be at peace in Helena's presence, even if they were concurrently terrified. Effie had witnessed the woman turn a grown man into mist with no more effort than she used to pluck a flower. It would be a mistake to forget who she was.

"She's not the only one." Lucian's words were for her alone, and Effie felt oddly exposed. *"You're just as powerful as she is, Effie. And no less magnificent."*

Her instinct was to contradict him, but she could feel the power rolling through her veins, the liquid lightning reinforcing his words. Even a week ago what he said might not have been true, but now? Now she was a Guardian, and not even the Mother's Vessel outmatched her.

Effie didn't know what to do with the discovery. It was so unexpected; so wholly opposite of everything she'd ever known about herself that she couldn't quite believe it was true.

"I apologize for barging in on you," Helena said, interrupting her thoughts. "It was unforgivably rude of me."

Lucian shrugged, a polite smile playing on his lips. "You're the Kiri," he said, as if it explained everything.

Helena shook her head, color blooming in her cheeks. "No, please don't make excuses for me. Believe it or not, I was raised better than that. Mother, I didn't even ask your names."

"I'm Lucian, Kiri," he replied in his deep rumble, giving Helena one of his rare, genuine grins.

Jealousy sizzled through her. Not because she thought Lucian had any romantic interest in Helena, but because until just now she'd never seen him grant that smile to anyone other than herself. She knew he could feel the shift in her emotions because he went still and then a flood of heat moved through her. Was he actually pleased by her reaction?

"Well met, Lucian," Helena said, returning his warmth and turning her head slightly to peer at Kael. "And you are?"

"Kael, my lady. The pleasure is mine." He gifted her with one of his dimpled smiles and bowed slightly.

Helena's smile faltered as her eyes returned to the place where the real Effie stood. Her voice was notably cooler as she said, "I don't suppose we require any introductions."

Sweat rolled down Effie's spine. The words, while not exactly a question, required a response. The only way she could do so, without undoing all of their carefully constructed illusions, was to reply in the same manner as the Triumvirate. Unfortunately, no one had explained how she was supposed to project her thoughts to those that weren't Guardians. So far, everything had just been instinctual. She had a thought she wanted them to hear—or sometimes not, as the case may be—and it was done.

But Effie should have known better than to worry. The Guardians were masters of subterfuge. Not even she could tell which of them it was that answered for her.

"At your service as always, Kiri."

Helena tilted her head, her eyes hardening. "Are you really? And all this time I thought I was just another one of your puppets."

The sound of crackling leaves filled the small room. The men were amused rather than offended by her sharp-tongued retort.

"We are all pawns to the Mother's plan."

Helena shook her head and sighed. "I suppose we are. In any event, I've intruded long enough. Effie,"—she turned to face Nord—"will you join me for dinner after the meeting?"

Nord didn't need any help anticipating Effie's reply. "Of course, Helena. I'm looking forward to it."

Helena beamed, hugging her doppelgänger once more. "I've missed you."

Effie couldn't contain her teasing reply, which Nord vocalized. "While you were on your honeymoon? I doubt it. Unless Von isn't nearly as skilled as I believe him to be . . ."

Lucian's gaze seared her with its intensity. *"And what do you know of his skill?"*

Apparently, she wasn't the only one feeling possessive today. Effie smiled beneath her hood.

Helena laughed, unaware of the conversation happening between them. "No need to fear on that front." She winked and then glanced at the men. "But perhaps that's a topic better left for when we are alone."

With a small wave, she backed out of the room, the door closing gently behind her.

There was a moment of silence before Nord dropped his illusion and Lucian murmured, "You can come out now."

"That was close," she said, pushing back her hood.

The Guardians nodded as one.

"Too close," Lucian agreed. "We'll need to be more careful about our practice sessions in the future."

Effie shrugged off the robe, looking at the runes still decorating her arms. Somehow she'd managed to make them appear like they'd been drawn on with shimmering dust. "What am I supposed to do about these?"

"Put them away," Kael offered unhelpfully.

She scowled at him. "Easy for you to say. How exactly do I do that?"

"The same way you made them appear," Nord said, moving to stand beside her.

Effie wanted to stomp on his foot, but was proud of herself for resisting the temptation. "That would make so much more sense if I knew what I did."

Nord shrugged. "It's simple. You wanted to see your runes, so you pulled them to the surface. Now you don't, so push them back down."

She frowned at his matter-of-fact tone. They were making it sound so easy. She risked a glance at Lucian, curious if he had anything to add, but he was leaning against a table, his arms crossed and his face neutral.

Frustration churned inside of her. Just when she finally thought she was making headway she started to drown beneath the weight of everything she didn't know. True, it had only been a few days, but these three acted as if it was supposed to all be so natural.

It wasn't.

Not even close.

Dealing with her visions was easier, and that had been an absolute fucking nightmare.

The only time Effie had ever felt like she actually had a grasp on her abilities was during her handful of sessions with Smoke. A surge of wistful longing caught her by surprise and she cast another furtive glance at Lucian.

For all that they were the same person, she couldn't help but miss her mentor. No matter how many times they might have butted heads in the beginning, Smoke had always made Effie feel truly understood. He was the one, after all, who'd made a point to break the anonymity of his station and actually talk to her.

Effie sighed. It was silly. Every interaction she'd had with Smoke had just been a conversation with Lucian in disguise. She hadn't actually *lost* anything, but a part of her still grieved. Now that she knew his secret, there was no reason for Smoke to reappear. No reason for him to use that campfire voice when he spoke to her. It was a voice she'd come to associate with security and comfort. She felt both of those things with Lucian, but if she was being honest with herself, it wasn't the same. Maybe she was simply too aware of him and who he was to her for those associations to be at the forefront now.

"Leave us."

Effie jerked, her eyes shooting up. Lucian met her gaze, his dark gaze unreadable as he studied her. It was then she understood that her thoughts hadn't been private after all. He'd heard everything as clearly as if she'd shouted it at him.

Again.

The realization only fueled her frustration.

Kael and Nord took one look at Lucian's expression and filed out of the room, though not before offering her looks she suspected were supposed to be reassuring. They only made her feel more on edge.

She crossed her arms, not meeting Lucian's gaze as she stared down at the tip of her boot. "I shouldn't have to censor my thoughts just because you can eavesdrop at will."

"No one asked you to," he replied, his voice unexpectedly warm.

Just as quickly, Effie went from righteous indignation to an uncomfortable sense of guilt. It had never been her intention for him to catch wind that she was mourning the loss of Smoke. He felt badly enough for deceiving her in the first place. She didn't mean to make him feel any worse.

"Turn around, fledgling."

Her eyes widened, and she glanced around the all-too-empty room. Turning away from him would have her facing the bed. Just what in the Mother's name was he up to?

"Why?" she asked, her voice betraying her nerves.

He pushed off the table and stared at her, letting his silence speak for him.

She did as she was told, knowing the quickest way to an answer was obedience. Even if it was begrudgingly given.

As soon as her back was toward him, Smoke's voice filled her mind. She stiffened for a heartbeat and then a shiver ran down the length of her back. Her eyes fell closed, and her breath left her in a soft *whoosh.* He was giving her what she'd craved, and without his overwhelming presence to distract her, Effie could buy into the pretense.

If it were possible, she fell even more in love with him. He'd given her what she needed—what she hadn't even thought to ask for—without hesitation.

"You know what to do. All the answers you seek are within you."

Effie focused on the voice, letting it silence all the other doubts floating through her mind.

"A Guardian's power is tied to their will. The stronger the intention, the more effective the results."

Nord had already said she'd been able to manifest her runes because she'd wanted to see them. If that were true, it really should be as simple as wanting them to fade.

"Call your power. Picture what you want in your mind, and then, once you are ready, impose your will on the world around you. Do not ask for permission; demand obedience. You are a Guardian. The universe serves at your whim."

"No wonder you're all a bunch of egomaniacs," she muttered with a small smile.

Smoke's rustle of laughter floated past, but his voice was stern when he replied. *"Focus. There is a room full of people gathering even as we speak, preparing to determine the course of Elysia's future. Don't you wish to be at the table helping to make those decisions instead of merely having to follow them?"*

"Of course I do." Her response was vehement. Immediate. After a lifetime of having to obey, being part of the team—a participant whose voice was actually heard—meant everything to her.

"Then remove your runes and let us go. You cannot join the others until you wear the form they need to see. If you cannot manage this small task, then you will remain here."

He'd struck a nerve. Of course he knew that being left behind was guaranteed to cause a reaction within her.

"The hell I will," she snarled, her power rising swiftly, filling her until energy all but crackled from the tips of her fingers.

He didn't need to speak again for her to sense his approval.

Holding the image of her rune-free skin in her mind, Effie released a breath and pushed her power out. Or at least she hoped she did. She was still working predominantly on instinct.

There was no sizzle of magic as the transformation took place. No flare of heat along her skin to tell her it was done. Opening one eye, Effie risked a peek at her arm. The subtle shimmer from the flowing marks was gone.

She let out a relieved huff of breath and was about to turn when Lucian was at her back, his hands warm on her shoulders.

"Well done." His breath flowed across the nape of her neck, the damp warmth causing goosebumps to explode across her skin. "I knew you could do it," he said, pressing a kiss to the top of her spine.

"I'm glad one of us did," she mumbled, distracted by the feel of lips against her skin.

He chuckled and pulled back slightly, the sudden cool rush of air causing her to shiver.

Effie turned to face him. "Luc?"

"Hmm?"

"Thank you."

His expression was tender. "I should have realized it sooner. The bond between a Guardian and their mentor is always strong." He let out a little laugh. "How could it not be when you practically live in each other's mind?"

She tilted her head. "But Smoke mentored me as a Keeper. It's hardly the same."

Lucian returned her inquisitive gaze. "Isn't it? Memories were experienced, concerns shared, guidance offered."

"I suppose so . . ."

He reached out and ran a knuckle over her cheek. "Never apologize for missing Smoke or what he represents for you. I know that there are few people you've been able to trust. I am happy to be that person for you whenever you need."

She grabbed his hand before he could pull it away. "Lucian, you are. I don't want you to think—"

He pressed a finger against her lips. "There's no need to explain. Smoke is part of me. It is no hardship to give him reign if it brings you peace. But," he leaned close, his eyes flashing molten bronze, "if it will make you feel better, I know how you can thank me."

Blood rushed to her cheeks and her mouth went dry at the heated look on his face. "Oh?"

He nodded, never once dropping his eyes from hers. It was so potent she could feel it racing across her skin. When he spoke, his voice was barely more than a rumble. "Tonight, once we're alone, I want you to wear your runes for me."

Her heart began to pound. "My w-what?"

"Your runes. *Just* your runes."

Her breath stuttered.

"You looked so beautiful standing there, practically glowing with your power. It was all I could do not to reach out and trace them. So tonight, that's what I want to do. Trace them. First with my fingers." He brushed his lips against hers. "Then with my tongue."

Effie's insides went liquid, her mind wiped of everything except Lucian. "Why wait?"

He pulled back. She would have thought he was completely unaffected by the exchange if not for the bitten-off growl and flash of longing in his dark eyes. "I'm sure our absence has already been noted."

Right. The Council. Effie forced out a ragged breath. "Later, then."

Lucian nodded and held out a hand.

She stared at it for a moment before wrapping her fingers around his wrist and tugging him toward her. The move wouldn't have worked if Lucian hadn't allowed it. He was entirely too big for the slight but insistent pull to have any real effect. But since their wills were aligned, he closed the small space between them.

"Just one more," she whispered.

He gifted her with one of those rare, stunning grins and pressed his lips against hers, lifting his head just enough to whisper, "For you . . . always."

CHAPTER 22

EFFIE

A storm was coming. She didn't need her gift of prophecy to tell her that. Tension filled the formal meeting room, heavy and thick. What was less obvious was when the storm would break, and who would be left standing once it did.

She glanced uneasily around the room. Four members of the Valen Council lined one ivory-colored wall. Helena, Von, Ronan, and Reyna stood facing them. Effie had made to join her friends, but one look from Lucian had her checking the impulse and remaining at his side. Thus, she stood with the three other Guardians in between the two groups, while Nord's illusion of the Triumvirate completed the square by hovering along the final wall.

Effie made a point not to look at the three robed figures. It was surreal knowing that nothing was actually there, and she was afraid she'd draw attention by staring. Not wanting to give the secret away, her attention bounced between the other attendees.

As far as she could tell, everyone who was coming was already present, but no one seemed to want to be the first to take a seat and officially start the proceedings. They'd spent the last few minutes standing around and eyeing each other without trying to be obvious about it.

Rather, most of them tried.

Trinity, a striking woman with red hair who Effie had only met in passing, openly glared at her. It had been awhile since anyone had displayed such outright hostility for her. She'd almost forgotten how physical a sensation it could be, and she fought the urge to squirm under the weight of it.

Effie had left much of her old life behind during her time with Helena and then with the Keepers, but those old insecurities were harder to shed. Especially when she was caught off guard. The best she could manage was to keep her expression carefully neutral, knowing better than to let Trinity see that her vitriol was working.

As always, Lucian missed nothing. From the corner of her eye she watched as he took in her rigid posture, then as he shifted his chin the smallest fraction to look at Trinity. His reaction was palpable. She almost flinched away from the icy rage, but then his fingers found hers, infusing her with his strength.

"You're a Guardian now," he reminded her. *"Own your space, fledgling. Show her that her petty games are beneath your notice."*

I am a Guardian, she repeated as she lifted her chin and returned Trinity's unwavering stare. This kind of blatant confrontation was heady. Before coming to the citadel, before her decision to never again be a mouse, Effie had rarely risked making waves. Especially when the other person was a stranger. When she'd been younger—and on her own—she hadn't wanted to draw attention to herself, lest she be cast out. But now . . . now she no longer stood alone. And even if she did, she was more than a match for anyone that would try to oppose her.

Pride from her fellow Guardians warmed her and Effie smiled.

The woman blinked, her cheeks turning a blotched crimson before she finally glanced away.

"Perhaps it is time to begin?" Helena finally asked. Her voice was frosty, her expression fierce. The Kiri hadn't missed the exchange either, and she was not pleased with the Council.

Helena had dressed for the occasion, no longer wearing her traveling clothes, but instead a lavender gown symbolizing her station, and her one-of-a-kind pendant. Its egg-sized, iridescent stone hung just above her breasts and was casting rainbows on the walls.

She was flanked on either side by Von and Ronan, with Reyna just to the right of the latter. Each one of them was a powerful leader in their own right, which only further emphasized the Helena's supremacy. She was not just a ruler in name. These three powerhouses had chosen to serve her, which meant they acknowledged her authority over them. It said a lot that three such people would willingly do so. A fact that was not lost on the Valen Council.

As one of the lost tribes, the people of the Vale were obviously struggling with this realization. They'd never shared space with anyone who had access to this amount of power in their very sheltered lives. Although in their defense, few had. Helena was the most powerful Kiri in living memory. Lucian might be the only man in the room to know her like.

An invisible wind lifted the ends of Helena's dark hair, and beside her Von's lips twitched in a smile. Helena's Mate was a gorgeous man with obsidian hair and silver eyes that were arresting even when he was clearly at ease. He was every inch the warrior Ronan was, although a bit less wild. Effie wouldn't go as far as to say Helena's love had tamed him, but Von was clearly more at peace these days.

Lucian cleared his throat, and Effie snickered. Someone wasn't a fan of her observation.

"I prefer a man with eyes that burn bronze, not silver."

Beside her he let out a low grunt, but his lips tipped up.

Oblivious to their exchange, a man with faded orange hair gestured for them to be seated.

Helena gave a regal nod, and Von smoothly pulled her chair back. Once she was seated, everyone else moved to follow. Except the Triumvirate.

The Councilman eyed them warily.

"We shall stand."

He cleared his throat. "As you wish."

Effie couldn't recall a time when the Triumvirate had ever done anything *but* stand when in a formal situation.

"The illusion is easier to maintain when movement is restricted. Especially up close," Lucian informed her, picking up on her thoughts.

Once they were all seated, Helena asked, "Guardian, what have we learned about the cause of the corruption?"

She may have addressed him by title, but there was no mistaking who she was talking to. Lucian loosely clasped his hands together on the table as he replied, "The Shadows are the source, Kiri. The remnants of Rowena's twisted magic still flows through them."

There was a small gasp from one of the Council members, but otherwise a few rustles of clothing were the only signs of distress.

Helena frowned. "So the Shadows survived her death and have found a way to pollute the land?"

"Not just the land." Lucian's shifted, sitting back and taking Effie's hand beneath the table. It was her only warning. "They can turn people as well. Until recently we did not believe there was a way to undo the damage."

Helena visibly paled, her eyes darting from Lucian to Effie and back again. "But it *is* reversible?"

"Only in the rarest cases, at least so far as we can tell. In fact, the method may not be replicable at all."

Her frown deepened. "Why not?"

"It has to do with how the Shadow's corruption takes root. As you are aware, they were created by a perversion of Spirit magic. Specifically, Rowena fed off the souls of her victims, draining them and their power to enhance her own. Most were less than hollow shells at the time of her death, but those with pieces of their souls intact survived. Just as Rowena's initial spell is tied to the soul, so too is the Shadow's magic. Over time it eats away at its host until nothing of them remains. The only way to reverse the damage is to pull out the corruption before it steals all of its victim's humanity, which is to say those things that make them whole."

"How did you learn this?" Helena finally asked, her voice frayed.

"When we first learned of the Shadow-touched we did not believe there was a cure. There was no way to sense the corruption before it was too late. It wasn't until one of our own was infected that we pieced the symptoms together. Unfortunately, by the time that we realized what was happening and how the corruption was spread, it was almost too late."

Von's expression was thunderous. "What are you saying?"

"Once the soul is gone, there's no salvaging the vessel."

"But you were able to undo the effects?" Von asked, looking at Lucian with more interest.

"Yes. Barely. With the help of the Valen Council I was able to locate a spell that enhanced my power enough to cast out the corruption and save her."

An undercurrent of tension thrummed through the near-silent room as the others processed what Lucian had just revealed.

It was Helena who pieced it together first.

"Effie," Helena whispered aghast. "Ronan had said that she'd been sick . . . but she was Shadow-touched. You managed to save her . . ." Her voice was breathless, and her eyes glittered as she turned them to Lucian.

He nodded.

"But if you managed to save her, why do you think we cannot save the others?" the Councilman asked, no longer willing to sit back and allow Helena to lead the conversation.

"On its own the spell still wasn't enough. While it allowed me to repair the damage to her body, it did not restore her mind. When she first woke, her memories were gone."

"Only at first?" Von asked, zeroing in on the words.

Effie stared at the table, not wanting to meet her friends' curious stares. Right now they were looking at her like she was some kind of fascinating creature.

She hated it.

Only Ronan fully understood what had been required to save her, although others likely guessed. Her eyes were a definite giveaway, but it had never been officially stated publicly.

It was almost amusing watching people jerk as Lucian answered as one of the Triumvirate, his spectral voice infusing their minds. *"We were able to restore Effie's memories because they had already been shared with us. The process, however, required she become a Guardian. Without those two elements, we wouldn't have been able to fully restore her."*

Helena slumped back in her chair. "We almost lost her?"

"Helena, I'm fine. I'm right here. We are at war. Isn't that the risk we all take every time we step onto a battlefield?" Effie forced herself to meet Von and Ronan's gaze. They were looking at her with respect. Even Reyna was nodding in agreement.

Helena's eyes lifted to Effie's, and she shook her head. "I took a damn vacation while you almost died."

"Rowena was defeated. You couldn't have known this was going to happen."

"Are there any other Shadow-touched we know of?" Von asked.

"Yes and no," Ronan answered. "Those we know of were lost with the citadel. As for the rest of the realm,"—he shrugged—"they are certainly out there, but we don't know where they are coming from."

"And there's still the matter of the land," Kael said. "Sylverlands and Caederan have both been affected. Not to mention Bael."

"Perhaps this is a silly question," the Councilman started, "but if it takes a bite to turn a person, how are the Shadows managing to turn the land?"

Effie didn't think it was a stupid question at all. She had been wondering the same.

Lucian had an answer for that as well. "We believe anywhere their blood has been spilled the land is altered."

The room fell silent as the information sank in.

Helena lifted her chin and spoke directly to the Councilman for the first time. "It would seem we are in your debt, sir. Your people helped save one I consider family when I could not. And it would appear that knowledge may yet help us save many more." She flicked her gaze to Lucian. "I want to go to one of the sites. I need to feel it for myself."

"Of course. Effie told us that you might have encountered

something like it before; that your magic might be able to reverse the effects without aid."

Helena shuddered, needing no additional prompting to know exactly what he was referring to. "The Forest of Whispers . . ."

"And Endoshan," Von added.

She looked haunted as she shook her head. "The signs have been there this whole time, but I didn't realize . . ."

"None of us did," Lucian said gently.

Helena twisted to face the Triumvirate once more. "Ronan's letters mentioned there was also the matter of a prophecy."

For a moment, Effie forgot the hooded figures were merely a trick of the light. Nord had the central figure dip its head.

"Many of these events have been tied to a prophecy known by most as the Shadow Years."

Another gasp, this time followed by Trinity lurching to her feet. "The Shadow Years?"

The way she said it, it didn't sound as though she was afraid, more like surprised. As if it were the oddest of coincidences.

"You are familiar with it?" Lucian asked.

She shook her head. "No, well, I mean everyone hears the stories growing up. It's just that you are not our first guest this month. We had another, a man who disappeared without a trace. He left behind his belongings. There was a note about—" She stopped abruptly, clearly searching for the right words. Snapping her fingers, she gave a little nod. "Markers. Something about the Shadow Years markers."

Lucian went rigid beside her, and Effie forgot how to breathe as a familiar pressure settled hard and fast in her chest.

"What did this man look like?" Lucian demanded, his voice dark.

Trinity blinked, visibly flustered. "Um, long hair, blond, green eyes."

Lucian shot to his feet, his chair flying out behind him. "That thrice-damned son-of-a-bitch!"

Helena's eyes were darting from Lucian to the panic-stricken Councilwoman. "Who?"

"Kieran."

Effie barely registered his snarled response. The room was closing in around her, stealing her sight as she plunged headlong into a vision.

~

KIERAN

HIS FINGERS BLED; his nails cracked and skin tore from digging in the earth in a desperate search for fragments of the crumbling stones that might send him home. Somehow he'd managed to find what was left of the gate. Perhaps it was dumb luck, or maybe the people of Eatos had once been traders with the Vale. Either was a possibility really, although neither did much to help him.

Kieran had found the ruin quite by accident. After learning what had become of Effie, his only instinct had been to run as far and as fast as he could. He was smart enough to know that there was no running from what he'd done, but at least this way there was no chance he'd risk coming face-to-face with the reality of it.

After days of nothing but endless desert and more of its false promises, something had changed. The atmosphere grew sweeter with a bit more chill and there was a new whispering sound in the air. Kieran had thought he'd finally lost his mind, but after half a day of walking—or so he guessed based on the sun's trek across the sky— he'd found the river.

He'd practically fallen face first into the cool water, lapping it up with no care for potential contamination. His thirst was all-consuming, and this was clearly a gift from the gods. Or the Mother. Kieran wasn't sure what—if anything—he believed in anymore.

Water also meant food. After a small feast of desert berries and sweet grass, he spent the night curled up on the river's muddied banks afraid that he'd wake to discover this had all been a cruel dream.

It wasn't.

Taking the time to bathe and fill up on more water and berries,

Kieran had made the decision to follow the river west. He had no plan and little in the way of prospects, but at least he had a direction.

It was another day and a half before he'd found it. There was a small copse of trees just beside an offshoot of the river. He'd blinked and rubbed his eyes at first, certain he was looking at another one of the Vale's mirages, but it hadn't blurred. After a few stumbling steps, he'd started running, not stopping until he quite literally tripped over one of the fallen stones.

The Gatekeeper hadn't been lying when she said Elysia's gate had been destroyed. If not for the markings etched into what was still standing of the original curved structure, Kieran never would have recognized it. It was hardly an arch, let alone anything resembling the stone sentinel he remembered.

That hadn't stopped him from kneeling before what was left of it, pressing his forehead to the sun-warmed stone and weeping like a child. It had to be a sign.

It had to.

Why else would he have found his way here?

So Kieran's search begun. Stones were scattered across the ground, most hidden beneath layers of grime and dirt. If not for edges jutting up just enough that he could either spot them—or trip over them—he may not have thought to look.

The hope that had fueled his frantic digging ebbed when after a day's search only a half dozen of the missing stones were located. That's when he realized the stones were only part of the problem.

Assuming he even managed to find them all, how exactly was he supposed to repair the gate? Kieran wasn't even sure how to begin going about putting it back together. Surely there was some rhyme or reason to the way they needed to sit atop one another? Or was it enough to simply stack them?

The longer he searched, the more inconsolable he became.

Discovering the gate hadn't been a blessing.

It was a taunt.

A reminder of all of Kieran's shortcomings. His numerous—and if he was being honest, quite spectacular—failures.

This was the universe's way of dangling hope before him only to snatch it right back and tell Kieran he may as well stop trying. That even now, in the presence of his one possible chance at redemption, he was going to fail.

Again.

He would always fail.

CHAPTER 23

EFFIE

When she could see again, the world was a mist-shrouded field. All around her delicate stalks of grass danced under a gentle breeze. It stretched on as far as she could see, which should have granted a sense of freedom, but only served to reinforce the sensation of being trapped. She was outside, true, but all she could make out in the distance was a wall of soft gray fog. Instead of being free, she was enclosed.

A part of her knew this was a vision, but it was unlike any she'd ever had. It was far too *pretty* to be one of her usual prophecies. She could feel the warmth of the sun even though she couldn't see it. There was a timeless quality about this place. It was neither morning nor afternoon, just an indeterminate sort of in-between.

"Hello?" she called, her arms extended on either side of her body as she started weaving her way through the waist-high grass.

"Hello, child."

Effie spun around, her heart caught in her throat as she searched for the owner of the unfamiliar voice. She hadn't actually expected a response.

No one was there.

Anxious now, Effie crept forward. Any peace this place was

supposed to impart vanished. Although she couldn't see anyone, she did not for a second believe she was alone.

"Would it make you feel better if I appeared to you thusly?"

Effie's eyes landed on the woman standing before her. She couldn't seem to recall how to breathe. Not that it mattered here.

The stranger was the epitome of ageless beauty. She had a flickering quality, as if she were constantly in a state of flux. One second, a young warrior queen—only to become a girl on the brink of womanhood in the next breath, and then shift once more into an ancient and gnarled crone. But always, no matter which form she was currently wearing, she was striking.

Her hair was the same spring-green of the field, her eyes a vibrant sky blue that shifted from pale storm clouds to the dead of night with each flicker of her visage. The woman's skin was the color of a silvery birch, and the soft pink of dawn tinged her cheeks and lips. As she rippled once more, no more substantial than a reflection swaying on the surface of the ocean, Effie caught sight of a crown of starlight ringing her brow.

"Do not be afraid, child. I've known you since before you were born."

"You and everyone else I come across these days."

If she was capable of forethought, Effie would have refrained from speaking the words out loud. This did not seem like someone she wanted to offend. As it was, she hadn't even realized she'd spoken until the woman's laughter flowed around them, filling the air with her mirth.

Effie squinted, staring hard at the woman as she tried to place her. She knew for a fact she'd never met her, and yet . . . something about her was so familiar. Frustratingly so. Almost as if they'd known each other a long time ago, or maybe even in another lifetime—as if such a thing were even possible for her to recall, if it were possible at all.

"You seem to have caught me at a disadvantage," she finally said. Her unspoken question echoed as loudly as the words she actually uttered. *Who are you?*

The woman beamed, and the beauty of it robbed Effie of breath. It was like bathing in sunshine. For no reason at all, tears pricked her eyes and it took more effort than it should have for Effie to keep from flinging herself into the woman's arms.

"You know me, child. Although perhaps you prefer to believe otherwise. The path I laid before you has hardly been an easy one. I know you place the brunt of the blame for that at my feet. Rightly so, I suppose."

The woman shifted again, and for one extended second, Effie thought she was staring into the face of her grandmother. Before she could react, the truth of her companion's identity slammed into her. Effie's knees went weak, and she sank to the floor, her body trembling with the shock of her discovery.

Suddenly, she wasn't sure where to look. Was it rude to meet her gaze? Should she genuflect? What was the proper way to greet a goddess? No, not just *a* goddess, *the* goddess. There wasn't time to land upon an answer before the Mother knelt beside Effie, cupping her face with both hands.

"My poor, sweet girl. How you have suffered and yet . . . still you rise. Time and again you thrive when so many others wouldn't know where to begin." As she spoke, she brushed away the tears that fell unbidden from Effie's eyes, her eyes gentle and her smile soft. "I know that you believe I had forsaken you, that I did not think you worthy to be one of my children, but that has never been the case. Your destiny was decided long before you were born."

Effie's throat was raw, and it was painful to pull the words forth. There was so much she wanted to say, so many questions she wanted to ask, and she didn't know where to start. There were countless nights when her tears had run dry and her heart ached, where all she could manage was a single word. One word that somehow encompassed all of the pain and betrayal that consumed her.

Why?

Why didn't you choose me?

Why don't they love me?

Why allow me to live at all when no one wants me?

"How my heart broke for you, watching what they did to you in my name. Every mother knows that she cannot intervene each time one of her children makes a mistake. At some point, they must find their way on their own. That does not mean I took any pleasure from your pain." She tilted her head, her eyes moving over Effie's face as her smile fell. "It was never that I didn't choose you, Effie. You must know by now that you've always been one of my daughters—a very special one, at that."

Resentment, anger, and decades-old hurt faded away. The explanation didn't undo the past, but at least now Effie knew that all of that pain had been endured for a reason. Somehow, that made it a little easier to forgive.

"I fear that your trials have only just begun, Daughter. You have an important part to play in the years to come."

"If that's so, why allow me to be Shadow-touched? You almost lost me entirely."

The goddess' ancient eyes were filled with apology. "I needed him to turn you. The only way to unlock your full potential was with a Guardian's power."

She couldn't help the little snort of disbelief that escaped. "You were sure counting on a lot of things to happen. What if Lucian hadn't found the spell? Or hadn't risked everything to try to save me?"

"There was never any doubt things would turn out this way."

"Maybe not for you."

The Mother smiled at that. "It is no accident Lucian ended up here in this time or place. He is my gift to you. Your reward for all that you have sacrificed."

It was such an absurd explanation. Effie couldn't wait to tell Lucian he was a goddess' gift to her. Her proud, independent Guardian would just *love* to find out he was nothing more than a pawn in someone else's game.

"I know it is hard for you to believe—that all of this needed to happen, in exactly this way. But it's true. The only way I could appear to you like this was with a Guardian's power running through your veins. Their ability to see the world as it truly is, combined with your ability to receive my warnings . . . no other before you has ever been so gifted."

Effie's brows dipped with confusion. "But . . . why me? Helena is your Vessel, so what can I possibly—" She was silenced with a finger pressed lightly over her lips.

"Helena holds my power, true. But you, Effie, you are my Voice."

Effie blinked. Whatever she'd been expecting, that certainly hadn't been it. "Oh."

The goddess gave her another smile, although this one was tinged with sadness. "For centuries I have been trying to warn my children about what was coming, to prepare them, but there are limits to what I can do, or perhaps more accurately, what they can comprehend. I protected them for as long as I could, but he's growing stronger, and I am out of options. I had to take matters into my own hands."

Foreboding surged through Effie, cutting through the wonder of the moment and providing a chilling sense of clarity. "The Shadow Years."

The goddess nodded, her expression fierce.

"So it's not a way for you to punish us?"

"You think I want this?" As she spoke, her voice cracked like thunder and the air whipped around until they were surrounded by the physical manifestation of her pain.

"Y-you mean you don't want to destroy the Chosen?" Effie stuttered, shocked by the venom in her response.

"What mother ever wants to see harm come to their children?"

It would seem not all mothers were cut from the same cloth in that regard. Effie still carried the scars from a past that provided a very bleak answer to that question. Her mother hadn't had any issue at all hurting her daughter.

Unaware of her internal recounting, the Mother continued speaking. "No"—she shook her head once, her expression dark—"this is not my doing."

"If not you . . . who?"

For the first time, true anger shone in the goddess' eyes. "Love and jealousy are not mortal emotions. What you experience is only the echo of the reality."

Effie blinked, wondering how exactly that was supposed to be an answer.

Sighing, the Mother added, "It takes two beings to create a child, even for one such as me."

Gaping, Effie stared at her. "But—"

A horrible tearing sounded in the distance, silencing her before she could finish the question. The goddess gave a start, her eyes widening as the sky at the edges of their little clearing turned black. Her next words coming out in a whispered rush. "He wakes. We're out of time. You need to go. Tell them what you've learned."

All the questions Effie couldn't seem to voice earlier poured from her now. "Wait, what? Who wakes? How do we stop what's coming? What am I supposed to tell them? Will I get to see you again?"

"I am always with you. The answers you seek are right in front of you. See the truth, trust your instincts, and you will find the way."

Before Effie could ask what that was supposed to mean, the goddess leaned forward and pressed her lips to the center of Effie's forehead. Light exploded behind her eyes, and she gave a wordless cry.

"Remember what you are, Daughter."

"What's that?"

"Mine."

The words echoed through Effie's mind as her eyes fluttered open and Lucian's face swam into view.

CHAPTER 24

LUCIAN

Startled gasps rang out as Effie slumped back in her chair. He was already kneeling by her side as her eyes rolled back into her head and her eyelids started to flutter.

"What's wrong with her?" Kael's concern was palpable through their mental link.

"She's having a vision."

"Are you sure? She isn't showing any symptoms."

Lucian frowned. That much was true. There wasn't so much as a twitching finger to suggest she'd been taken over by her Keeper's gift. But instinct told him that was definitely what just happened. Ignoring everyone else in the room, he brushed his hand over her forehead, shamelessly using his power to try to see whatever it was she was experiencing. A bolt of lavender light practically blinded him and he grunted in pain as he removed his hand.

"It's definitely a vision, but none like I've ever seen."

"Should visions even be possible now that she's a Guardian?" Nord asked, joining the telepathic conversation.

Lucian didn't have an answer, so he ignored the question. Instead he wove an arm beneath Effie's legs and wrapped the other around her back, easily lifting her as he stood. "Visions can be very disorienting," he said by way of explanation. Not that he owed one to anyone.

"I'll go with you." Helena was ready to surge to her feet, Von's hand on her shoulder the only thing keeping her in place.

"I think Effie would appreciate a bit of privacy when she comes to. I'll send for you once she's ready for company," Lucian assured her.

Helena was clearly not used to being told no. His lips almost twitched up in amusement, but Effie gave a low groan in his arms. As he glanced down, her eyes snapped open. Lucian shuddered as power surged through him. That was not particularly uncommon except that he wasn't the one who called it forth. Something—Effie—was drawing his power to the surface.

Eyes glowing with lavender fire, she stared straight through him. "He wakes," she intoned in a deep, resonant voice that sounded nothing like her own.

"Who wakes?" Lucian demanded. In all his years working with the Keepers, none had ever spoken while still under the effects of their vision. He wasn't sure if she could hear him, let alone respond in a meaningful way, but he couldn't have stayed silent if he tried.

Her eyes pulsed, growing even brighter as she answered, "*Tul Mort Jateh*." As soon as the foreign words left her lips, the lavender light extinguished and Effie fell limp in his arms.

There was a high-pitched cry followed by the sound of wood scraping against stone. Lucian's head snapped up, but Nord was two steps ahead of him, keeping the Triumvirates' pretense intact.

"What do you know, Night Stalker?"

Reyna swallowed, her already pale skin the color of chalk. Lucian had not seen much of her since the incident with the lajhár, but it was obvious she still hadn't made a full recovery even though the others had weeks ago. Her skin had a waxy sheen and there were dark purple smudges beneath sunken eyes. She was breathing fast, the sound of her shallow pants practically booming in the anxious silence.

"We're waiting."

Reyna flinched, the involuntary move speaking louder than any words. For the Night Stalker to be so obviously terrified did not bode well for whatever she was about to say. But then, when had anyone had good news to share lately?

Her tongue darted out as her eyes swept around the meeting room. Lucian didn't think it was his imagination that she was looking not at the people in the room, but the shadows. "Just as the Chosen have their children's tale, so too do the Night Stalkers. Instead of the Mother and her Shadow Years, we have our own story. One that is told only in whispers."

Lucian exchanged a questioning look with Kael. *"Do you have any idea what she's talking about?"*

Kael discretely shook his head. *"I know as much as you. If this is part of their lore, they've never disclosed it."*

"Do you know about this?" Helena asked, swinging her attention to Nord's illusion of the Triumvirate.

"No, Kiri. We are not privy to the secrets of the Night Stalkers."

Her eyes narrowed. "How can that be? I thought you three knew everything."

He bit back a bemused grin, her frustration a clear echo of his own. It never ceased to surprise him that immortality still wasn't long enough to provide someone with all the answers.

"We are not omnipotent. We know only that which is shared with us. The Night Stalkers were all but forgotten since they were the very first tribe to be cut off from the Chosen and given the title of Forsaken. Until you sought them out, we've had no contact with any from the tribe. As for the archives, there are very few references to the Night Stalkers beyond their roles as skilled assassins and the protectors of the forest. There is nothing in our books about their cultural beliefs."

"But that name, Tul Mort Jateh, it means something to you?" Helena pressed, now seated beside Reyna with her hand resting on the other woman's knee.

Reyna nodded, her tongue darting out to wet her lips. "All Night Stalkers know the name. He is the monster beneath our beds. The thing we all blame for keeping us awake at night. Tul Mort Jateh," she whispered, her throat bobbing as she swallowed convulsively. "The Lord of Death."

"Do you know what she meant by 'he wakes'?"

Reyna gave a sharp nod. "It means that the spell keeping him bound to the dream world has weakened."

"What happens if it breaks completely?" Ronan asked.

"What do you think happens when the Lord of Death walks the realm of the living?"

Effie stirred in his arms. Tightening his hold on her, Lucian tuned out the sound of the others. *"Fledgling?"*

"Lucian," she whispered, her blue eyes with their flecks of sapphire roaming over his face. "You're never going to believe what I just Saw." Wonder filled her voice, but before she continued, she frowned. *"Why are you holding me?"*

"Effie? Are you all right?" Helena asked.

"What did you See?" Ronan added.

Lucian inwardly sighed. *"This is why. I was trying to spare you."*

"I'm fine," she murmured, answering their question before demanding along their bond, *"Set me down."*

He raised a brow. *"You sure?"*

She dipped her chin. *"They're not going to let up until they hear what I Saw."*

Lucian was tempted to sit with her in his lap, but it would only serve to be a distraction he could ill afford. He gently placed her back in her chair and took his seat beside her.

Effie glanced around the room. "I feel as though I missed something. How long was I out?"

"Not long," Kael assured her.

"Do you remember speaking?" Lucian asked.

Effie's eyes widened, and she shook her head.

"We're never going to get anywhere if we have to keep stopping to go back and repeat things," Ronan growled.

Lucian's temper flared and a soft roll of thunder sounded in the room. Everyone assumed it was the Triumvirates' displeasure and turned uneasy gazes on the three robed figures.

Effie took his hand beneath the table and gave it a squeeze, a silent reminder to rein it in. Lucian knew it was only concern for Reyna that had Ronan so riled. He was intimately familiar with the coiled impatience that settled deep inside of him as a result of being unable to do anything to help Effie. It had been living inside him for the better part of two weeks.

"We all want to get to the bottom of this," he forced himself to say.

Helena shot Ronan a warning look and then nodded her agreement. "Clearly whatever Effie Saw is related to the Night Stalker's tale. We need to hear one in order to understand and appreciate the warning in the other. It might also help if we understood what triggered the vision in the first place."

Lucian's brows furrowed as he thought back to what had happened immediately preceding Effie's vision. A low snarl escaped as it came back to him. In the resulting chaos, he'd forgotten about Kieran.

Ronan's thoughts seemed to be traveling in the same direction. "You'd mentioned your guest had left some belongings behind. Could you bring them here?"

Trinity nodded, the composure he'd observed during their prior interactions notably lacking. She was clearly shaken by everything that had happened. "I'll be right back." She all but ran from the room, the door slamming shut behind her.

His hands flexed, itching for a weapon. An innocent man wouldn't be on the run. Somehow Kieran was connected to all of this, and Lucian intended to get to the bottom of it.

There was nowhere the blond bastard could run that would keep him safe. Not from Lucian. Certainly not once he began the hunt.

Effie shot him a curious glance, likely picking up on the simmering anger inside of him.

"Later," he told her, not wanting to derail the conversation further by giving voice to his realization.

"All right. While we wait for her to get back, Effie, why don't you tell us what you Saw."

She pressed her lips together, her eyes shifting to Lucian for a second before she obliged. He'd seen her do something similar before. Whenever she was buying time. *She's not going to tell them*, he realized. At least not everything. It looked like Lucian wasn't the only one keeping things to himself for the moment.

"My grandmother appeared to me," she began.

Lucian wasn't sure if he only sensed the lie because he was waiting for it. No one else seemed to have any trouble believing her story.

"She told me that the Chosen had not heeded the warnings. That the Keepers couldn't fully comprehend the Mother's voice through the veil of their mortality and that we were running out of time."

This sounded true. No one could fake that sort of quaver in their voice.

"What warning?" Helena asked.

"The Shadow Years. They are very much real, but they were never about the Mother's judgment."

The way she emphasized the word Mother gave Lucian pause. "If it's not the Mother, then why is it happening? Who's causing this?"

Effie bit her lip and gave a little shake of her head. "I didn't get a name exactly, but I think . . . I got the impression that the Mother did not create the Chosen on her own?" She glanced at Helena. "Is that even possible?"

"I've never heard any Chosen creation story refer to anyone but the Mother. If there is another god out there, it's news to me." She looked to the Triumvirate as if waiting for one of them to contradict her.

"The Chosen have the Mother, but the Forsaken . . . they have the Father." Reyna's voice was flat, devoid of all emotion. "We just know him by another name. Tul Mort Jateh, the Lord of Death. But there was a time when he was known as the Father of Dreams."

EFFIE

She could tell by the troubled looks on everyone's faces she was the only one who didn't fully understand what was going on. Before Reyna could elaborate, the door flew open and Trinity sprinted in, dropping a leather-bound book onto the table.

Lucian reached out, his hand hovering above the cover.

"Is that . . ." Kael started to ask.

Lucian nodded. "From the archives. Yes."

"How did this Kieran manage to sneak a book out of the archives without the Triumvirate or their Guardians knowing?" Helena asked. There was no censure in the question, but the Guardians visibly tensed.

"It shouldn't have been possible," Kael answered as Lucian opened the ancient book.

"May I?" Trinity asked, still hovering by Lucian's shoulder.

He gave a terse nod, and she reached out, flipping through quickly before stopping on a dog-eared page with notations scrawled in the margins. "Here. This is the page it was open to when we found it."

Everyone moved around the table to get a closer look. Effie recognized the passage immediately, although she'd never seen this book before. It was the same one Smoke had shared with her when they'd connected the massacre in the jungle to another marker.

"TMJ prophecy? What's that?" Von asked, looking to the Triumvirate for answers.

Lucian was very still beside her, his jaw clenched. Whatever it meant, he was familiar with the reference.

"The Mother's Judgment?" Helena offered.

It was a smart guess. Given what they'd been told of the Shadow Years, it certainly fit.

"No," one of the Triumvirate answered. *"It's a much older prophecy."*

"Obscure and long forgotten."

"Named, it was believed, for the one who Saw it."

"Do you think you could manage to recall it?" Von asked. Despite being phrased as a question, it was clearly not a request.

Lucian bristled, but no one save Effie was looking at him. Everyone else was staring hard at the three robed figures. It was hard for her to remember to carry on with the charade when she knew who was actually speaking.

The silence in the room stretched, and Effie was starting to think the Guardians wouldn't—or possibly couldn't—respond. But they did, their spectral voices harmonizing as they answered as one.

"The slumbering one comes. The spell that holds him suspended no match for the depth of his wrath. None will be safe when his lies return to the realm of the living. The shackles will break, a sign to mark each passing. When the last is broken, he will walk the world once more."

Goosebumps rose along her skin and Effie's heart began to race. It was too similar to what the Mother had shared with her to be a coincidence. "These marks refer to the markers we've attributed to the Shadow Years," she said, her voice low but steady.

Lucian looked grim as he nodded his agreement.

"Your prophecy wasn't named for its bearer," Reyna said with a harsh laugh. She leaned across the table and slammed her finger down to point at the notation. "TMJ: Tul Mort Jateh. None of your Keepers recognized it because they weren't familiar with the title. This prophecy is about the Lord of Death. He's coming for us all."

"Why are you so sure it's about him?" Lucian asked.

"Besides the initials? Every element points to him. The sleeping, the shackles, being trapped between worlds . . ." Reyna trailed off. "The Night Stalkers recognize the Mother, but we do not consider ourselves Her children. We are born of night, as are the gifts we are blessed with. Who do you think my people served before he was bound and we were freed? We were his assassins. His spies. His slaves."

"So why serve him at all?" Helena asked.

Reyna scoffed. "We were not given a choice. He is our creator. The Night Stalkers would not exist if not for the Father of Dreams. But he was not a kind Father. Legend has it that the Night Stalkers were created out of a jealous bid for attention. When the Mother's focus shifted from him to her Chosen, he lashed out. Began destroying them just to hurt her, as she had hurt him. We were the instruments of that destruction. Why else do you think we were banished alongside him? The first of the Forsaken tribes."

The mingled gasps of their indrawn breath was the only noise in the room. This was not the history the Chosen had been raised with. Not even close. Even the people of the Vale looked shocked by Reyna's tale.

"If you belong to him, why are you afraid of his return?" Kael asked.

"How do you think he was captured? Bound? It was with our help that he was trapped in the dream world, the place that joins the realm of the living to the land of the dead. If he returns, my people will be punished for that treachery even though any wrongdoing happened many lifetimes ago. The Mother cast her spell with our help, trapping him in between worlds so he could no longer torture her favorite children. Not that it stopped the Father of Dreams. In the end, he is the lord of that domain. Even bound he was able to reach out; to find someone who could set the necessary events in motion."

"Time means nothing to an immortal," Lucian murmured.

"Exactly so. All beings were immortal before the Lord of Death," Reyna said with a small shrug. "Once he brought death into the world, mortality was inevitable. He might be trapped, but that is a gift that can never be taken back."

"As dire as this sounds, it doesn't really change anything . . ." Effie said slowly.

"How can you say that?" Reyna asked, looking stricken. "If he is freed, death as you know it would be a mercy compared to what he will do to you—to us all."

"We already knew that the Shadow Years meant the destruction of the Chosen. All that's different now is that we know it's not some vague notion, but an actual being. Beings can be fought and defeated. And either way, Shadow Years or your Lord of Death, if we can find a way to stop the final markers from coming to pass, then we're in the clear, right? He'll still be trapped, and we get to keep living."

The room fell silent once more but some of the tension ebbed. It was not much as far as plans go, but it provided something they'd been sorely lacking only seconds prior . . . hope.

Kael scrubbed a hand over his head before leaning forward on the table. "Easier said than done, unfortunately. There's one, *maybe* two markers left if we're lucky, and that's assuming there aren't any out there we don't already know about."

"I think there has to be at least one more—otherwise my vision would have said he's here, not he's coming . . ."

"Fair point," Lucian said softly.

"Well, there are still any number of events that could be markers, most I should add, that we have no way to predict," Kael said.

Instinct had Effie turning to Reyna. "Do your legends say anything about what the final marker could be?"

Reyna shook her head. "No, I'm sorry. That is as much of a mystery to us as it is to you."

"Without knowing what else to watch for, our best and only option is still to go after the Shadows," Lucian said. "Any remaining marker is likely tied to them."

"All right, so that's our next move," Helena declared.

"Where do you suggest we start looking?" Effie asked.

Helena looked thoughtful. "I still think we need to go back to the citadel. There may be something there that points us in the right direction."

"Is there anything the people of the Vale can do to help?"

Helena turned her aqua eyes on Councilman Vance. "Are there any other spells that you know of that might help us cleanse and repair the land? We'll likely need to split our resources in the days to come, so anything that gives more of us the ability to counter the effects of the corruption would be welcome."

"I already provided the Guardians with the main spell, but I will have the Council search through all our records. Perhaps there is something we overlooked."

"Thank you, Councilman. As always, our best chance of survival lies in working together."

"Agreed, Kiri. When do you leave?"

"At first light," Von replied. "We'll take the night to prepare and travel by Kaelpas stone in the morning."

Just that easily the plan was set. Suddenly there didn't seem to be much else to say. The mood shifted from heated debate to quiet contemplation. Depending on what they discovered at the citadel, all of this could be over in a matter of days . . . maybe even hours now that Helena was with them once more.

For the first time in months, Effie felt optimistic about the outcome of this war. Between her newly acquired Guardian abilities, Lucian's steady presence, and Helena's return, they were as ready as they could ever be for the battles to come.

There was little doubt in her mind that's where they were heading —into battle.

After all, this was still a war . . . and the stakes had never been higher.

❧

KIERAN

HIS EYES DANCED beneath his eyelids as he dreamed. Kieran's sleep was restless, the dreams far from peaceful. Even now his fingers twitched as if staving off invisible foes.

After days of digging for fragments of the gate, his search was more trickle than flood, and it was weighing on him. There was no escape from his failure.

Not even in sleep.

A MAN'S *voice sounded in his mind. Cruel yet undeniably sensual. No matter where he cast his eyes, Kieran could manage to make out no more than a towering shape concealed by shadows.*

The man was speaking, and yet it was not to him. There was another here. A woman. She was kneeling in the center of some sort of cathedral, the light of the moon surrounding her with its milky glow through a massive circular window high in the wall behind what could only be an altar.

She was wearing a hood, her face shrouded, and yet Kieran knew the timbre of her voice. It was melodic, in the way that things born of the wild were melodic. He could easily picture the rustle of leaves, and the dappled play of light filtering down into an ancient forest. She was a child of the woods, a daughter of night, a huntress.

"You should not be here," she said, steel lacing the words.

Kieran's heart began to race. Did she speak to him? Could she see *him? But no . . . it was the other one she spoke to.*

"It is not for you to decide," the man replied, thunder rolling through his voice.

Kieran felt an answering tremor work its way through him. He may not be able to see the man, but he was not immune to his considerable power.

"This world is not your own. You are an intruder."

The mysterious man's voice cracked like a whip. "This and every world is mine for the taking. I own everything."

"Claiming ownership does not mean you actually possess anything. Some things can never truly be owned. Have you learned nothing these past years?"

If Kieran had a physical body his knees would have been weak. How was it this woman showed absolutely no fear?

"Perhaps the real issue is that you have forgotten," he said, the anger in his voice unmistakable.

"My people never forget."

"Oh? Then how is it we find ourselves here?"

Her answer was immediate. "Wounded pride and an inability to admit defeat."

"Yes," the man crooned, and the shadows trembled. "Never has there been anything more delicious than breaking one down to the basest of human instincts. Mortals are so predictable when you know which strings to play."

The darkness rippled once more, and when the man next spoke, Kieran knew he was speaking directly to him.

"I have one last job for you. In order for us to complete what we've started, you need to return to the place where it all began."

Fear surged through Kieran, closing his throat and making it impossible to voice the questions racing within his mind.

"Bring me that which I seek, and this will all be nothing more than a dream. Fail, and well . . . trust me when I say, you really *don't want to find out what happens if you fail."*

Finally, the shadows shifted, peeling away to reveal the last face he ever expected to find.

His own.

CHAPTER 26

EFFIE

She closed the door behind her and leaned against it with a low groan.

"You okay?" Lucian asked, looking up from the boots he was in the middle of untying.

Giving him a tired smile, she nodded.

"Side effects of your vision?"

"No, I don't think so," Effie said slowly, making her way over to their bed. "The vision was only mildly disorienting. For once it didn't feel like my head was about to explode. I wonder if that has anything to do with being a Guardian now," she mused, turning back to face him when he didn't immediately weigh in on the idea.

"You going to tell me why you lied to them?" Lucian asked instead, his head tilted as he stared down at her. There was no censure in his eyes, only curiosity.

Pangs of guilt gnawed at her. She should have known he wasn't going to let her get away with that. "It wasn't a lie. Not exactly."

He lifted a brow.

"Everything I told them was true. I just modified one of the details . . ." she trailed off, trying to find a way to explain the bone-deep certainty that it was not yet time to make public all that the Mother had revealed to her.

Lucian moved closer, his hand lifting to smooth the crease that had formed between her brows. "If your instincts are telling you to keep it to yourself, you should trust them. They haven't led you astray before."

As she considered his words, Effie realized that the thought of revealing her vision in full to him caused none of the same warning bells to sound off within her. He was not the one she needed to tread carefully with.

"No," she murmured, "I think you should hear this. Lucian, it wasn't my grandmother that appeared to me. It was the Mother."

His eyes flared, and he went very still. "The Mother?"

She pressed her lips together, nodding as she held his gaze. "Everything I shared with the others was true. She said the Shadow Years were not her doing, and that the Chosen had misunderstood Her warnings. That everything that happened to me needed to, including my becoming a Guardian, so that for the first time She could deliver her warning in person. It was the only way She could directly communicate with me. She said that I was her Voice."

Lucian's eyes never left hers, and if not for the thrum of tension pulsing through her along their link, she wouldn't have had any idea how he was taking her news. His face was completely blank.

He finally blinked, running a thumb along her lips as his expression turned serious. Threads of worry wove themselves through her, replacing the tension.

Effie reached out, his stubble prickling her palm as she pressed it against his cheek. "What's wrong?"

Connected as they were now, there was no way for him to pretend everything was fine. His eyes darkened, reminding her of a storm rolling in from the horizon. The danger was heading straight toward them, and all they could do was hope to outrun it.

He let out a soft breath and rested his forehead against hers, his eyes briefly closing. "For her to appear to you in person, to make a point to warn you about what's coming . . . it does not fill me with ease. I don't know what's waiting for us at the citadel. Hardly anything was left standing, but—" Lucian broke off and shook his head. "I just have a bad feeling."

"You just reminded me not to ignore those kinds of instincts. If you're worried, you likely have a right to be."

Lucian was silent, his eyes boring into hers as his fingers idly traced a pattern along her neck and jaw.

"What is it?" she finally asked, on edge as his emotions continued to batter her.

"I can't lose you," he whispered fiercely.

Pushing up to her tiptoes, she kissed him, promising, "You won't."

He gave her a half-grin but it didn't reach his eyes. She was still being pelted by his fear, but at least now she understood the true cause. It was a twin of her own.

"I think I've proven by now that I can hold my own in a fight. Meaner things than you have tried to cut me down and haven't succeeded. There's no reason to believe they will this time. Not when you'll be right there beside me."

His throat bobbed, and his eyes went tight, as if her words caused a nightmare to come to life behind his eyes.

"I've failed you before."

Effie shushed him. "Am I standing here in your arms?"

His brows puckered. "Yes."

"Then how did you fail?"

"I—"

She put a finger on his lips. "Luc, stop. I'm right here. Whatever happens tomorrow, we'll face it together. No matter what is waiting for us, those are the best odds we can ever hope for."

Lucian's body quaked as a tremor raced through him, and his relief rained over her as the emotional storm within him broke.

"I don't deserve you," he whispered, cupping both of her cheeks with his hands.

Effie tilted her head, unsure whether to tease or to soothe. She decided on honesty. "The Mother said you do."

He pulled back slightly. "What? She spoke to you of me?"

"Mmhmm. I asked her why she almost let me die if she needed me to be her Voice. Her answer was that all of this had to happen, and that *you* were my gift for enduring it. So," Effie said with a shrug, "stop trying to weasel your way out of being with me. I earned you."

Lucian stared at Effie for one long moment. Shock etched in every line of his face before he threw his head back and laughed. His arms dropped to wrap around her waist, and he lifted her high, kissing her hard.

"I guess that settles it," he said, his eyes soft and warm.

"Finally," Effie said with a smile, still lightheaded from his kiss. "I love you, Lucian. I think I've always loved you."

Kissing her once more, softer this time, he breathed against her lips, "Not as much as I love you. Now, let's go to bed so I can prove it."

~

EFFIE STARED INTO THE MIRROR, focusing on the man still sleeping behind her. Lucian was sprawled out, one arm folded behind his head, the other curled on top of his chest. One of his long, tanned legs was hanging off the side of the bed, the other concealed beneath a hunter green blanket that did very little to hide his impressive bulge.

She'd spent the last night having her way with Lucian until the sky turned pink with the dawn and they'd collapsed beside each other in a sweaty tangle of limbs.

Her cheeks heated as her eyes roamed over his sculpted body. Lucian as a lover was every bit as demanding and attentive as Lucian in every other aspect of his life. Effie selfishly wished they could ignore the rest of the world and spend the day, or even the entire week, in bed. They'd only just found their way back to each other, and barely had more than a handful of hours to enjoy it.

"You keep looking at me like that, love, and I'll haul you back in here, responsibilities be damned."

Her eyes found his in the mirror, and she gave him an impish grin.

"Between the other Guardians, Ronan, Von, and Helena, I'd like to see you try."

His answering smile was potently male, and she was far from immune. Her belly tightened, and her breath caught as he slowly sat up, bracing himself on his elbows. "You really think even if they combined forces they could prevent me from doing anything I wanted to do? Do you think so little of my ability, fledgling?"

"Of course not," she managed to rasp. "But that's a lot of people for you to overcome on your own."

"Shall I prove it?"

"No," she answered quickly, though every fiber of her being screamed a resounding *yes*.

"Spoilsport," he said, giving her a playful pout.

Effie was discovering that playful Lucian was her favorite. He so rarely gave into that side of himself, or maybe it wasn't giving in as much as having an opportunity to relax enough to experience it at all. Either way, she cherished these moments with him.

Who was she kidding? She cherished *all* her moments with Lucian. Every second she had with him was precious. After what they'd been through to be together, they'd more than earned their right to enjoy life's simple pleasures. Like eating a meal together, or waking up together, or losing themselves inside of each other. Effie would gladly face any number of chores or mundane tasks if he was at her side.

A knock sounded on the door.

"Last chance," Lucian said with a lift of his eyebrows as he swung his legs over the side of the bed.

She stared unrepentantly, getting an eyeful as the blanket fell to the floor. "Mother have mercy," she whispered, the temptation to tackle him replacing any other thought. She was still sore from last night's festivities, but it only took a look at him and she was already ready for another round. Or ten.

He laughed at her, pressing a kiss to her shoulder as he bent to pick up his pants where they'd landed the night before. He was in the middle of pulling them on when the second knock came. Mostly decent, Lucian opened the door with a barked, "What?"

"A month ago you'd have my arse if you had to come hunt me down the morning of a job," Kael's amused response came.

Lucian didn't bother to apologize as he slammed the door closed in his blade brother's face. He held his hand flat against the wood and turned to wink at her over his shoulder with a hushed, "Let him wait."

Effie laughed, stepping under his arm and prying the door open just enough to peek through the crack. "We'll be right there."

Kael's dimples flashed as he smiled knowingly down at her. "If it's longer than five minutes, I'm coming in, and I won't bother knocking. Keep that in mind if there's anything you don't want me to see."

"Two minutes," she promised with another laugh.

Lucian was pushing the door closed as she spoke, letting her know he could have prevented her from opening it in the first place if he'd really wanted to. She turned, angling her body between him and the exit.

"Not a morning person?" she teased.

His smile turned wicked, and he leaned forward to nip at her bottom lip. "I think you know exactly what kind of person I am in the morning."

It was difficult to remember what she was going to say. Her body went molten, and her eyes shifted back to the bed. Yes. Yes, she absolutely did.

Lucian's eyes burned bronze as he leaned down and stole her breath with a mind-numbing kiss. Eagerly, she wrapped her arms around his neck, loving the way his body pressed against hers as he deepened it.

The door vibrated against her back and Lucian moved so quickly she didn't understand what happened until Kael's laughter floated through the wood.

"Let's go you two," he hollered. "Everyone's waiting."

Lucian's palm was above her head, holding the door closed. "Ready?"

She knew without needing any sort of psychic connection that if she said no he'd stay with her until she was, no matter who was waiting. Heart full, Effie cast one last longing look at the bed. "I guess."

He leaned close as his hand dropped to his side. "I was really hoping you were going to say no." Stepping away, he winked at her before he turned to finish getting dressed while she laced up her boots.

"Here, you'll need this," he said, moving back into her line of sight.

Effie looked up, her eyes widening at his offering. "Where did you find that?" she asked, awestruck.

His smile was almost shy when he responded. "You'd told me that I owed you a weapon more substantial than your daggers. I made it for you using one of my old blades, but didn't have the chance to give it to you before . . ." he trailed off, but she had no trouble filling in the blanks. He'd had it since before he'd realized she'd been turned. Shrugging, Lucian held it out a little further. "Anyway, I've been carrying it with me ever since. It's time for you to have it."

Effie reached for the hilt, lifting it up and inspecting it. The sword was as thick as her arm and just as long, but as light as one of her daggers. The metal was as pale as moonlight, and seemed to glow with its own inner light. Runes were etched into the blade, the same ones that marked her as a Guardian.

"Lucian, it's perfect."

He moved to stand next to her, his finger gliding along the markings. "These runes are imbued with our power. They will protect the blade."

"Protect it how?"

"It will never dull or rust, but more importantly it is indestructible."

Lifting to her toes, Effie pressed a kiss to his scruffy cheek. "Who knew a weapon could be such a romantic gift?"

He laughed, his amusement rolling through her. "Come on, fledgling. We should probably go before Kael comes barging in."

"Oh, it wouldn't be so bad. All he'd discover is us in the middle of a little swordplay." Effie lifted her brows meaningfully, shoulders shaking with laughter.

Lucian shook his head, lips fighting a smile as he moved toward the door. "That was a terrible joke."

"No, it wasn't. It was hilarious. Admit it."

"Never," he said, but his eyes were twinkling with suppressed laughter.

They were both still smiling as they walked out of the room hand in hand.

~

She wasn't smiling anymore as she stared at what was left of the citadel with open-mouthed horror. The beautiful city with its mist-colored buildings was nothing but ash. She'd hardly been coherent for the better part of the battle, but even with Lucian's warning she hadn't been prepared for this level of destruction.

The City of Light was gone. A few crumbling buildings were all that was left to mark where it once stood. Effie hadn't been one of its citizens long, but it was the first true home she'd ever had. And now it was gone.

Lucian squeezed her hand, his grief a mirror of her own. *"You okay?"*

Effie pressed her lips together and gave a tight shake of her head. Rationally, she knew this wasn't her fault, but she still felt guilty. What little she could remember of the battle was bloody. Some of that blood she was responsible for spilling. As far as her emotions were concerned, that meant she was culpable for the resulting chaos.

"We did our best, but the Shadow Fire was impossible to control."

She bit the inside of her cheek, the jolt of pain helping steel her nerves. "It's a miracle there were any survivors at all."

"Letting it burn was probably the kindest thing you could do for the fallen," Helena said behind them. Effie and Lucian turned to face her. They must have looked dubious because she added, "Fire purifies."

"Even Shadow Fire?" Effie asked.

Helena's eyes cast out over the ground, her voice a little flat as she replied, "Well . . . it certainly ensures that there's nothing left to corrupt, so there's that."

Effie wasn't so sure that was true. Ever since stepping foot through the portal, a creeping sense of wrongness nagged at her. This place may be little more than soot and ash, but there was something else . . . something *other* that had staked its claim in the wreckage. She could feel it even now, sinking itself deeper into the earth, taking root.

Effie shivered, not sure where the certainty came from, but not about to question it. She had two separate gifts now, both tied to knowing. The Guardians gave her the ability to see the world as it truly was, while the Mother had simply given her the ability to See. It's only natural that she would start to sense things others couldn't. This would hardly be the first time she'd had a premonition without understanding what exactly her instincts were trying to warn her about.

"There's something wrong with this place."

"You feel it too?" Helena asked, her brows lifted in surprise.

Effie nodded, turning to glance at Lucian. "Do you?"

The flecks of bronze in his eyes flared and he gave a terse nod. "It's tainted. The place reeks of corruption."

"This is the feeling you associate with the corruption?" Helena asked, her head tilting and her eyes going iridescent.

A muscle spasmed in Lucian's jaw as he gave another jerky nod.

"I've felt this before—twice now—but hadn't recognized it for what it was," Helena said, studying their surroundings with more interest.

"How could you? You didn't know it was a possibility," Lucian replied.

Helena's lips were a flat line. "Even so."

Von stared at his Mate from across the clearing. He was half-listening to Kragen, Helena's Sword. He along with her Master, Joquil, had joined them this morning—his attention clearly not on the conversation. Joquil, however, listened with rapt attention, taking notes in a small book as he nodded along with whatever Kragen was saying. The two Circle members had been waiting for them in a tamer part of the jungle. If they'd been waiting awhile, they didn't make a point to mention it.

Effie allowed her attention to briefly shift over the rest of their party. Nord had stayed behind to maintain the Triumvirate's presence with the Keepers—and as a failsafe in case anything happened—but Kael had come with them. He was currently staring in her direction with curious green eyes, Ronan and Reyna beside him. The Night Stalker's arms were wrapped around her body, and her dark eyes darted from side to side as if she was waiting for something to jump out at her. Ronan was talking to her, his voice pitched low and his icy eyes flashing with intensity. Apparently, no one was feeling entirely at ease being back here.

That was it; the extent of their hunting party. Effie didn't mind admitting that each of these people individually were more powerful than most armies. Together they were a damn force of nature. The thought should have been reassuring, but all it seemed to do was reinforce the fact that they needed an army in the first place. The last two times she'd been on a battlefield that necessitated this kind of manpower, she'd lost two of the people she'd held dear. And those were both battles their side had actually *won*.

Effie clamped down on Lucian's hand. She'd be damned if she said goodbye to anyone else she loved.

She must have been transmitting her thoughts because Lucian returned the vise-like grip with one of his own. *"I'm not that easy to kill, and I have a whole lot more to live for than anything we might face in the days to come. You never need to worry about losing me."*

His conviction was appreciated, but she'd thought that before and been proven wrong. Effie was pretty certain that when something vital was on the line, there was no choice but to worry. And for her, Lucian was absolutely vital.

Because he was expecting it, she gave his hand another squeeze and tried to muster an authentic smile. That was the best she could manage under the circumstances.

Not wanting to dwell on everything that could go wrong, Effie returned her attention to the woman beside her. Helena's eyes were still glowing, an invisible breeze lifting the strands of her hair until it flew around her face like a chestnut halo. She took two determined steps forward, her voice swollen with power as she said, "I may not have been here to stop it, but at least I can put it to rights."

"Wait." Effie stopped her with a hand on the wrist. She hadn't realized she was going to speak until the word burst out of her. The weight of the stares the others leveled on her made it almost impossible to continue, but she couldn't ignore the sudden pressure settling in her chest. "I think there's something we need to do before you cleanse the land."

Helena turned her brilliant eyes on Effie, and it was all she could do not to flinch. She'd come a long way from the mouse of a girl she used to be, but when faced with the other woman's sheer power, it was really hard to remember that.

"What makes you say so?"

Effie placed a hand on her chest, just above her heart. "Just a feeling."

Lucian cleared his throat. "If I may, Kiri?"

Helena nodded for him to continue.

"Effie's sight has manifested as premonition in the past, the most recent happening right before the citadel was attacked. I think it would be wise to heed her warning."

"Of course. It would be foolish to ignore any of those the Mother has blessed with such a gift."

Lucian placed his hands on Effie's shoulders, his thumbs brushing up and down the knotted muscles just below the base of her neck.

"I'm not sure what we're supposed to do," she admitted, feeling silly that they were taking her so seriously when she didn't have anything more substantial to offer.

"Your instinct has always been a good guide. What is it telling you to do now?"

She chewed on the inside of her cheek as she considered the question. If cleansing the land would remove something crucial, then what could they do to find it first? The question hadn't even fully formed in her mind before Effie had her answer.

Who better than a Guardian to search and see?

"We need to follow the threads."

Lucian didn't need to ask what that meant. From the flare of emerald in Kael's eyes, neither did he. Almost as one, the three Guardians summoned their power.

In the same breath, Effie really wished she hadn't.

Bile climbed up her throat and the acidic taste of it made her gag. She was grateful there hadn't been time for her to break her fast that morning. If there'd been anything in her stomach, it would be littering the ground.

What she could only sense before as a prickly unease was now visible in all its horrific glory. The land was rotting. Like an overripe pumpkin that had caved in on itself and started to ooze. The extent of the decay was such that other than a few defiant strands there was nothing left for them to salvage.

Everywhere she looked, oily black fibers strangled anything that shone with feeble light. Even now, the darkness beneath their feet seemed to swell and grow, as if it was working its way up from the bowels of the earth to consume an unexpected treat. Them.

Not safe. Not safe. Not safe.

The need to run tore through her, but safe or not . . . they had a job to do. The only thing running would accomplish was sealing their fate.

Swallowing back her nausea, Effie released her power and turned to Lucian and Helena. "If we trace the corrupted threads, we can use them as a means of tracking the Shadows. They should lead us straight to one of their nests."

Lucian stared over her shoulder, his expression sending skitters of fear down her spine. "No need . . . they're already here."

CHAPTER 27

EFFIE

She didn't need to bother turning around to see what Lucian was staring at. A quick glance at the horizon told her everything she needed to know. The Shadows and their Shadow-touched victims were swarming all around them.

They were surrounded and badly outnumbered. She watched in a sort of horrified awe as they crept out from behind the ruined buildings, their numbers multiplying faster than her brain could process. While the Keepers had been in hiding, the Shadows had been busy creating an army.

A part of her wished she could feign surprise at the ambush, but she'd known they were walking onto a battlefield before they even stepped foot on this cursed land. It had always been a matter of time.

Effie's mouth went dry as she watched dozens more of the Shadow-touched crawl out from behind the wreckage.

"Is that . . ." The question died in her throat as her eyes widened in horror.

The Chosen were no longer the Shadow's meal of choice. Half-decomposed creatures—which had been terrifying in their own right—were now slithering among their ranks. Effie could make out a caebris, one of the gray and lavender striped jungle cats that could turn itself invisible, as well as the scaled body and sharp-toothed maw of a crokolisk.

"What are they waiting for?" Ronan bit out, an ax in each of his hands.

The sky ripped in two, seeming to respond to his question, the crack of thunder making the earth shudder.

"Whatever it is, I don't intend to stand around and find out," Lucian growled, his own weapon drawn, its edges blurred with tendrils of smoke.

Clouds rolled across the sky, angry and black, turning day to night. It was an unnatural storm, fueled entirely by the woman who ruled them. Effie could feel the pulse of the Kiri's anger in the air, pushing her, driving her to answer its call. It tasted of soot and smelled of smoke. It promised vengeance . . . and death.

Effie pulled her sword free, just barely making out the silvery-blue markings as she slid into a defensive stance. Beside her, Helena lifted her hands, orbs of Fire blazing brightly in her palms. She looked like a warrior goddess with the flickering flames reflected in her eyes and embers crackling at the ends of her hair.

"This ends here," she cried, her voice a layered chorus as it boomed all around them.

There was a flash of lightning, so bright that for one frozen moment they were cast back into day before the growl of thunder joined in and all hell broke loose.

The Shadows surged forth, moving with an inhuman speed as they broke ranks. Effie felt Lucian beside her, and she could just make out some of her friends in her periphery, but she was wholly focused on the abomination heading straight for her.

It had been human . . . once. Now it was a creature that existed only in nightmares. There were more bones visible than flesh, one slinking eye was hanging from its socket, and it walked with a distinctive lurch, although that didn't seem to slow it down at all. Its tattered black robes filled in the rest. This thing had once been a Keeper, but the Shadows had managed to keep the poor soul alive long enough to turn it. Given the state of its appearance . . . the Keeper had likely been begging to die long before they were done with him.

Effie tightened her grip on the pommel of her sword and charged. The Shadows may not have put the poor man out of his misery, but she would.

Its sibilant voice reached her before she was within striking range. "He wakes."

"Yeah? Tell me something I don't know," Effie replied, her blade already swinging high as she prepared for a killing blow.

The Shadow reached for her, bony fingers curled into claws. "There is a traitor in your midst. One who aligns themselves with the darkness."

That gave her pause.

"Effie, look out!"

While the Shadow had been distracting her, two more had snuck up behind her. She hissed in pain as razor-sharp nails raked down the back of her right arm. As she turned to deal with the threat, Lucian beheaded them both with one powerful swing of his blade.

Knowing he would protect her from further sneak attacks, Effie twisted back to face her enemy, her eyes narrowed into slits. "*If* we have a traitor, I'll gladly show them the same courtesy I'm going to give you." Her blade was already moving, looking like a beam of light as it arced through the air. Before the Shadow could speak further, she was slicing through his neck with no more effort than one would use to spread jam on toast. As his mangled head fell from his body, she wiped her blade on the side of her pants. "Even an enemy should appreciate a quick death."

She looked away from her kill to see that the rest of the mass had met up with them. Sliding into position, she was lost to the dance of the blade. Effie was covered in ichor and filth, but she only ever stopped long enough to identify her next target. If she'd realized how far away she'd gotten from the others, she might not have allowed herself to become so lost to the battle.

But by the time she noticed, it was too late.

⁓

LUCIAN

HE MOVED with a warrior's grace, the act of battle so finely ingrained in him he reacted without conscious thought. Around him others hurled balls of fire and ice, using their magic in combination with their weapons. For all that they were outnumbered, it was a slaughter. Helena alone managed to cull half the enemy's force by raining fire from the sky.

But still the Shadow army came, undaunted by the ease with which their fellows had been dispatched.

The air was thick with smoke and the smell of rotting flesh. Lucian's eyes watered, but his steps were sure. The ring of Kael's blade met his ears. They fought as they had for centuries: back to back. From the sound of it, his blade brother was doing just fine.

He spared a second to eye the battlefield, searching for the familiar blonde head that was supposed to be just in front of him.

Effie was nowhere to be found.

Jaw clenched, Lucian tightened his hold on his blade and became a flurry of movement, working his way through the sea of bodies to the place he'd last seen her. He'd almost lost her once. There was no way he was going to allow it to happen again.

"Lucian, hold on. Luc, wait!" Kael's frustrated shouts sounded behind him, but he didn't stop. Kael was a warrior born and bred; he could hold his own.

Lucian ducked as a ball of sickly green acid was lobbed his way, and then dodged as one of the Shadow-touched caebris appeared directly in his path. The beast bared its teeth, saliva dripping from its long fangs as it let out a deep growl.

He bared his teeth and returned the growl with a roar of his own. The beast lunged, claws extended as it sprang toward him. Lucian was ready, his blade sinking clean into the massive cat's belly and then up

212

through its chest, cleaving it in two. Warm blood spurted on his hands and face, but still he did not stop.

As he raced ahead, he caught brief flashes of the others. Helena and her Mate were wielding Fire, creating a smoldering wall of flame that cut off the Shadows on two sides. It provided Joquil a safer place to stand while he called forth his own powerful magic. Ronan was pulling an ax free from some furred beast Lucian didn't recognize while Reyna hurled dagger after dagger into the throat of an approaching Shadow. Meanwhile, Kragen was crushing the skull of one of the fiends between his massive hands.

But still no sign of Effie.

He hesitated to call out to her through their mental link, lest it startle her during a crucial moment. For any of the other Guardians, there would have been no hesitation. They had spent years preparing for those exact circumstances in order to coordinate with each other during attacks without being overhead. Effie had yet to venture into that level of training, and Lucian refused to be the liability that saw her harmed.

That didn't stop him from muttering a string of stinging expletives as he imagined with crystalline clarity all of the horrific things that could have happened to her. He used his fear to stoke his rage and swung his weapon with brutal force. Lucian could just make out a distinctive sizzle over the screams of the fallen when his sword connected with flesh, cauterizing wounds as it created them.

He let out a low grunt as he pulled his weapon free from another caebris when a flash of wheat-colored hair caught his eye. His relief was so potent he was momentarily lightheaded. Effie used her height to her advantage, easily ducking beneath one of the Shadows' arms as it attempted to strike, darting around its body to land her own deadly blow.

Lucian recognized the move. He'd taught it to her.

Effie caught his eye and gave him an impish grin.

He returned it with one of his own, pride swelling inside of him just as the ground began to shake. There wasn't even time for him to catch his balance before the world dropped out from beneath him.

$\backsim$

EFFIE

THE EARTH GROANED as it was bent in two. She could only watch in stunned disbelief as Lucian disappeared into a sinkhole that had grown right where the citadel once stood.

"Lucian!" she screamed, running forward to be stopped short by an arm around the waist.

"Effie, damn it, wait."

"Kael, let me go," she gasped, struggling in his hold. "He could be hurt. He needs me."

"It's not safe. If you get too close, you could fall in too."

She twisted in Kael's arms, her voice feral as she spat her words at him. "No matter the danger he would never give up on me, nor I him. Now, let. Me. GO!" With the last word, she shoved his arm away, finding a strength she didn't know she possessed.

As soon as she was free she shot forward, the ground continuing to quake as more dirt and rubble fell into the ever-growing hole. Reaching the edge, she began to slow, dropping to her knees when she'd gotten as close as she dared.

"Lucian?" she called as she risked a look down into the massive pit.

For one terrible moment there was nothing, and then a labored, "I'm here!"

Her relief was so intense it was almost painful. She may not know the state of his injuries but at least he was conscious. "I'm going to get you out of there!"

Tears stung her eyes as she tried to figure out a way to follow through on her promise. *Think, Effie. Think.* As it was, Lucian was so far down she could barely make him out in the gaping darkness. Even then he was only a ripple in the gloom.

Around her the battle raged, but it felt muted now. Her entire being was focused on the man below. And then her heart stopped beating as a terror she'd only experienced during two of the worst moments of her life took hold of her.

"Effie . . . I don't think . . . I'm alone down here."

The darkness seemed to slither and swell, coiling in on itself even as it stretched higher. Icy sweat rolled down her back as a high-pitched shriek of absolute fury swelled from below. The sound grew in intensity as the darkness climbed higher, its formless mass taking shape.

Effie barely scrambled back in time as a monster surged up out of the hole, Lucian dangling from one of the scales on its back, his weapon nowhere in sight.

She had no name for the creature towering above her. It looked like some kind of corruption-mutated wyrm. The monstrosity was the color of midnight, its cylindered body covered in blue-tinged scales. Its eyes were red slits on either side of its narrow head, and its mouth was pointed. When it opened it up to shriek again, Effie noticed row after row of deadly teeth and a long gray tongue that dripped with slimy black saliva. A drop of the acidic spit fell and Effie dodged just as the viscous black fluid splashed on the ground, melting through the debris.

The wyrm began to buck, clearly not appreciating the man hanging from its back. If the creature hadn't been so tall, Lucian could have easily dropped to the floor, but extended to its full height as it was, her Guardian was four or five stories high. A drop from that altitude could be fatal.

"Lucian, hang on!"

That he didn't bother with a smart-assed reply only emphasized how much effort it was taking him to cling onto the writhing creature.

Her mind raced, frantically seeking some vulnerability they could exploit to slay the monster without risking Lucian. There was no obvious answer.

In an act more desperate than brave, Effie swung her sword, praying it was sharp enough to cut through the body of the beast. Her arms vibrated from the force of the blow, but she didn't so much as scratch it. She did, however, piss it off even more.

No longer worried about Lucian, the wyrm's head swiveled and its mouth opened on another petrifying shriek. Effie was blasted with a wave of breath so hot and putrid it must have come straight from the bowels of hell.

Mother, if you have any tips to share, now would be a really great time to enlighten me.

She stood frozen as the monstrous head began to dip down in her direction. "Oh no, I didn't get this far just to become wyrm food," she muttered, starting to run.

The creature gave chase, slithering along behind her with more speed than anything that size had a right to. She risked a glance over her shoulder and almost stumbled as she noticed Lucian shimmying up the thing's back.

"What in the Mother's name are you doing?"

"Trying to save your life!"

"Maybe you should be more worried about your own."

"Speak for yourself."

Effie bit off a curse and kept running, heading straight for a wall of Shadows. If it came down to fighting them or the thing chasing her, she'd much rather test her luck with the plague bringers. At least she knew how to kill them.

"Effie!" Ronan roared.

She didn't dare look back. She pumped her legs harder, jumping over piles of rubble and bodies like she'd been doing it her entire life. Effie had no clue where she was running, but she knew as soon as she stopped that thing would strike. Maybe if she kept it distracted long enough the others could figure out a way to put it down.

The Shadows snickered as she drew near them. She was close enough now to make out the snaking black lines in their eyes.

Sudden instinct told her to dodge left, so she did.

The ground trembled as the wyrm cried out. Effie threw her body over a half-crumbled wall and landed in a graceless heap. She'd just managed to cover her head with her arms when more of the deadly black spittle flew from its mouth, landing right where she'd been heading—right where the Shadows were still standing.

Their wails of pain were a deafening chorus as the acid ate through their skin. She stared in horrified fascination as what was left of their flesh and bones melted away. One by one the group of Shadows dropped to the ground, their bodies writhing in pain until their cries grew silent and their bodies still.

Those that had not been hit by the acid wasted no time fleeing. As far as wins went, it was a questionable one, but at least there was only one foe left for them to deal with.

Her body aching with protest, she pushed herself up from the ground, the tip of her sword scraping against the dirt and ash as she rose. The wyrm twisted its head, its hellacious eyes finding her due to the tell-tale sound.

"Mother's tits," she rasped. There was no way she was going to defeat this thing on her own, but a little bit of a break would have been nice. Even if the temporary safety was only an illusion.

The wyrm reared back, preparing for another strike. Effie was grateful that her hands were steady as she lifted her sword. If the damn thing wanted to eat her, it was going to feel her blade sliding down its fucking throat. Determined, she steeled herself, preparing for the attack.

"Don't you *dare* give up now," Lucian roared, swinging around the creature's neck, his arm cocking back. With a savage battle cry, he swung his fist and slammed it straight into the wyrm's demonic eye.

Effie was knocked to her knees as the creature let out a deafening screech, the earth trembling in response to its outrage. Her mouth fell open on a soundless scream as Lucian was flung from its neck. She started to crawl, pushing herself up with some misguided notion of trying to catch him.

His arms windmilled as he fell through the air and time slowed to a crawl. Heart in her throat, Effie threw out her arms as if her will alone could hold him suspended in the air. As she did, she prayed.

When Lucian didn't crash into the earth, Effie blinked and then blinked again. It worked. He was still falling, but it was a controlled, graceful descent. Shaking, she looked at her hands, wondering if this was some newly discovered Guardian power.

Lucian's voice was a bit breathless as it filled her mind. *"I hate to disappoint you, fledgling, but you aren't the one responsible for this."*

Wide-eyed, she glanced from Lucian to the man whose hands glowed a soft blue. *Joquil.* The Kiri's Master of Magic had managed to use his power to control Lucian's freefall. Tears spilled from her eyes as she let out a grateful hiccup.

The sudden silence finally registered, and Effie spun back to the wyrm. Why wasn't it pressing its attack?

The answer pulled another startled laugh from her. It was frozen, completely coated in shimmering ice crystals.

Effie darted forward, flinging her arms around the Master. "Mother bless you," she gasped, squeezing him as another tear slipped down her cheek.

Joquil returned the embrace with an awkward pat on her back. "I would have helped sooner, but we were a little tied up."

Lucian stood beside her, blood dripping from a gash in his head and entirely coated in sweat and grime. To her eyes, he'd never been more handsome. He pulled her up in his arms, grunting when she wrapped herself around him.

"Stop *doing* that," she hissed.

"Doing what?" he murmured, burying his face in her neck.

"Almost *dying.*"

"I told you, I'm very hard to kill, especially now that I have so much to live for." He lifted his face, his dark eyes scorching her as he let the words sink in.

Effie pulled his head to hers, lips aching to claim his.

Crack.

As one, they turned back to the wyrm as it somehow managed to break free of its icy prison.

"No!" Effie cried out in exasperation and shock, even as a part of her knew it had been too easy.

Lucian lowered her to the ground, and they raced away, Joquil on their heels. Helena and the others were running toward them, expressions grim.

"I think you're going the wrong way," she panted when their group was reassembled.

Helena gave her a humorless smirk. "Someone has to deal with that thing."

"You say that like we weren't trying."

Her smile turned genuine. "You were just wearing it down for me."

Effie barked out a laugh and used her arm to push her sweat-dampened curls off her forehead. "Exactly."

Another loud *crack* shook the earth, and with a savage screech the creature flung off the last of the ice.

Bracing herself, Effie turned back to the wyrm. "Any great ideas, Vessel?"

Thunder and lightning chased each other across the sky as Helena lifted her arms. "One or two."

A bolt of lightning struck the wyrm, then a second and a third, throwing it up high and illuminating its interior like some kind of scientific drawing. The creature spasmed and the air was permeated with the scent of burning meat.

It crashed to the ground, and the sense of expectation was palpable. Tiny currents of light still danced around the creature born of corruption and darkness. Just when it felt safe to breathe, the wyrm's slitted eyes flew open and it screamed.

"I think you made it angry," Kael announced.

"What do you think it was before?" Effie asked, heart pounding.

"Hungry."

Not wanting to give the monster a chance to strike first, Von and Kragen sprinted forward, blades in hand. Effie's heart sank. Their weapons were useless against those scales.

Kragen swung first, his mighty axes glinting in the pale light. He could have been using wooden toys for all the good they did. Both weapons bounced off, utterly harmless.

Von struck almost simultaneously, his flaming sword aiming for the sliver of space between two of the scales that covered the wyrm's belly. The strike was true. The wyrm's scream of pain infused their small group with renewed purpose.

"Fire!" Lucian shouted. "It's not immune to fire."

Helena's lips lifted in a cruel smile, her eyes sparkling with iridescence. "Fire I can do," she murmured in the harmonic voice of her power.

Effie's eyes lifted to the sky, expecting fiery bolts to rain down and crash into the wyrm. Instead, Helena pulled her arm back, a spear of flame forming in her hand. She hurled it with perfect aim, using Air to guide it to its target.

The wyrm's jaw opened once more, each glistening row of teeth on display as the spear flew upwards into its mouth and buried itself in the creature's brain. Helena wasted no time, lobbing ball after ball of Fire until the monstrosity was no more than a pillar of flame.

There was one final, horrific screech and the wyrm toppled to the ground, completely consumed by the inferno.

They edged closer, watching as the fire burned and the sky started to clear. The light of the flames danced on their faces and in their eyes as the fiendish beast turned to smoldering ash. Heat lapped at her skin and sweat trickled down her body, making her battle leathers stick to her skin, but she relished the burn and the almost perfect silence.

Today they had won, and this time, Effie hadn't lost a single person she loved.

Or so she thought.

Looking around, Effie's victorious smile faded. Not all her friends were among their ranks.

"Uh . . . where are Ronan and Reyna?"

CHAPTER 28

RONAN

*R*onan raced to the edge of the trees, his axes lifted defiantly as he chased the escaping Shadows. When the last of them disappeared into the jungle, he finally stopped giving chase.

"Run you fucking cowards," he spat. "But know that I will find you. So long as I draw breath, you'll never be safe." The crack of a branch had him spinning around, weapons held high. "Mother's tits, Reyna. Are you trying to get yourself killed?"

She blinked at him with her forest-colored eyes, the multi-hued orbs glittered with suppressed mirth. "I thought you could use the assistance. Apologies for treading on your fragile ego, Shield."

Ronan grunted.

She tilted her head, her eyes flitting from him to the place where the last of the Shadows had disappeared. "Why *did* you think it was a good idea to go after them on your own?"

"Helena will make easy work of the wyrm, and it didn't sit well, the thought of these abominations running free once more. We allowed it last time and look what came of it."

"There are far fewer among their ranks after today," Reyna pointed out.

"Aye, well. One is too many, especially now that they can multiply."

She let out a soft murmur of assent and fell into step beside him. "We have the means to track them now. They will not hide from us for long."

Ronan supposed she was right, but it still rankled.

Another snap sounded to his left, and he gave her an amused grin. "For a Night Stalker, you sure make a lot of noise. I thought your kind were exceptionally gifted at sneaking up on your prey."

Reyna gave him a haughty look that had his pants tenting uncomfortably. He mentally calculated the last time he'd lain with a woman. When the number of days surpassed the better part of a year, he decided it had been entirely too long.

"If I hadn't wanted you to hear me coming, Shield, trust that you wouldn't have known I was there until my blade was sinking into your heart."

Ronan would be lying if he said the thought of it didn't make him want her more.

"Feel free to try, kitten." Her nose wrinkled at his choice in name, but before she could react, he continued, "But don't be too disappointed when you are the one that ends up pinned by my blade." He gave her a fierce grin, letting the double meaning of his words pulse between them for one long heartbeat.

Color stained her cheeks and her eyes flashed with desire. The color looked good on her. Healthy. Ever since the lajhár attack, she'd been less herself. Less vibrant in some indiscernible way. Multiple healers had inspected her, and in every way that mattered she was healthy. But she was a shadow of her former self. Just as fierce, but more fragile now.

Ronan knew better than to mention it. She'd practically stabbed him in the thigh with her dinner knife the last time he'd tried to bring it up. Reyna did not appreciate being called out on her weakness. Fair enough. Neither did he.

He started walking once more, letting the moment between them pass unacted upon. They would have their time together. Soon. But this was hardly the place for seduction. And Reyna deserved seduction. A woman such as her deserved every skilled move he could lavish upon her.

Snap.

Ronan laughed and looked over his shoulder. "Now you're just doing it on—" He broke off when the only thing he found was trembling branches. "Reyna? Reyna, stop fucking around."

Even as he tried to tell himself she was just playing games, trying to prove a point, he didn't believe it. His heart spiked as he combed through the nearby foliage. His movements became more frantic as he tore through the jungle.

There was no sign of her. Not so much as a scrap of cloth hanging from a nearby branch to indicate which way she'd gone.

He dropped to his knees as the air left his lungs.

Reyna had vanished.

~

*E*FFIE

HER HEART FELL AS A LONE, heart-wrenching cry pierced the air. There was no mistaking the sound of her friend's anguish. "Ronan!"

Their group sprinted toward the sound, already preparing for a fight. They found him not far from the remains of the battle, just on the edge of the jungle on his hands and knees in the dirt.

Von was the first to reach him, dropping down beside his best friend. "What is it? Where are you hurt?"

He was inspecting him for some sign of a wound, something that would have justified such an awful sound to be torn from him. Effie could have told Von he needn't bother with his search. She recognized the grief that had etched itself in the lines of Ronan's face and body. This was no physical wound. This was loss, in its purest form.

Her voice was so quiet it took the others a moment to realize she had spoken. "Ronan, what happened to Reyna?"

He looked up, and Effie gave an involuntary shiver. His eyes were colder than shards of ice, and they were entirely devoid of life.

"She's gone."

"Gone?" Helena asked, eyes narrowed as she scanned the horizon.

Ronan gave a brittle nod. The man was barely holding himself together. He was practically vibrating under the twin forces of his rage and grief.

Lucian exchanged a look with Effie, picking up on the direction of her thoughts. He knelt down on the other side of the Shield, his hand braced on the other man's shoulder. "Gone as in dead or taken?"

Even though the Guardian's voice had been gentle, Ronan flinched violently. "Taken."

Lucian nodded, glancing up at Helena. "Say the word, Kiri, and we can begin a search."

Her eyes swirled with power, her lips twisting down in a frown. "There's no need. Reyna isn't here."

"How do you know?" Kael asked, his own eyes glowing emerald as he scanned the jungle using his power.

"I know what her power looks like. There is no trace of it here. Wherever she is, she's no longer in this jungle. Likely not even in Bael."

Ronan's jaw clenched, and his hands fisted into the damp ground as if he could strangle the truth out of the earth itself.

Effie's head shot up as the Shadow's hissed words came back to her. "One of the Shadows spoke to me. I didn't pay much attention to it. I just thought he was trying to distract me at the time, but he said we had a traitor among us."

"Reyna would never," Ronan growled, his eyes wild.

Effie held her hands up in a placating gesture. "No, you misunderstand me. I wasn't suggesting she was the traitor, but perhaps someone else orchestrated her abduction?"

Her gaze darted around as she studied each member of their party in turn. Could it be true? Who among them would dare to betray one of the Guardians, let alone the Kiri herself? And how? Who had the means in addition to the death wish?

"Impossible," Helena declared, her voice thick with power. "None of the Circle would dare betray me."

"Not all among us are bound to you," Von murmured, his silver eyes dark with suspicion as he studied Lucian and Kael. Beside him Kragen cracked his knuckles and Joquil's eyes narrowed.

Lucian returned Von's look with a bland one of his own. "The Guardians are sworn to the protection of this realm and all who inhabit it. We could not betray our vow even if we wanted to."

Effie bristled at the implication, offended on Lucian's behalf. No man who walked this earth was more honorable.

He slid his hand into hers and squeezed. *"I appreciate your concern, but he would not be doing his job if he didn't voice the possibility. He is sworn to her, as I am sworn to you. Her safety comes before all else."*

"Your loyalty should never have been in question in the first place."

Lucian chuckled. *"I don't think anyone has ever been so fiercely protective of me and my honor before."*

Effie gave his hand a squeeze of her own. *"Well, get used to it."*

"Peace, fledgling. You can soothe my wounded pride with your kisses later." His words were light, but she knew he was touched by her declaration.

"Just your pride?"

Her Guardian's eyes flared hot. *"To start."*

"If it's not one of us, who else could he be speaking of?" Kael mused, bringing them back to the conversation.

They eyed each other uneasily, trying to think who else could have the ability to do anything to compromise their mission.

"The Valen Council?" Kragen asked.

Lucian shook his head. "It doesn't feel right to me. What do they have to gain from such a move? Besides . . . things were going on that haven't sat right with me long before their involvement."

Effie didn't disagree with him. There had just been one too many coincidences for the events of the past few months to feel unconnected. She searched through her memories, trying to recall the first event that truly felt off. It wasn't their visits to Sylverlands or Caederan. There was nothing about what happened while they were there that felt like a personal attack.

She bit her lip, memories racing through her mind. The lajhár attack. That was the first time that things didn't quite add up. Kieran's vision had sent them to the site of the slaughter, and they'd all agreed there was something odd about the manner in which the jungle cats had been killed.

That trap in the jungle. The one they'd found *after* Kieran's vision about the missing Keepers. She'd assumed it had been the Shadow-touched, but while lucid, they've never been particularly strategic . . .

Heart pounding, Effie's thoughts turned to the attack on the citadel. Someone had to lead the Shadows to the portal; they never would have found the entrance otherwise.

She sucked in a breath as the answer came to her.

Just like a key sliding into a lock, pieces fell into place. Things that hadn't made sense at the time were suddenly glaringly obvious.

Lucian was rigid beside her, each one of her thoughts broadcasted to him and Kael via their Guardian's bond.

"Kieran," he snarled. His face was twisted in fury, his eyes practically black with rage. "He's the one who's responsible for the markers being fulfilled. He orchestrated the whole damn thing. If we can find him, perhaps we can stop any more of them from coming to pass."

Ronan looked up from the ground, his eyes murderous. "Is it possible Reyna is the key to unlocking the last binding?"

Lucian considered the question and then slowly dipped his chin. "If the Night Stalkers are tied to this Father as she says, it's certainly possible."

"Then perhaps it's time we pay the ex-prince a visit," Ronan snarled, pushing to his feet.

"How will we find him?" Kael asked. "We have no clue where he went after he fled the Vale."

"Leave that to me," Helena said in a voice that was not wholly her own. "If he's truly behind these atrocities, there's nowhere he can hide."

Effie shuddered. It was a voice she recognized. One that belonged to the Mother herself. It was the voice of justice . . . and bloodshed.

Kieran's reckoning was at hand.

CHAPTER 29

EFFIE

There was one last thing they needed to do in Bael before they could hunt down Kieran.

"Now that we have locked on to the corruption's signature, it's time for me to heal the land."

"Us," Lucian corrected, interrupting Helena without apology. "It's time for *us* to heal the land. There is no doubting your power, Kiri, but if we have any hope of outrunning this blight, we'll need to split our forces. Working together now will ensure we all understand the nuances of the task before us."

Helena considered him, a small smile playing about her mouth. Her eyes darted to Effie, and she cast her voice low, speaking as if no one else could hear her. "I can see now why you say he's so aggravating." She let her eyes return to Lucian and travel up his body. "And why you tolerate it."

Effie blushed as Helena smirked and then broke out into peals of laughter at her Mate's scowl. For his part, Lucian merely crossed his arms, causing the muscles in his biceps and chest to flex in the most deliciously distracting way.

"Aggravating?"

"Impossibly so."

A smile ghosted her Guardian's lips, gone as quickly as it appeared.

"All right, Guardian," Helena murmured. "We'll try it your way."

Lucian was gracious enough to look as though he was honored by her concession, although Effie didn't think anyone was fooled into believing he would have allowed matters to go any other way. Even surrounded by other alpha males—and females—he had no trouble establishing dominance.

"Are we supposed to be helping you? Because I'd feel remiss if I didn't point out that besides Helena, you're the only other person who's done something like this before."

Kael's dimple flashed at Effie's impertinence. *"Ye of little faith."*

Effie quirked a brow. *"What? Am I supposed to just magically know how to go about sending the corruption to this Nether place?"*

"In a manner of speaking." Came Lucian's amused reply.

The other Guardians were already moving into place, standing to the side of Helena. Effie trailed behind, trying to figure out what she was missing. When she reached him, Lucian ran his thumb along the crease between her two brows.

"Do you remember how I taught you to access your power?" he asked, his voice tender in her mind.

"By sharing your first experience of it."

"That is how you will learn the ritual we are about to use."

Effie couldn't help but feel a little slow. He had already explained the Guardian's shared pool of knowledge to her. She'd been on the receiving end of it more than once now, both in her position as a Keeper and also since becoming a Guardian. She should have realized one of them knowing something was essentially the same as all of them knowing it.

His touch was featherlight against her skin, but the memory was just as powerful as before. Colors twirled and shifted behind her eyelids until she was witnessing Lucian perform the ritual. It was more than a little odd to see her body chained to the wall as he moved around speaking the words of power. More so once she was splayed on the floor.

Effie wanted to pull away, not quite ready to face the truth of how far gone she'd been, but unable to stop it.

When it was over, the knowledge was hers, as if she'd performed the spell a hundred times before.

"Do we have everything we need?"

"Helena can manifest every element, the only other thing we require are the words."

Effie gave a little nod, clearing her mind to help center herself. She was still new when it came to performing magic, and this was a massive undertaking. She didn't want to be the one to fuck it up.

Helena looked over at them, her brows furrowed. "I'm not used to doing this as a group effort."

It soothed a part of Effie's soul to hear such a powerful woman admit that there were still things she didn't know. It made her feel like less of an imposter. If the Mother's Vessel was still learning after all this time, then it was only natural Effie would have a learning curve of her own.

"If you focus on strengthening the unbroken strands, we can cast out the tainted ones," Lucian said.

Helena's brows puckered further. "I don't see the land through these strands you speak of. To me it is a myriad of colors."

"Do these colors allow you to distinguish that which is salvageable from that which is already lost?"

There was a beat of silence as Helena's eyes sparkled like twin prisms. "Yes," she murmured, her voice layered.

"Repair what ails. We will weed out that which cannot be salvaged. Then together, we will replace what has been lost."

Helena looked intrigued. "Ready?"

Lucian's eyes burned bronze. "Aye, Kiri."

There was no need to speak incantations or call upon the elements. Helena embodied them all, and she was more tied to the Mother's five branches than any other living being. As soon as Lucian finished speaking, Helena began to glow with power.

Effie couldn't begin to imagine what it felt like to Helena, the force of all those elements rising within her, but for her, joining with her power was like being truly alive. As she merged with that limitless potential, for one perfect moment there was no fear. No shame or doubt. Just pure, wondrous ability.

The last time she used her power to view land, the earth lost its color and transformed into a wasteland comprised almost entirely of oozing, noxious black fibers. This time, however, Effie could also see vibrant strands of light. They were flowing out of Helena, sinking their way deep into the ground and reinforcing the threads that were little more than feeble protests against the choking corruption.

Tendrils of darkness shrank away from the purity of Helena's power and from the life she was reintroducing to the land. Together, the Guardians focused on those tainted filaments, using their power to assert their will.

It was the first time Effie had really tried to modify the essence of a thing. She may be casting the corruption out, but she was also reshaping reality itself. Telling the land which pieces were allowed to stay and thrive, and which must be eliminated. It was heady, that kind of power. So easily could she rebuild the entire world to her liking. Getting rid of the plants and beasts that annoyed rather than delighted. But every ecosystem required balance. Destroy too much, and nothing would survive.

All of this she knew, and yet the temptation flickered there until the very last of the tainted strands were gone.

When they were done, the citadel was still missing, but so were the ashes and scent of despair that had clung to the land. It would take years before the repairs were finished, but at least the Keepers would have a homeland to return to, if they wished.

A sense of peace washed over Effie. She had helped do this. In her own way, she had managed to save the place that had become her home.

Lucian threaded his fingers through hers. There was no need for words. She could feel the contentment flowing off of him and cascading over her skin. Effie breathed deep, savoring the feel of his happiness, allowing it to reinforce her own growing contentment.

Perhaps it was not the citadel that had made her feel at home, after all.

Sneaking a peek at him, Effie could only grin when she discovered him staring down at her with burning umber eyes.

No. Home was never a place at all.

"THERE'S no need to race off into the night, Desda." Lucian's voice was thick with exasperation, but his eyes twinkled with good humor.

Effie loved watching the shopkeeper boss her Guardian around, almost as much as she loved how he allowed it. It gave her hope that one day she'd be as lucky.

Desda waved his comment away with a snort. "We've imposed on the people of the Vale for too long. It's time for us to go home, to reclaim what is rightfully ours. You know as well as I that nothing heals the heart better than a purpose."

Lucian gazed down at the older woman with affection. "Fair enough."

"Besides," she added with a shrug. "You lot will go running off again, and it's not right the rest of us don't do our part."

Effie bit back a laugh as Lucian held up his hands, clearly outmanned. "You've made your point, Desda. In our absence, I think you'll be the perfect person to lead the charge. I can ask the Kiri to escort any who wish to return to Bael before we continue on our journey."

"Absolutely not," Desda scoffed. "We are more than capable of traveling for a few days. No need to waste time on an unnecessary task when more important things are yet to be done."

"The woman is impossible."

"I think you mean incredible. I'm taking notes."

Lucian couldn't quite contain his groan. *"Just what I need. More sass from you."*

"Admit it, you love my sass."

He winked at her. *You know I do.*

Effie's cheeks warmed, and her stomach gave a low flutter.

Helena joined them, a dirty satchel and book of prophecy held aloft. "I have what I need to track him. Oh—sorry, I didn't mean to interrupt."

"No bother at all," Lucian said with a quick grin. "You're saving me, really." Turning to Desda, he said, "Let me know if there's anything you require for your journey."

She held her arms open. "Just a proper goodbye."

Effie fell a little deeper in love with Lucian for the way he didn't shy away from the demand for affection. So many men pretended to be put off by such requests, but not him. He gathered the woman in his arms and pressed a kiss to her weathered cheek, his voice turning gruff. "Don't go and do anything stupid while I'm away."

Desda laughed and patted him on the cheek. "I love you too, sweet one. Now, where's that pretty girl of yours?"

Effie blinked in surprise, startled by the request. "Me?"

"Aye, lass. Lucian may not have come from my womb, but he's more of a son to me than any who share my blood. It's only right that I get to impart some wisdom on his life mate."

It warmed Effie, this display of familial loyalty. Her family was also comprised of those that she had chosen versus any she'd been born to. She could appreciate the strength of the ties, and how important it was for Desda to give Effie her blessing. Lucian may not give two shits about such things, but she relished the idea of having a mother figure's approval.

She stepped forward, and Desda grasped her shoulders, her grip surprisingly strong. "There now. You're a beauty, aren't ya? But it's not your looks that matter, dear. No. Only a woman strong in mind and spirit could ever be a true match for my Lucian. Look after him. Don't be afraid to put him in his place when he gets too bullheaded. And I expect lots of grandbabies, you hear?"

Flushing, Effie managed a strangled sound that Desda took as agreement. Lucian, however, was completely unfazed by her declarations about their future.

"You seem surprised."

"Grandbabies?" Effie sputtered.

"We have our entire lives to raise a family. There's no rush. Although I must admit, I enjoy the thought of making a child with you."

As soon as he said the words, the image of a sweet-faced girl with blonde ringlets and her papa's dark eyes flashed into Effie's mind. Had you asked her two minutes prior, she'd tell you she had no intention of bringing a child into this world, but now that the child held some of Lucian's features? Well . . . perhaps she could be persuaded.

Desda pulled Effie into a tight embrace, brushing dry lips against her cheek. "That boy doesn't know how to love, save with his entire being. He may look tough, but he feels deep. No man will be more loyal to you or love you more fiercely."

Unexpected tears pricked Effie's eyes, and she gave a choked nod. "It's the same for me."

"Aye," Desda smiled, and it took years off her lined face. "I see that it is."

She let Effie go with one last squeeze, turning her face to Lucian as she started to shuffle away. "Don't forget you owe me a store's worth of artwork. How else am I supposed to make my living?"

That earned a snort from Lucian. "I'll get right on that. Somewhere between saving the world and rebuilding the citadel."

"See that you do," she called, waving at them over her shoulder as she walked away.

"I like her," Helena declared, eyes bright with suppressed laughter.

"Don't tell her that," Lucian replied dryly. "You'll only encourage her."

"I didn't mean to interrupt the moment, I just thought you'd like to know that we're ready to go as soon as you are."

"No worries, Kiri—"

"I'm going to have to insist that you call me Helena. Effie is practically my sister, any life mate of hers is thereby family." Helena's aqua eyes twinkled.

For the second time in as many minutes, Effie was overcome by emotion. She'd been rendered nearly speechless when Helena had declared her as a friend the first time, but to be claimed as a sister? She didn't think she'd ever be able to convey how much that meant to her.

Intimately familiar with the darkness of her past, and the scars that still hid in plain sight, Lucian wrapped his arm around Effie's waist, bolstering her as always with his strength.

"You honor me, Helena."

She waved the words away. "Just make her life a happy one, Lucian, and I will consider any debts paid in full."

Lucian's emotions seeped into her, although his face betrayed none of them. Her Guardian may appear stoic, but he was not unmoved by Helena's words.

"That is my greatest wish as well," he replied.

"You two need to stop this or I'm going to start weeping like a child."

Helena smiled. "There are worse things in life than to be surrounded by people that love you."

Effie was at a loss for words. It was such a foreign notion. "Don't we have a rat to catch?" she finally blurted.

"That we do," Helena replied, eyes flashing with iridescence. "I was able to discern the unique look of Kieran's magic through his belongings."

"I know that all magic leaves a trace, but Kieran's power is linked to his dreams, so how is that possible?"

"He is still a creature of magic at his core. That means a trace of it will linger any place that he spends a significant amount of time, a bit like a fingerprint." Helena looked between Effie and Lucian. "Surely Guardians can pick up on it as well?"

Lucian gave Helena one of his enigmatic grins that was neither admitting nor denying her statement, but she didn't seem to actually be waiting for an answer.

"Once I was able to identify his signature, for lack of a better word, it was really just as simple as walking around until I locked onto the freshest imprint. It looks like he fled through the northwestern exit," she finished with a little shrug.

"Any direction he went, he's alone, on foot, and traversing through desert. He couldn't have made it very far, even with such a significant head start," Lucian murmured.

"Oh, it wouldn't matter regardless," Helena said, her smile turning mean. "Nothing can outrun a Talyrian."

CHAPTER 30

KIERAN

A cloud floated in front of the sun, providing him with a welcome respite from its unwavering glare. As he'd done every morning since discovering the gate, he'd woken with the dawn, trying to take advantage of the cooler hours to continue his search, before breaking mid-day when the sun was at its zenith in the sky. For all that there was—a river and a smattering of what only the most optimistic could call a copse of trees—it was still the desert.

Kieran ran a forearm across his forehead, wincing at the sting. His fair, unblemished skin was a thing of the past. Now he was roughly the shade of a beet—at least the parts of him that were exposed to the elements. Portions of his face had already started peeling, and there were now a smattering of tiny blisters across the bridge of his nose and cheeks that could have passed for freckles had they been any darker.

Not even the salty tracks of his sweat brought any relief. In about another ten minutes he'd have to abandon his work for the afternoon and trudge back to the riverbank to soak his battered body.

Kieran peeled a strand of sun-bleached hair off his neck and wrapped it back around the sweaty tangle atop his head. No one who saw him now would ever mistake him for royalty. A farmer, perhaps, but certainly not a prince.

Instead of continuing on its journey across the sky, the cloud never moved past the sun, leaving him cast in a hazy shadow. Beads of sweat dripped down his body but he shivered with sudden chill. Dread pooled in his stomach as wind began to howl in the distance.

Twisting around, Kieran peered up at the sky, if for no other reason than to assure himself it was in fact just a cloud.

"Elder's sagging sack," he gasped, terror robbing him of breath and causing his limbs to quake. The rock he'd used to help dig tumbled from his hand as his mouth fell open.

While it was white, there was no confusing the winged creature zooming toward him for a cloud. Kieran had never laid eyes upon one of the famed felines of the north, but there was no mistaking it. Especially not once it opened its mouth and spewed forth molten jets of flame.

Talyrian.

How his mind managed to supply the word was a miracle in itself. Kieran couldn't even manage to remember how to breathe properly, so intense was his shock. But why was it here?

Then he noticed the woman mounted on its back, her chestnut hair whipping around her face. He'd seen her before in his dreams. The one who caused fire to rain from the sky and had battled a maelstrom and won. The Kiri. The Mother's Vessel. The instrument, it would seem, of his demise. For why else would she have come for him?

The ex-prince of Eatos wanted to sink to his knees in submission, but he was frozen in place, fear holding him captive. One wrong move would surely see him eaten, or worse.

Sand flew up in a series of tiny storms as the Talyrian's massive black wings beat, keeping it aloft. Helena studied him from her perch on its back, her eyes glittering with barely concealed wrath.

"I take it there is no need for introductions," she stated, her voice booming like thunder.

Kieran flinched and gave a quick shake of his head.

"Good."

When she said nothing further, he began to fidget under her

scrutiny. *What is she waiting for?* His eyes darted to the sides, instinct pushing him to search for an escape.

"I wouldn't risk it if I were you. There's nothing Starshine loves more than to chase down her prey, and no one, not even the Kiri herself, can stand between a Talyrian Queen and her next meal."

He couldn't muster a shred of shame as a damp stain spread down the leg of his pants. Helena wrinkled her nose but refrained from commenting.

Several heartbeats passed without either of them making a sound. Just when Kieran was about to find his voice, several familiar figures crested the horizon.

"Sorry it took so long," Lucian said. "So much of this land looks the same."

A man with obsidian hair scowled at the Guardian, his voice little more than a deep growl. "I showed you the image exactly as she sent it to me."

A blur of red was Kieran's only warning before Ronan tackled him and sent him crashing to the ground. Kieran's back slid across a sea of stone and sand as a fist stronger than iron clamped around his throat, pushing his head back into one of the many holes he'd dug.

"Tell me what you did to her!"

Kieran struggled to breathe, his eyes bulging as he blinked, trying to process the rapid shift of gravity and loss of air.

"If you expect him to tell you anything, you'll need to let him go."

Even trapped as he was, Kieran couldn't help the spark of temper Lucian's voice set off within him. Ronan may have him by the throat, but his hatred was reserved for the dark-haired Guardian.

Black spots were dancing in his eyes, but Kieran was still just barely able to make out Ronan's clenched jaw and flaring nostrils. His hand tightened around Kieran's throat and a pathetic gurgle escaped from his lips before Ronan released him with a snarl.

"Where is she?"

He sat up, coughing hard as tears rolled down his face.

"Answer me!" Ronan snarled as he kicked him.

Kieran saw stars. He wasn't surprised at the distinctive snap of one of his ribs breaking. "I-I don't know," he stuttered, his voice little more than a harsh rasp. "She was with you."

That only seemed to enrage the Shield more. "And then you took her from me, so where the fuck is she?"

Kieran was truly confused. The last he'd heard the Guardians had locked Effie in a cell. "H-how should I know? He's the one that locked her up."

Ronan's brows lifted, and he twisted back to address Lucian. "What's he talking about?"

He couldn't see anything except Ronan looming over him, and he didn't hear anyone respond.

"Stop fucking around and tell me what you've done with Reyna."

"Reyna?" Kieran blinked, then he started laughing at the absurdity of his situation. They were blaming him for the loss of a woman he hardly knew, but had said nothing of the woman he'd unintentionally destroyed. "How the hell should I know?"

"Unless you want me to rip your balls out through your throat, you should probably tell me what you know about Reyna being locked up."

One quick glance at the absolute rage in the Shield's eyes told Kieran he wasn't exaggerating. Gulping, Kieran shook his head, his throat on fire as he struggled to speak. "Not Reyna. Effie. He locked her in a cage."

Ronan's eyes frosted over. "How do you know about that?"

"Overheard."

"And then decided to run away because of the part you played in putting her there?" Ronan accused, hands flexing as if he was barely restraining himself from beating Kieran to a pulp.

He glanced away, unable to meet the other man's eyes any longer. *When did I turn into such a fucking coward?*

"Yeah, we know all about the part you played in the attack on the citadel."

He could hear his teeth grinding as he glanced back up at Ronan. "None of that was supposed to happen. It was never supposed to go that far!"

"So you are a fucking traitor."

"You said . . . you said you knew . . ."

"We suspected and you just confirmed."

Elder's piss in a pot.

"How could you do this, Kieran? The Keepers were your family; they gave you a home."

Kieran's body froze, his heart spasming in his chest when he recognized the voice he never thought he'd hear again. The one he first heard in his dreams. *Great, now I'm hallucinating again.*

Shaking his head as if to clear it, he blinked up at the small figure standing beside Ronan. When he rubbed his eyes as the illusion didn't vanish, Kieran scrambled to his feet, arms outstretched. "Effie? Effie, you're alive!"

She scrambled back out of reach, her voice dripping with anger. "No thanks to you."

Ronan slammed his hand into Kieran's chest, keeping him in place. "That's close enough."

Kieran was openly crying, his relief momentarily blocking the pain. Finally, he'd have a chance to explain. To make things right. "I-I didn't mean for you to get hurt. It was all a way to prove myself to you. That I could be the man you wanted. Everything just went so wrong, and no matter what I did, you never noticed me. You never even gave me a chance to prove myself to you. All you ever saw was *him*." There was no hiding the petulant cast of his voice as he spat out the last word.

Effie let out a startled bark of laughter. "You thought destroying the citadel, my *home*, would make me fall in love with you?"

"No!" Kieran cried out in frustration, smacking himself on the side of his head as his bloodied fingers knotted in his hair. "I just wanted you to *see* me. To show you I could be what you need. A hero . . ."

"Some hero you turned out to be. Do you even know how many lives you ruined? How many people you killed?"

"Effie, I—"

"You are *pathetic*."

"But I just—"

"You are the worst sort of villain. You actually believe your actions were justified."

Anger bubbled up as she continued to speak over him. Kieran couldn't have held back the words that burst from him if he'd tried. "You all think you're so fucking untouchable. Well I proved you weren't, didn't I? You should thank me for teaching you how to see more clearly."

"Thank you?" Effie snorted with derision. "You're lucky we don't kill you where you stand."

Kieran saw red. No matter what he did, what he said, she would never listen to him. Never understand him. All of this was for nothing. "That would require you to get your hands dirty and you don't have what it takes," he snarled, spit flying from his mouth as he lunged for her.

Instead of flinching away, Effie countered the attack, stepping into his arms and then gliding around him before Kieran could fully process the movement. He was too distracted by the fresh rose and honey scent of her hair. Even now, when he hated her as much as he loved her, she consumed him.

"Effie," he begged, trying to touch her.

"Try it," she said, her voice hard as she pushed the blades held at his throat and groin in a little deeper. "Give me a reason to gut you like the swine you are."

"This has gone far enough," Helena said, dismounting from the Talyrian as if the massive cat wasn't still hovering three feet off the ground. "Lucian, bind him. Make sure to gag him, too. I'm tired of listening to the vitriol he spews."

"With pleasure," Lucian said, his grin too filled with violence to be mistaken for a smile.

Kieran struggled in Effie's hold, trying to get free. He'd rather die than endure any kind of degradation at the Guardian's hand. He tossed his head back, hoping to headbutt her, but she was too small for the blow to land and all he'd managed to do was cut himself on the edge of her blade. The fiery sting did nothing to stop his frenzied movements.

"Enough!" Ronan roared, punching Kieran so hard in the face that stars exploded behind his eyes and he slumped to the floor practically unconscious.

"Was that really necessary?" Helena asked.

"Yes."

There was a sigh from somewhere above him and then everything went dark.

When Kieran came to, he was bound and gagged. In addition to the ones around his hands and feet, one was also looped around his neck.

Lucian hovered above him, not bothering to hide his grin. "Now, be a good boy and stand up," the Guardian practically purred as he gave the chains around his waist a sharp tug, forcibly lifting Kieran to his feet.

He growled low in his throat, saliva dripping down his chin.

"What was that? I didn't quite catch it," Lucian said, dropping his ear down as if trying to hear better.

"Untie me and let's settle this like real men!" Kieran said. Although what came out sounded more like, "Ung e'n l'til iss hic eel min!"

Lucian laughed and pushed Kieran stumbling forward. "Why didn't we do this sooner? I like him so much better this way." He bucked again, but Lucian pulled the chains so tightly he couldn't breathe. "Don't mistake my amusement for leniency. The only reason you're still alive is because she demanded it."

Kieran's eyes darted over Lucian's shoulder toward Effie.

Lucian's smile stretched, his dark eyes glittering with malice. "No, not her. Effie asked if she could be the one to kill you. It is the Kiri who claimed the right to enforce your punishment. She is the one that requires you to live."

Kieran's throat bobbed as Lucian released him and pulled him forward to stand before the queen of the Chosen. Ronan and the man he didn't know stood on either side of her, their expressions murderous. But it was Helena that made his bowels loosen.

Her eyes glowed, and her voice thundered, the sky churning like a deadly storm. "Kieran of Eatos, you have been found guilty of treason against the realm of Elysia. Since you cannot return to your own realm, you will live out the rest of your days locked deep within the Palace's dungeon. You will rot down there long after we've forgotten your name, but you will never forget mine"—the sky exploded with thunder and lightning—"I am justice, I am vengeance, and I am here to collect what is rightfully mine. Your life in exchange for all of those you damned with your selfish greed. Take a good look at the sky, Prince, for it's the last time you'll ever see it."

CHAPTER 31

EFFIE

"Considering you likely just pulled Elysia back from the brink of annihilation, you don't look very victorious, or happy, for that matter."

Effie spun around, Lucian's deep voice shocking her from the stasis she'd been locked in ever since returning to the Palace. The last time she'd been here she'd buried her grandmother, and these halls, while exquisite, were haunted. She couldn't wait to leave.

"Just a lot on my mind," she murmured, turning back to the window she'd been staring out of, not that she was actually enjoying the view of the Kiri's gardens below.

"Want to talk about it?"

"Want? No, not really . . ." Effie sighed, wrapping her arms a little tighter around her waist.

She stiffened for the briefest moment as Lucian rested his hands on her shoulders before melting into his warmth. Somehow his mere presence made the air a little less oppressive. Not that she was about to admit it to him. His ego was big enough already.

Lucian brushed a kiss to the back of her neck, his voice dryly amused as he spoke in her mind. *"I heard that."*

Her lips twitched and a little more of the melancholy faded away.

"I just can't shake the sense that this isn't over," she finally admitted. "We've captured the man responsible for setting off the markers, imprisoned him to ensure he cannot continue with his nefarious deeds, learned how to track the Shadows and repair the damage to the land, and yet we're no closer to discovering who took Reyna, *and* we still—"

"Shhh," Lucian breathed against her ear, cutting off the torrent of her words. "It's always impossible to believe a war has been won when you've been in the thick of it for so long. True peace takes time. Just because a war is over doesn't mean the work is done. So, yes, you are right. There are still more battles before us, but with Kieran imprisoned and unable to set off the last of the markers, the worst has passed. With him out of the way, we have the time that we need to set everything else to rights. You'll see."

His words eased some of the pressure in her chest. It would take time, but together they would deal with the Shadows and cast out the last of the corruption. Then, perhaps, Elysia would finally know peace once more.

"I'm worried about Ronan," she admitted, voicing the other concern weighing heavily on her heart.

Lucian's hands squeezed her shoulders. "I wish I could say that there's no need for your worry, but I know better than most what it does to a man when he thinks he might lose the one he loves."

Effie turned to look at him. "We don't even know where to look for her. How can we help him when we don't have a path?"

He ran his knuckles over her cheek. "You cannot save everyone yourself." She opened her mouth to protest, but he placed a gentle finger on her lips, continuing, "Helena can search in ways we cannot. Let her lead the hunt while we take care of other matters. She will summon us when she needs us. We will be there for your friend when it matters the most."

Sighing, she nodded.

Lucian dropped his hand, tilting her chin up. "We all have our own parts to play in life's battles, Effie. Just because you are not leading the charge does not mean you do not play an important role."

One side of her mouth lifted in a reluctant smile. "Spoken like a true warrior."

"With centuries of experience. You'd do well to listen to my wisdom."

"Is *that* what this is? Oh, well then . . ." They fell into a comfortable silence, a small smile playing on her mouth. "She wants to throw us a parade, you know."

Lucian chuckled. "Mortals love to celebrate their continued existence, brief as it might be."

"You could try to sound a little less elitist when you say that, old man."

His hands tightened on her as his lips moved back to her ear. "Who are you calling old?" he growled, setting off a wave of tingles low in her belly. "Do I need to remind you just how virile I can be?"

She squirmed, a flash of desire making it impossible to remain still. "Maybe . . ."

He caressed her cheek, turning her face so that he could lean down and steal her lips in a spine-melting kiss. It started soft, just the featherlight touch of his lips over hers before he deepened it.

Her Guardian growled low in his throat when a knock sounded at the door. "Ignore it," he demanded, searing her with another kiss.

The door swung open, and their visitor loudly cleared his throat.

Lucian groaned, pulling away from Effie to close his eyes and rest his forehead on hers. "Remind me to start removing doorknobs from now on."

Nord scoffed. "Like that could stop me." Lucian glared at him, and the blond man held up his hands, laughing. "At ease. I just came to see if the two of you were ready."

"Ready? Ready for what?" she asked, looking between them.

Nord didn't bother to hide his amusement. "You didn't even get around to telling her yet, did you?" Shaking his head, he ran his hand over his beard, giving it a little tug. "How are you two supposed to be trusted to follow through on your duties when you can't seem to keep your hands off of each other?"

Lucian shifted his attention back to Effie, his grin wolfish. "He might have a point."

Her cheeks were on fire with the heat of her blush. "Speak for yourself. I was just standing here minding my own business when you accosted me."

Lucian raised a brow, his eyes hot. "Is that so? Would you care to wager who could go longer without *accosting* the other?"

"No," she blurted, her refusal adamant. She'd waited long enough for the Guardian to give in to his feelings for her, the last thing she wanted was to ever go back to the days when she was dazed with lust and all but vibrating from her unfulfilled desire.

Nord and Lucian roared with laughter.

"I suppose it's a good thing there are three of us then. Kael will just have to be the responsible one for the next few hundred years or so while we get over this incessant need to touch each other." He waggled his eyebrows in such an un-Lucian-like fashion that Effie snorted with laughter. He pulled her close and nipped her ear. "Not that it's likely I'll ever get over it no matter how many centuries we spend together."

Effie's heart swelled, and she melted against him before something he said snagged her attention. "Hey!" she chided, lightly slapping Lucian's chest with the back of her hand. "You forgot to include me."

Lucian's brows furrowed. "I did?"

She nodded emphatically. "You said 'good thing there are three of us,' but Elysia has four Guardians now."

His expression cleared. "Ah, actually that's what I was coming to talk to you about."

Now it was Effie whose brows dipped into a deep vee and sudden panic sent her heart racing. "Is something wrong?"

He caught her hand in his, giving it a comforting squeeze. "No, nothing like that. Nord has put in his request for a transfer."

"Nord?"

His ringed fingers were covering his mouth, doing little to hide his grin as he peeked at her with twinkling blue eyes. "I'm afraid it's true."

"But . . . why?" she asked, her heart aching at the thought of having to say goodbye to someone who had become the older brother she'd never wanted. "Where will you go?"

He dropped his hand and shrugged, his teeth flashing behind his beard. "That's the beauty of it, isn't it? One of the greatest adventures in life is the not knowing. For far too long I've been trapped in that citadel upholding the illusions necessary to keep our secret safe. But now, with you here, I finally have a chance to go out and discover my true purpose. It's time."

Effie blinked back tears, not about to try to stand in the way of anyone and their destiny. "Will you at least come visit?"

Nord's grin softened, and he held his arms open for a hug. "Don't worry, little sister. This is hardly the last you'll see of me."

She rushed forward, curling herself into his embrace. "Be safe?"

His chest vibrated beneath her cheek. "But where's the fun in that? Who doesn't love a little danger?"

Effie pushed back and glared up at him through watery eyes. "Nord Amadeus Ragnarson!"

Nord stared down at her with wide eyes before sputtering with laughter. "What did you just call me?"

"When I was in trouble, people always used my full name."

"But that's not my name," he pointed out.

"Well I don't know your full name, so I just gave you one. Deal with it."

His expression softened, and he pulled her back in for another hug, giving her a brotherly kiss on the forehead. "I promise to keep myself safe. You don't need to worry about me."

Effie squeezed him hard. "That's not how family works. I'll always worry when we're apart."

She heard Nord draw a startled breath before he rested his cheek on the top of her head. "Ah, *lillesøster*, I do not deserve you."

Effie stepped back, trying hard to keep her voice steady. "When do you leave?"

"Today."

"So soon?"

He nodded.

"Well what about the Triumvirate? Can you really leave when there's no one to replace you?"

"That's what I wanted to talk to you about," Lucian said, moving back into her line of sight. "How would you feel about officially joining us?"

A high-pitched ringing started in her ears and she shook her head, not certain she'd heard him. "Me?"

"Who else would I ask?"

"I don't know, I just assumed someone else from the Brotherhood would be sent to take Nord's place."

"Why send for someone else when you're already here? Unless that's what you want. I won't force this upon you."

Effie took less than a second to consider what a lifetime of secrecy and leadership at Lucian's side would be like. "I'll accept on one condition."

He raised his brows.

With a devilish grin, she projected her terms to Lucian and Nord through their link. She knew they weren't going to like what she wanted to do, but the same impulse that had her request the condition in the first place was pushing her to ensure it was met.

There was one stunned moment of silence before Lucian laughed. "You can't be serious."

"I know it's a lot to ask, but hear me out. By the time I'm done, I think you'll agree with me."

Lucian crossed his arms, exchanging a look with Nord before leveling his dark eyes back on her. "Go ahead, I'm listening."

EFFIE WAS ODDLY nervous as she knelt on the floor, Kael, Nord, and Lucian, standing around her wearing the scarlet robes of their position.

Lucian hadn't said much about what would be required of her once she took her formal vows. As with everything else that happened to her in the last year, she'd have to learn as she went. Thankfully, she at least had his memories to help provide a little bit of context for what was about to happen.

"*Initiate, state your intention.*"

"I come before you—clear of mind, pure of heart, and free from the ties of my past—requesting a place among you."

As she spoke the words, Effie realized they were true. For quite possibly the first time in her entire life, she was not wholly defined by her past and the way other people saw her. Of course those old aches would always be a part of her, but they no longer had the power to cut. Darrin, her grandmother, her parents: they were the storms that tempered her, but she was the one who learned how to rise from the ashes. They had made her, but they no longer defined her.

"*The Triumvirate are eternal.*"

"*They are the memory of the past.*"

"*The watchers of the present.*"

"*The guides of the future.*"

The spectral voices rose around and within her, stirring her pulse and calling up her power with the majesty of their inflection.

"*The Triumvirate are unified.*"

"*They have no names.*"

"*They have no faces.*"

"*They have no desires outside the protection of those they serve.*"

Effie bit back a smile. That might be true of the Triumvirate, but she had it on good authority that the Guardians were not so limited. Thankfully, becoming one did not preclude her from being the other.

A voice of smoke and crackling embers filled her mind. "*Focus, fledgling.*"

"*I thought I was an initiate now.*"

Lucian's amusement coursed through her, soothing her with its warmth and infusing her with its love.

"*It is not a path for the weak of heart or mind.*"

"*It is not a path for the selfish or self-serving.*"

"*It is not a path for the prideful or those filled with doubt.*"

"*Do you believe you are worthy to walk it?*"

Effie hesitated. Not because she was unsure of her answer, but because the sudden image of a mist-shrouded field and a woman with a crown of stars filled her mind. The woman smiled, and just as quickly as it came, the vision dispersed.

"I do." The voice that left her mouth was not her own. It was both ancient and ageless, filled with the power of a thousand storms and yet as gentle as morning dew.

Cloth rustled around her as the men shifted in surprise.

"Then stand, Sister, and take your rightful place among us."

Effie stood, her movements graceful and sure. As she did, her gown of simple blue cotton transformed into a robe of deepest scarlet. She lifted her arms and the sleeves fell back, revealing pale arms that were covered in navy runes. Grasping the edges of the hood that was settled around her shoulders, Effie looked at each man in turn.

"I vow upon the Guardian blood that lives in my veins, this hood shall be my crown. It is not merely a reminder of the duty that binds me, but it is a tribute to the people that I serve. A promise that I will spend the rest of my life fulfilling."

When she was done speaking, the hood rested over her head, concealing her within its warm folds.

"Witnessed," Lucian said, his voice steady and filled with pride.

"Witnessed!" Kael and Nord repeated.

Deviating from tradition, Lucian pushed back his hood and gave her a blinding grin. "Welcome to the Triumvirate. May your people be infused with your grace, kindness, and wisdom. May your reign be long and uneventful. But most importantly, may the Mother bless us with the strength to withstand the systematic unraveling of millennia worth of tradition you're about to subject us to."

"Uneventful?" Kael asked, nose wrinkling. "Have you met the girl?"

Lucian broke the circle to step forward and wrap her in his arms. "I have, which is why I know we're in for the ride of a lifetime."

"I feel like I should be offended, but you're likely right. You know how I feel about stupid rules. You gave me a position of power; I'd be remiss not to use it to my benefit."

"I'd have it no other way."

Effie beamed at him, knowing that while Lucian may not be able to see her smile, he could feel her joy.

"So what are we waiting for?" Kael asked with his signature dimpled grin. "I believe your entry to our esteemed ranks had conditions. Are you ready to collect?"

"Now?"

"We're nothing if not men of our words," Lucian said.

"But—"

Lucian was already pushing her to the door. "Oh no . . . there's no backing out now. You asked for this. Demanded it, actually."

"Why are you suddenly more excited about this than I am?" she asked, suspicious of their overenthusiastic willingness to indulge her.

Lucian exchanged a wordless glance with the other two men who quietly left the room. Her question had been playful, but there was nothing playful about the way Lucian was looking at her. He dropped his eyes, taking her hand in his.

"For too long you've stood in the shadows, content to hide while others stole the glory. It is time for you to claim your place in the light. Today you will show the people who matter most to you what I long ago learned to be true. You are a force to be reckoned with. A woman without equal." His eyes burned bronze as he finally raised them. "After today, no one will ever dare dismiss you or your will again."

Effie was rendered momentarily speechless. Ever since she'd looked into his memories, she'd known but perhaps not fully understood. Lucian wasn't just offended on her behalf; he had been carrying the scars of her past abuses as if they were his own. He wanted—needed—this moment for her. This public demonstration of her power.

After everything he'd given her, everything he'd done to save her, Effie would be the last one to ever refuse him anything. Especially if it would bring him peace.

"Then let's not leave them waiting."

CHAPTER 32

EFFIE

There was nothing to announce the arrival of the Triumvirate in the throne room save the startled gasps of the Chosen as they set eyes upon the infamous red robes.

Helena was seated, a five-point crown resting on her brow. She looked bemused, but not by the arrival of new guests. She was resting her chin in her hand, talking in low tones with her Shield. Her Mate sat beside her, his crown of onyx and diamonds glittering like the night sky.

"I know the timing is not ideal, but you know I must go."

"Ronan."

"I cannot remain here while she is out there."

"Ronan."

"Her life could be in danger. Hell, she could already be d—"

"Ronan!" Helena finally snapped.

Her Shield lifted his chin, his expression unreadable from the back of the room.

"I agree with you. No one is trying to stop you from finding Reyna. In fact, if you'd actually allowed me to get a word in edgewise, you might have heard me offer to help you."

"You'd do that?"

"Ronan," she groaned, "how could you ever doubt it? You are not the only one who made vows. The Night Stalkers are our allies. They need their queen, but more importantly, we owe it to our friend. Of *course* I intend to find her."

Effie didn't need to be able to see Ronan's face to know that he was struggling to contain his emotions. He'd been unraveling ever since Reyna had been taken. She hoped for everyone's sake that she was alive when he found her.

Helena finally seemed to notice the trio standing in the back of the room. Her eyes slid over them as if searching for someone else.

"She's looking for you," Lucian said.

"Then I guess it's show time."

Effie took a step forward, Kael and Lucian flanking her on either side. *"We request a private audience with the Kiri and her Circle."*

Helena lifted a brow. "Leave us."

The others in the room scurried to obey, casting awed glances between the Triumvirate and their ruler. Effie didn't need to be telepathically linked to them to read the question burning in their eyes. Who would dare command the Mother's Vessel to do anything? Who had the right?

Helena did not speak again until the massive metal door shut with a soft boom.

"I can only assume that your presence here means you intend to deliver another of your vague warnings."

It took more effort than it should have for Effie to keep from laughing out loud at Helena's barbed comment. She knew just how exasperating conversations with this particular trio could be.

Dipping her head as she'd seen Lucian and his brothers do so many times before, Effie replied, *"It is not a warning so much as a reminder and goodbye. It is time for us to go. There is work yet to be done."*

"Far be it from me to keep you. Will your Guardians be joining us in our efforts to cull the last of the Shadows and repair the damage?"

"They go where we demand."

Helena's jaw clenched. Von did not move, but his eyes narrowed slightly as if he'd picked up on the undercurrent of tension in his Mate and was prepared to strike if necessary.

"I see," she said.

"Do you?"

Helena gave a terse nod. "If it's not already too late, I'd like to at least say goodbye to Effie before you depart."

Effie lifted her arms and slowly pulled back the hood that had concealed her face. Helena was careful to keep her expression neutral as she stared unblinkingly into the black pits that represented her eyes. Between one tense breath and the next, Effie released her illusion, allowing the Circle to see her true form.

Helena's mouth went slack.

There was a whisper of cloth as Lucian and Kael pulled back their hoods behind her.

The Circle's collective reactions were beyond amusing. Ronan looked thunderstruck. Kragen, quietly amused. Von's expression was alert but impassive. Timmins was clearly fighting back a tidal wave of questions, while Joquil only seemed mildly intrigued.

"What's the meaning of this?" Helena asked, her eyes never once leaving Effie's.

So that they would know this was not some kind of trick, Effie continued to speak telepathically using her real voice. *"This is the Triumvirate's most closely guarded secret."*

"You were one of them? This whole time?"

Effie shook her head. "There was a recent opening, and I accepted the position upon the condition that I could share this truth with you."

Helena looked back to Lucian and Kael. "If this is such an important secret, why agree?"

"Effie made a compelling argument," Lucian muttered.

"That I can believe," Helena said with a laugh. "She's been known to put my Circle in their place a time or two."

Lucian and Kael chuckled.

"I'm glad we aren't the only ones," Kael said.

"What was the argument?" Helena asked, leaning forward slightly.

"It's something I Saw in a vision. Actually, I'd like to share it with you if that's all right?" Effie asked.

Helena's brows lifted in surprise. "With me?"

Effie nodded.

Helena started to push herself up.

"There's no need. I don't need to touch you to share this vision."

There were a few murmurs of surprise. Even from behind her. Usually, the Triumvirate needed physical touch to establish a connection, but Effie's intuition was assuring her that they already shared the necessary link for this to work.

Closing her eyes, she replayed her time with the Mother for Helena. When they were done, Helena's eyes shot to hers.

"Do you understand now?" Effie asked.

Helena nodded, flickers of her power flaring in her eyes.

"It would be great if you could fill the rest of us in," Von said in a bland tone.

Effie laughed. "Helena and I are connected in ways we never expected. Two halves of a much greater whole. We—all of us in this room—are protectors. There is no question in my mind that you will safeguard that which we've revealed to you. If for no other reason than your vows precluding you from it. In fact, your vows as the Circle are not that different than ours as Guardians. While it is important that the rest of the world continue to believe in the strength and unfailing power of the Triumvirate, it's also important that we are united, not just as Elysia's protectors, but for what we—together—really are: the Mother's ultimate weapon against the darkness."

"You speak as though you anticipate another war," Von said, leaning forward.

"I know only what the Lady deigns to tell me, and that for the first time in history both the Mother's Vessel and her Voice walk the realm, each of us in positions of immense power, Helena as Kiri, and I as one of the Triumvirate. Between the two of us, there is more power and knowledge at our disposal than ever before. Moreover, these positions by their very nature rely on the combined strength of those that are bound to us. Helena has her Circle, and I"—Effie gestured to the men behind her—"have the other Guardians. That is no insignificant thing. Nor do I believe in coincidences, not with all that has come to pass. There is a reason we've been brought together. We may not yet know what trials lie ahead, but it is without question that it will take all of us, united, to face whatever it is. That kind of trust requires full disclosure. So it was my request—"

"More like demand," Lucian said in her mind.

"—that there be no secrets between us. They will only see us divided at a time when we can ill afford discord."

Effie smiled then as silence stretched through the room.

"And you have Seen this?" Timmins asked.

"I don't need to See it. The Mother speaks through me as she wills."

Timmins opened and closed his mouth a few times, looking like a gasping fish.

Effie couldn't help but grin at the handsome older man. "I know . . . it takes a bit of getting used to."

He shook his head and gave her one of his fatherly smiles. "Your grandmother would be proud of you. She always told me you were destined for wondrous things."

Her throat felt tight with emotion, but she managed a wobbly smile and nodded. "Me too. I should have known better than to doubt her."

"So I guess this means our goodbye is only temporary," Helena said as she stepped off her throne and moved toward Effie.

"Aren't they always when it's between friends of the soul?"

Helena's expression softened, her eyes looking a little glassy as she pulled Effie in for a hug. "I guess they are. Will you stay in touch? Let me know how you are doing?"

"Yes, of course. Perhaps my letters will actually reach you this time?"

Helena gave a watery laugh. "If not, use one of their portals and find me."

"It's a promise," Effie agreed with a final squeeze. "Until we meet again, Helena." She let go and gave the others a little wave before starting to turn away.

"Efs, what will you three do in the meantime?"

Effie paused in the act of lifting her hood and looked over her shoulder. "I'm going to finish what we started." With a last smile, she turned away and headed for the door.

"We," Lucian said in her mind. *"We are going to finish what we started. Together."*

She allowed her fingers to brush against his as she moved past him. *"Are you referring to what Nord interrupted upstairs or—"*

He let out a choked groan. *"I am now."*

Twining her fingers through his, Effie gave him a little squeeze. *"How about both?"*

"Do I get to pick the order?"

"I think Sylverlands can use our help first . . . but after?"

"Count on it. In fact, clear your calendar. I'm claiming the rest of the year. It's going to take at least that long to do everything I have in mind."

"I never thought I'd say this, but I already miss Nord." Kael sighed and shook his head. "I may not be able to hear what you two are saying, yet I feel like I need to take a shower just walking next to all those hormones."

"Just open the damn portal already," Lucian griped.

"Hey, Brother, just because you're suffering from a case of blue balls doesn't mean you can take it out on me."

Effie snorted with laughter as Lucian cuffed Kael on the back of the head.

"Fine, fine. No need to be so *testy*." Kael winked at Effie before ducking through the shimmering portal he'd seamlessly summoned.

"Arse," Lucian grunted.

"Think of it this way," Effie offered, giving his hand a small tug toward the entrance, "the sooner we get this over with, the sooner we can—"

She didn't get a chance to finish before Lucian pulled her through, her squeals of laughter ringing out and echoing down the hallway long after it vanished behind them.

EPILOGUE

The Lady of Light sat in her garden and watched the approaching nightfall with no little sense of dread. She knew what the portent brought; what it meant for her children.

He had finally returned, and he was coming for her.

The vibrant blooms she'd just plucked withered and died in her hand. It should have been impossible. She was the mother of creation, and death should not exist in her sanctuary. Yet the proof was impossible to ignore.

There was no time to cry out, no time to hide—not that either would have done any good.

He was here.

"Luna."

She'd held so many names throughout her immortal existence, but he still remembered her first. That one word uttered in his cold and sensual voice held entirely too much meaning. She'd been named for the moon, the mother that watched over her creation. He'd been named for the night, the endless expanse that held the moon in its glittering darkness.

"Erebos."

Letting her dead flowers drop to the ground, she looked up, trying hard not to recoil at the sight of him. How could someone so evil look so perfectly beautiful?

"I told you I would return for you, *wife*."

She held her body rigid, promising herself that she would not give him the benefit of a reaction. There was little that the Mother feared . . . but she was desperately afraid of him. Of what he would do to her and her Chosen.

He stepped closer, trampling the lavender and gray petals as he moved to stand right before her. Fingers that felt like ice brushed her cheek. "Did you really think you could keep me from you for eternity?"

Despite her promise, Luna shivered. She was too shaken to know whether it was from lust or fear. With him, it was always a mix of both.

"Everything I've ever done has been to protect them."

His fingers tightened painfully on her chin, and his eyes of swirling black flashed. "Maybe you should have been more concerned with me." His expression cleared, and he looked almost giddy. "No matter. I've decided to forgive you."

"Forgive me?"

He released her chin and nodded, his smile rapturous. "Oh yes, darling. You see, I've finally managed to even the playing field as it were."

Closing the distance between them, he brushed his lips over hers. Her body reacted immediately; her nipples hardening and her breath coming out in shallow gasps. It was just as it had always been. She was helpless to resist the feelings he lured to the surface.

Her eyes fell closed as a tear splashed down her cheek.

"Ah, Luna. I've always loved the sight of your tears," he whispered, licking the salty bead off of her cheek. "But there's no reason for them."

"How can you say that? You're going to destroy everything that I love."

"No, wife. I am merely teaching you a lesson. Really, you've brought this on yourself."

"You are underestimating my children."

"Perhaps you underestimate mine."

Luna scoffed. "The Night Stalkers won't turn on the Chosen because of this. If anything, it will only strengthen the ties that bind them."

The Lord of Death smiled, and it was both cruel and terribly beautiful. "Ah, but you're already forgetting, wife. You might have your Vessel . . . but now I have mine."

Deep within the bowels of the Palace, the Dreamer opened his eyes.

~

THE LORD OF DEATH IS COMING.
ARE YOU READY TO FIND OUT WHAT HAPPENS WHEN
THE GODS GET INVOLVED?

PRE-ORDER YOUR COPY OF PRISONER OF STEEL & SHADOW,
BOOK 1 IN THE FORSAKEN TRILOGY. COMING SOON!

ACKNOWLEDGMENTS

It's no secret that writing can be an incredibly lonely job. We create entire worlds in our heads with only a computer screen to share them with, at least until we hit that publish button and our stories go out into the world. Then we just sort of feel nauseous and pray that people would love our worlds as much as we do. It is why so many authors, especially indies, talk about finding their tribe. Without one, there's only an inevitable sort of madness that would consume us.

I've been so lucky to have found my tribe. (I'm still not entirely sure how I snuck my way in, but they haven't kicked me out yet!) THANK YOU. No, seriously. Thank you. You motivate me every day to drag my butt to the computer and just keep going. Whether the words are flowing or not, you ladies are there to listen to me talk through plot holes and character arcs, celebrate the days of brilliant prose and work through the clunkers, or just count down the hours until its socially acceptable to drink wine. And I don't even have to get out of my pajamas. More than all of that though, you make a point to check in on me, if not daily definitely multiple times a week, just to say hi and see how I'm doing. You guys genuinely care, not just about me as a writer, but me as a person. You SEE me, and I love you for it, because there's no judgment there. Only love. Only acceptance.

When I started this series, I'd just joined your daily sprint group, and I feel like you guys are as much a part of this as I am. Thank you for helping me bring Lucian and Effie to life, and for drooling over Lucian with me when he says something particularly delicious.

I love you so much and am thankful every day for each and every one of you.

THE CHOSEN UNIVERSE

THE CHOSEN SERIES: THE COMPLETE SERIES

(VON & HELENA)

A FATED MATES HIGH FANTASY ROMANCE

MOTHER OF SHADOWS

REIGN OF ASH

CROWN OF EMBERS

QUEEN OF LIGHT

THE CHOSEN BOXSET #1

THE CHOSEN BOXSET #2

THE KEEPERS: THE COMPLETE SERIES

(LUCIAN & EFFIE)

A GUARDIAN/WARD HIGH FANTASY ROMANCE

THE DREAMER (A KEEPER'S PREQUEL)

THE KEEPERS LEGACY

THE KEEPERS RETRIBUTION

THE KEEPERS VOW

THE KEEPERS BOXSET

~

THE FORSAKEN: THE COMPLETE SERIES

(RONAN & REYNA)

A REJECTED MATES/ENEMIES-TO-LOVERS

HIGH FANTASY ROMANCE

PRISONER OF STEEL & SHADOW

QUEEN OF WHISPERS & MIST

COURT OF DEATH & DREAMS

ALSO BY MEG ANNE

BROTHERHOOD OF THE GUARDIANS/NOVASGARD VIKINGS

UNDERCOVER MAGIC

(NORD & LINA)

A SEXY & SUSPENSEFUL FATED MATES PNR

HINT OF DANGER

FACE OF DANGER

WORLD OF DANGER

PROMISE OF DANGER

CALL OF DANGER

BOUND BY DANGER (QUINN & FINLEY)

THE MATE GAMES

A SPICY PARANORMAL REVERSE HAREM

CO-WRITTEN WITH K. LORAINE

OBSESSION

REJECTION

POSSESSION

TEMPTATION

STANDALONES

MY SOUL TO TAKE: A FORBIDDEN LOVE MEETS FATED MATES PNR

ABOUT MEG ANNE

USA Today and international bestselling paranormal and fantasy romance author Meg Anne has always had stories running on a loop in her head. They started off as daydreams about how the evil queen (aka Mom) had her slaving away doing chores, and more recently shifted into creating backgrounds about the people stuck beside her during rush hour. The stories have always been there; they were just waiting for her to tell them.

Like any true SoCal native, Meg enjoys staying inside curled up with a good book and her cat, Henry . . . or maybe that's just her. You can convince Meg to buy just about anything if it's covered in glitter or rhinestones, or make her laugh by sharing your favorite bad joke. She also accepts bribes in the form of baked goods and Mexican food.

Meg is best known for her leading men #MenbyMeg, her inevitable cliffhangers, and making her readers laugh out loud, all of which started with the bestselling Chosen series.